WICKED SAVIOR

STELLA BRIE

AUTHOR'S NOTE

This book is a spin-off from The Killian Blade Series and includes fictional characters and places introduced in that world with little explanation or backstory. I highly recommend you read those books prior to this one.

Please note—this book contains references to magic, death, sex, graphic violence, and cursing. It also includes religious references to angels, demons, and overall Christianity. If this is not your thing, please SKIP THIS BOOK! I mean it. It's more of a side story and does NOT have to be read to continue on with the series.

Take care of yourself and read at your own discretion. Recommended for 18+ due to mature content.

Playlist

"Heavy is the Crown" - Daughtry

"Who I Am" - The Score

"Bad" - Royal Deluxe

"Born Ready" - Zayde Wolf

"Indestructible (feat. Jung Youth)" - Sam Tinnesz

"Chosen One" - Valley of the Wolves

"Champion (feat. Nicole Serrano)" - Tommee Profitt

"Wicked Game" - Daisy Gray

"All This Power" - WAR*HALL

"SOS" - James Arthur

"Can't Hold Us Down (feat. Sam Tinnesz)" - Tommy Profitt

"The Fear" - The Score

"Pull Me From The Edge" - Like A Storm

"Only Love Can Save Me Now" - The Pretty Reckless

"Masquerade" - Lindsey Stirling

"We Go Down Together" - Khalid, Dove Cameron

"Victorious" - The Score

Playlists for all my books can be found on
youtube @authorstellabrie

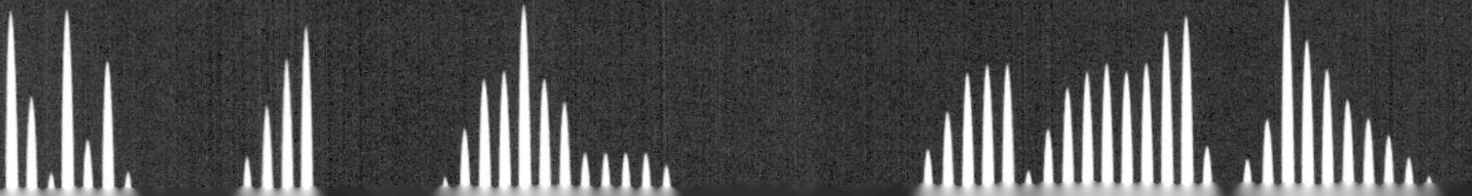

DEDICATION

*To all the fabulous readers who loved the Killian Blade Series and
who have returned to read Lucifer and Evren's story.
Thank you! You are the BEST!*

LUCIFER

The bone is smooth and worn beneath my fingertips, and with every stroke, satisfaction thrums through me. Easily seven feet tall and four feet wide, my throne of bones is a vicious reminder of my ruthless rise to the top and my continued reign of the Underworld. Magic weaves the bones into the chair, giving them an eternal resting place under my ass, an honor I only extend to the most powerful or treacherous of enemies.

The bone under my right hand was the first and most important, and the reason I'm here in this world, and not above with the other archangels. Satan's right arm. The one he raised against his creator, and the one I cut off when I struck him down, ending the angels' rebellion. A noble act for the one I served. And yet, unknowingly, the ultimate act of betrayal against us both. An inflection point more powerful than the act itself.

Black marble stretches from one end of the great hall to the other. The shiny surface directly beneath my feet is a mirror for the bone white throne and the golden figure sitting upon it. I ignore the reflection and sweep my blond hair back behind one ear.

Smooth black obsidian walls rise high to the ceiling above where they meet arches made of real gold and encrusted with gems. Huge, elaborate chandeliers made of the same metal drop low, casting candlelight across every surface. There are no windows to break up the shadows here. It was designed by a predecessor who abhorred the sunlight, and it's the embodiment of the creatures it serves—the Underworld.

A loud voice interrupts my thoughts, and I realize the first case is being called. Every month, I hold court to listen to the conflicts and grievances of my people. In the beginning, these sessions were necessary, a control mechanism for establishing order in a world where none existed.

A couple of demons from two different Houses of Sin step forward to present their case. Lord Envidia, an envy demon, and Lord Gula, a gluttony demon. Both reflect the characteristics of their house. Envy is styled perfectly from head to toe. The nymphs call him tall, dark, and handsome. In contrast, Gluttony is a large, rotund man, indicative of all the excess he consumes, whether it be food or power.

It's easier for me to call them Envy and Gluttony, although I try not to do it to their faces. Daire tells me rulers need to be PC these days. I try. At least my new nicknames are better than the old ones, which were variations of asshole one, two and so forth.

The Houses of Sin were originally created by the Seven Princes of Hell to give their worshippers a place to congregate, thereby building a massive power base to perpetuate their sin… lust, gluttony, greed, sloth, wrath, envy, and pride. Now, most demons are born into their houses.

Human philosophers, theologians, and historians like to attribute the Seven Princes of Hell to the angels who rebelled against Heaven. But this is pure propaganda handed down from above. I should know, I was there. The princes, vanquished by angels during Satan's rebellion, existed long before angels were created. Their legacy continues to exist thousands of years later.

Lord Gula places an artifact on the table in front of my throne. It must be an ownership dispute. Typically, these types of cases bore the fuck out of me, but when I look closely at the object, a glimmer of interest sparks in me.

On a bed of black velvet, a golden torque gleams in the candlelight cascading down from the chandelier above. I look for a magical aura, but there's nothing to indicate it's anything but what it seems—a piece of jewelry made of hammered gold and twisted into an arc. Designed to wrap around the neck, they were common among noble men and women, who wore them to proclaim their rank and status, or by warriors, who considered them good luck charms.

This particular torque has an engraved Celtic spiral on each end, indicating its provenance and age. As a historical piece alone, it's magnificent, the ancient symbol indicating its age to be sometime around the tenth century BCE. To a human, that would generate awe, but Underworld possesses artifacts much older than this piece.

My interest wanes.

The two lords drone on and on, each one methodically presenting their case with the hope of swaying my opinion, neither realizing they lost my attention within the first five minutes.

I sigh.

At the sound, the one in front of me stutters to a halt.

I wave a hand for him to carry on.

Restless, my eyes drift around the packed room. Demons, hellhounds, sirens, and other Underworld citizens dressed in all manner of clothing from different eras, including the modern one, fill the hall, half of them waiting to present their own case, while the other half are simply spectators here for the show.

Or for me, I concede, meeting the eyes of a brunette in a purple silk dress. Her luscious breasts are thrust in my direction, and a small smile plays on her pouty lips. She confidently winks, then slowly raises one eyebrow, a silent, sensual invitation. For the briefest of seconds, I consider her offer. A nymph is the perfect companion to spend a few pleasurable hours with, but my body refuses to twitch in response.

The crowd cheers, and I turn my attention back to the demons in front of me. The one speaking smiles broadly at the crowd in the back before addressing the stern-faced group sitting on my right. The council. Another one of my great ideas.

I glance over at them. Or not.

Most of the council members are pompous bastards, only interested in promoting the agendas of Underworld's elite. Right now, they're vigorously nodding in agreement to the points being made by the demon speaking in front of me. It almost reads as if they're giving him their approval, something that immediately makes me suspicious. Their greedy eyes are locked on the torque.

I'd been quick to dismiss it earlier, but the council isn't swayed by insignificance, and two lords wouldn't be arguing over the artifact's ownership if it weren't valuable.

Returning my attention to the torque, I narrow my eyes to study it further. Faint marks glimmer in the light. It could be scratches, but my intuition says it's not, and I raise my hand to bring the object closer.

The demon's eyes widen, and he steps forward to object, but it's too late.

The second the torque connects with my hand, my power rumbles, and spikes, multiplying and increasing tenfold, expanding rapidly inside me until it fills every square inch. My jaw locks and my muscles strain to keep it under my control. Tremors shake my body. It's one thing to gain power over time, but quite another to exponentially gain it in the span of seconds.

Unused to this much higher level, I pull on the strength of my people to help me contain it. My body flexes as I stand. The wings in my back pop out, spanning the width of the hall, and the crowd stumbles back in fear. Using the tremendous power and strength I've acquired over the years, I do everything I can, but it cannot be physically contained.

The excess power rips through my magical barriers, shredding them like tissue, until it's free. It collects into a shimmering, semi-transparent cloud near the ceiling. Shifting first one way, then the other, it suddenly rolls out like a tsunami and crashes against the obsidian walls of the hall. The stone contracts and expands, cracking under the immense pressure. The crowd screams in fear, but the spelled walls hold, containing the force.

Warily, I eye the cloud, wondering how to disperse it, when it suddenly moves again.

The power, seemingly sentient in nature, slithers along the surface of the walls and ceiling, sliding into every crack and crevice as it actively searches for a way out. When it finds nothing, it shoves away from the walls and heads toward the back of the hall. Along the way, the shimmering cloud briefly touches the denizens of Hell, and they moan with pleasure from the extra boost of power.

Suddenly, the double doors at the back of the hall fly open, and the power shoots into the Underworld.

Fuck me.

Thunderous, I look down at the torque and immediately manufacture a glove to shield myself from it.

An amplifier with the ability to increase any power, no matter how great.

Who could create such a weapon?

Equal parts pissed off and intrigued, I bring it closer to examine the markings I noticed earlier. They're definitely not scratches. I inhale sharply. There's a spell engraved between the lines of the spiral, but that's not the most interesting part. The words are written in a language, called Viridian, that was spoken before the Great Flood, but lost to history when everyone perished.

The only ones who speak it now are the ones who spoke it then—the angels and other ancients like us. Viridian was the first language we learned. Its true origin is unknown, but the complex language was often used to create powerful spells.

Yet here it is on a human piece created in tenth century BCE. I rub the tip of my glove across the words. It's been so long since I've seen or spoken the language. Not since *that* day. I shake my head and push the thought away before reading the words.

I frown. The spell doesn't make sense. It calls for the blood to rise up, not magic.

Focusing on the two lords in front of me, I note the fear on their faces.

They should be afraid. The fallout from power of that magnitude on the loose in the Underworld will be catastrophic if I don't find it quickly. It pisses me off that they brought such a volatile artifact into my palace without warning.

My wrath wraps around them, squeezing tightly, and I lean forward. "My patience left the palace along with my power." My words drop softly into the quiet room. I raise a hand when one of the demons starts to speak. "I'll ask the questions. You'll give me succinct answers. If you state anything but the facts, I'll eliminate you and keep the object for myself. Got it?"

Swallowing hard, they both nod.

I loosen the invisible hold on them. "Where did you get it?"

The Lord of Gluttony steps forward. "The Duke of Malevolentia's estate sale. It was in a trunk."

The court inhales a collective breath at the name. Level one demons rarely perish, especially dukes, but treason will not be tolerated.

Disbelief rings in my voice. "You bought a trunk from the estate sale, and it contained this artifact?" What are the fucking odds?

Lord Envidia, aka Envy, raises a shaking finger. "We bought the entire estate, your Majesty."

The court erupts into whispers while I silently whistle at the fortune they must have dropped to procure Malevolentia's estate.

The duke had been around since the beginning of time. Literally. Who knows what the wily bastard had in his possession? Something I should have foreseen when I ended his existence. An oversight that requires immediate correction.

With a single raised finger, the general behind me, steps forward, listens to my orders, then dips his chin and disappears to carry them out.

Ahem. "Given the nature of your purchase, I want a complete inventory list in my hand tomorrow. Understood?" The flinch in response to my order immediately confirms the treasures they've already discovered must also be of significant importance. Wealth means nothing to them. Power is the only commerce of value.

This is a bigger problem than I expected.

Cormal, the uncrowned king of the criminal underworld—or knowing his ambition, the king of criminals everywhere—appears with the general on my left. The crowd shuffles uneasily when they see the dark-haired man. Fear typically reserved for only the top of the food chain flashes across their faces. It's warranted. The power he's amassed is impressive and terrifying... and none of it was his in the beginning. He accumulated it from ancient and unnatural sources, and let's just say his methods were unconventional.

I smile. He's perfect for this task. Not only does he have the power to retain possession of the object, but he runs Underworld's black market. It will be easy for him to broker deals for the use of the torque.

The general bows, then disappears to follow my other order.

Cormal quickly assesses the situation in front of him. When his eyes spot the object, they flicker, not with greed, but knowledge and a glimmer of emotion.

Interesting.

I turn to contemplate the two lords in front of me, then focus solely on Envy. "Why do you want the artifact?"

He looks at the crowd and grimaces. "I want to give it to my daughter's new husband." With a shrug, he continues. "Her mate is a level four lust demon."

The court titters at his confession.

Angry at their ridicule, he flicks power at the worst offenders, but it dissipates as quickly as it leaves his hand. He swivels to confront his friend but finds his knees cracking against the hard floor before he utters a single word. His hiss of pain is music to my ears.

"Nobody uses power in my court without my permission," I remind him.

Turning to Lord Gula, or Gluttony, I repeat the question. "Why do you want the artifact?"

"To gain more power," he answers simply.

An expected response. The issue? Gluttony demons can't stop. It's not in their nature.

They purchased the estate together and, therefore, are joint owners of the piece. But when they brought it into my court and asked me to assign ownership, they relinquished their rights to me. I'm sure they intended ownership to go to one of them, but unfortunately, that won't be happening.

I slide a glance to Cormal, who steps to my side.

Realization hits the Gluttony first, and he angrily steps forward, only to hit the ground with his knees less than a second later.

"Not one word. I don't have time to listen to your protests, because I have to hunt down the power unleashed in my court today before it does any damage." My voice booms, wrath and power coating every word, reminding them of their offense. And who they offended.

I take a deep breath, then continue speaking in a controlled voice. "For finding this artifact, I'm going to reward you both by giving you exactly what you want."

Their eyes dart to me with a look of confusion.

I gesture to my left. "You will lease the artifact to Cormal for an indefinite period. In exchange, you will have access to it for the reason you stated. After that first use, you will continue to have access, but Cormal will extract payment."

Both demons look ill at the thought of negotiating with Cormal in the future, but they nod in agreement.

I smile in return. "For the aggravation you have caused me, and the disruption to my court, Cormal will also get to use the object for free..." I narrow my eyes at Cormal. Allowing him to use the object also eliminates any debt I would owe to Cormal for doing me this "favor." "One time. Agreed?"

Amusement sparks in Cormal's bright blue eyes along with anticipation. "Agreed."

Done with the whole charade, I raise my voice and gesture to the room. "Excellent. Now get out. Everyone except Cormal. Immediately." A wall of power pushes the demons and the crowd toward the double doors in the back.

My head swivels to the right. The council stares back at me, their eyes heavy with speculation, but none of them move toward the exit.

Irritated at the assumption that they are exempt from my order to leave, I contemplate disbanding the council, but a sliver of patience cautions me against any rash moves right now. Instead, I wave a hand and deliver them outside the gates of the palace.

I'll keep them for now, but their days are numbered.

Once everyone is gone, I turn toward Cormal. "Tell me what you know."

<u>LUCIFER</u>

Cormal arches an eyebrow but says nothing.

Stalking toward him, I show him the true extent of my anger. "I don't have any patience for your games. This torque amplified my power. I contained some of it, but a significant fucking amount escaped. It's out there. Wreaking havoc. In my kingdom."

A flash of surprise and something else shows on his face, but it's quickly gone.

He shoves his hands in the pockets of his pants. "It's not, actually. The torque is only an amplifier, a tool to generate more power. Nothing more or less." Knowledge simmers in his eyes. "The power is waiting for you to call upon it. It comes from you, and therefore, cannot be used by anyone else. Some may get a small boost from it, but it wears off quickly."

I study him for a solid minute to assess any potential

agenda. The tension slowly eases from my shoulders. "You have knowledge of this torque, haven't you?"

He dips his chin. "Yes."

I smirk at his reticence. "Have you used it in the past?"

"Yes," he admits gruffly, his voice strained with irritation.

"Did you know the Duke of Malevolentia had possession of the artifact?"

Anger sparks in the depths of his blue eyes. "No." Hands clenched, he paces back and forth. "And before you ask, yes. I owned it before him. It's mine. A... gift given to me long ago. But it was stolen around a thousand years ago. I always suspected him, but none of my spies could ever find a hint of its location." He jams his fists on his sides.

Another piece to the puzzle. "Well, he's gone, and it's back in your possession," I state firmly, watching him nod in satisfaction. "What's the history of its origin?"

He stops pacing and swivels to look at me. "A Celtic warrior was given the piece in 1020 BCE as a reward for his bravery."

The answer fits the design of the piece, but not the language of the spell on its surface. "Was he human?"

"Yes," Cormal replies shortly.

"What does the torque do to humans?"

He shrugs.

"The torque increases power. Humans have no power," I state, watching him closely. His brows lower and jaw clenches. "Or I should say, the common human has no magical power. Witches acquired magic during that timeframe, but their spells and magic were simple."

He runs a hand through his hair, an air of frustration surrounding him.

"There is one group of humans who had access to magic and power before the witches... Druids," I say, watching him stiffen. "In fact, I seem to recall they appeared around ninth or tenth century BCE. Was the warrior a Druid?"

He shrugs.

Power swells along with my irritation, and the air becomes charged. Maybe a small display will get me the answers I need.

Reading my intent, he raises a hand. "The warrior was the first Druid. The torque was given to him."

"By whom?"

Uncomfortable with revealing so much information, he runs a hand down his face. "History is vague and inconsistent on this account. Some sources say it was an angel from heaven, others say the power came from the divine, and yet, others report the piece was found buried in the ground. Nothing indicates which one was the truth. Maybe your library will offer more answers."

A master of misdirection, I weigh his words, unsure whether to believe him or not.

He smirks. "It's true. Most of the information has been lost or destroyed, so the facts are scarce. Even among the Druids." He pauses when I frown. "If you recall, I requested access to your library several times but was denied. It's one of the oldest in existence and likely your best source of information."

My library is one of my most treasured possessions. Built by my predecessor, and extensively added to by me, it houses the best collection of ancient scrolls, books, and artifacts across the supernatural worlds. The only other library that comes close to competing is the one built by the Dark Fae King.

I don't know how much of the Druid history was documented and collected, but if there's anything, I'll find it.

I've never given a thought to how Druids might have acquired power. At the time, it seemed natural, like an evolution of species, but over the years, their power lessened, and others, including myself, easily dismissed them.

Some of what I thought must have shown on my face because Cormal laughs derisively. "Masters of their own demise. Unwilling to share power with other humans, they isolated themselves, only marrying and reproducing with other Druids. Today, they're almost extinct." He exhales slowly, his hooded eyes concealing his thoughts. "If you discover the truth, let me know. I'm sure the few remaining Druids would like to know their heritage."

Druids are known for their secrecy. Guess he hasn't lost that trait. Probably the foundational cornerstone of his criminal empire. Looking at Cormal, I realize he's worried. "You forget how long I've existed. I know more than you can possibly imagine but care little for it. Your past is your own. Besides, you're a long way from your roots now, aren't you?" I smirk, referring to his immortal status.

He nods sharply, the only sign of gratitude he'll extend.

I rub my chin. "Tell me. What language did the Druids speak?"

He arches an eyebrow in response. "A variety of languages, depending on their origins, but the common one was Gaelic. They didn't speak Viridian."

He knows the language of the spell. That actually doesn't surprise me. Cormal's thirst for knowledge is an extension of his thirst for power.

"I'll have the scribes pull our resources. In the meantime, I know the torque will be in good hands," I say, walking back over to sit on the throne. "And just to make sure we're on the same page, I expect this to be the most expensive service you offer. Agreed?" When he reluctantly nods, I continue. "The last thing we need are Underworld citizens running around with copious amounts of stupidity and power."

He waves a hand. "I'll send over the spell and associated tools for calling the power. Unfortunately, the power is not a pool you can draw from bit by bit. It's a one and done explosive hit. There is no time limit, though. You can call it a millennium from now, and it will answer."

My lips firm. I wonder if that's how he gained enough power to change his mortality.

With an extremely shallow bow, he asks, "Is that all, Your Majesty?"

"For now," I reply. "Once I have the inventory list, I'll let you know if I need your assistance for anything else."

He stares at me for several seconds. "Thank you." Then disappears.

My teeth slam together to prevent a stream of curses from spilling out. Except for a select few, nobody should be able to enter or leave my palace at will. Certainly not Cormal. I sigh. I don't know why I'm surprised.

During a recent battle with the light Fae, Cormal supplied critical insider knowledge of guard rotations and palace floor plans for the attack. It stunned most of the rulers in the room, including myself. When I returned, I upgraded my entire system with wards and spells. Apparently, it wasn't enough. Somebody's head is going to roll.

A chuckle escapes.

He's too smart to reveal his access unless it suits him. Cormal's either happy to have the artifact back in his possession, or it's a distraction. Maybe both, knowing him. He lives and breathes strategy. Short plays, the long game, you name it. With this "favor", he won't owe me for the torque.

I sigh. It's still another task to add to the long list on my desk.

With a wave of my hand, I summon a scholar. "Pull everything we have on Druids. From their origin to the present. I want to know it all. Source all libraries, not just mine."

Surprise appears on his normally placid face. "As you wish, Sire. Anything else?"

A thought occurs to me. "Have someone examine all of the artifacts in our inventory. I want to know if any of them have spells written in Viridian."

"I'll get a team on it right away," he says with a deep bow.

"Thank you. That will be all," I tell him.

The general returns a few minutes later. Tall and lean, with blue hair and the lightest green eyes, most mistake him for a scholar or a merchant, not the lead general in the Underworld army and my third-in-command. It's served him well over the years. A vicious fighter, he's impossibly fast and always strikes with the intent to kill.

"It's done. All the other estates have been destroyed, and the contents moved to your warehouses."

"Thank you, Ishkova," I reply with satisfaction before dismissing him.

My previous second-in-command, Alain, along with the Duke of Malevolentia, tried to lead a coup against me last year. It didn't end well for them or their followers. Treason is not tolerated. I've already lost one kingdom because of betrayal. I won't lose another.

My lips press together. I'd intended to disperse the estates to my most loyal supporters, but the auction and today's events changed everything. To the victor go the spoils. I snort.

THREE

LUCIFER

The current second-in-command, the normally unflappable Commander Vargas, paces back and forth in front of my desk. Heavy sighs and the occasional unintelligible, but clearly dissatisfied, murmur spills into the air, conveying his frustration with the status quo. My hand clenches with the need to remove him from my sight, but guilt stops my action. After all, my blood is the reason he's in this predicament.

When I exchanged blood with Vargas to ensure his loyalty, I never realized how differently demon blood would react to mine. Angels have been exchanging blood with humans from the time of their creation in order to create the guardian bond. Only the angels felt the bond, and when the human died, the bond died too.

Exchanging blood with a demon created a similar bond—

but one that went beyond its established boundaries. My genetic makeup altered my bond with Vargas in an unforeseeable way. I'm eternal, not immortal. When Vargas died in battle, his physical body turned to dust, but his spirit was given a choice: life or death. Since his mate is Fae and still very much alive, he chose to embrace life. Unfortunately, it means he has to find a new body to inhabit. Something that is clearly proving hard for him to do.

I eye the almost translucent image in front of me. Right now, his spirit retains the physical attributes from his old body, even wearing the same black leathers and t-shirt. As a Chaos demon, he was unusually tall and stacked with muscle, which typically indicates Lesser Demon blood and an ugly fucking mug. Vargas somehow won the genetic lottery with a strong jaw, dark hair and eyes, and enough swagger to win his equally beautiful mate. He used to say his darkness only allowed Solandis to shine all the brighter.

"Vargas," I state softly, pausing until I have his full attention.

He stiffens at the sound of my voice, having clearly forgotten my presence, then jerkily turns to face me.

"I'm guessing this one didn't work either?"

With a resigned shrug and a negative shake of his head, he fills me in on his latest attempt to find a new body. "Powerful, but ugly. Solandis would never glance twice at the bastard. I don't understand why it's so hard to find a dead demon who's tall, good-looking, magically powerful, a good fighter, and swings a decent size cock. I can find one, maybe two traits on a good day, but none of them comes close to fitting my needs. I'm running out of time. Solandis is set to go to the light Fae Court with Meri soon. She's going to need protection from those golden aristocratic pansies." His translucent image shudders at the thought of Solandis alone with the Fae.

Raising an eyebrow, I remind him, "She's the Princess of the Light Fae with considerable powers of her own, and she grew up in that environment. I'm sure she's well versed in the machinations and politics of the court."

His lips compress, but he dips his chin in a respectful nod of semi-agreement. "She's my life, my reason for everything. My mate. Ours isn't a romantic, pretty love. It's raw and powerful. Fire and ice. A demon and a Fae, an impossibility, and yet the fates decreed us joined. In this world of lost souls and destruction, I need her light to balance the darkness in me. It's brutal living without her."

While he agrees with my logic, Solandis is his mate, and he's almost feral when it comes to her. Having loved once, I use the memories to dredge up some patience.

"I—"

A prickling awareness, unlike any other, invades my body. Time grinds to halt for the briefest of moments, then resumes in a silent roar of protest. My mind sorts through the possibilities, knowing there is only one answer.

This is the third time I've felt this sensation over the last two days. Twice I ignored it, but this one was significantly stronger. This death has more power.

The aether beckons, whispering of answers. I resist for a second, but time is of the essence, so I slip into the stream. Images flash by without rhyme or reason. The past, present, and future bound together with silvery strands, with no indication of when or where. Shadows wrap around me like old friends. Forcing myself to relax, I push the wordless request from my mind into their darkness.

Layers of grey nothingness undulate in front of me. The images speed up until they're nothing but a blur, then stop. One image floats in front of me. The answer to my request.

The scene appears to be an alley from the world above.

Brick rises high on each side and in the back. Dumpsters line one wall. Dirt and grime cover every surface. I frown. Everything looks normal except for the body lying dead on the pavement. The image turns in response to my request, but no matter where I look, the body remains pristine. There isn't a single mark to indicate General Balith's cause of death. I need more info.

Bracing myself, I cast a new request into the shadows surrounding me. They writhe in excitement, sliding across my body, searching for payment. A hundred cuts. Blood drips. The shadows consume my power.

"Enough," I boom, closing off their supply. "Show me."

Images flow backward in time, then stop.

Tall, ethereally beautiful, an angel and warrior all the same—General Balith—strolls down the sidewalk, bright blue eyes focused on the woman in front of him. An aura of menace and danger surround him. A predator stalking his prey, he waits for the best moment to strike.

Tall and lithe, with gorgeous dark red hair, the woman strides quickly down the street in front of him. She nervously glances behind her in an attempt to discern the location of her stalker, but her green eyes skip over him as if he's invisible. Her pace picks up. She may not know where her stalker is, but she feels his presence.

The entrance to an alley provides him with the perfect opportunity. He strikes, shoving her into the dark interior. White wings snap open until they're brushing the brick sides of the surrounding buildings, completely cutting off any chance of her escape.

Golden light arcs into the night and fills the alley, blinding and bright.

She raises her arm to shield her eyes against the light.

Gripping his sword, he raises his to strike her down but comes to an abrupt stop at the pinnacle. The perfectly symmetrical face full of arrogant confidence suddenly changes to confusion, then astonishment, before morphing into disbelief.

The hand holding the sword falls limply to his side, and the golden light withdraws. His body folds, like a lifeless puppet, to the ground. Eyes bright with life dull and their glow fades. The once-magnificent warrior met the death he sought to deliver to another.

The aether tugs at me, offering to show me more, paving an enticing path of secrets and visions, but it's a trap. If you stay too long, the way out closes. With careful shifts, I slip through a gap, extricating myself from the strands of knowledge.

Vargas' relief is almost tangible when my presence fully returns to the Underworld and my office. He's unable to tap into the aether and hates the risk I take when I use it.

My body sways.

Vargas curses, his current predicament preventing him from physically helping me.

I raise a hand. "Stop. I'm fine. My power is only temporarily drained. A few minutes in this world will restore me." Even now, I feel tendrils of power, full of fresh sin and free will, slithering through the halls of my palace making their way to me. My drained reserves fill rapidly.

Normally, I utilize other methods to obtain critical pieces of information, but the event warranted the risk.

"What happened?" Vargas

"An angel died."

<u>LUCIFER</u>

Vargas' eyes gleam with satisfaction and pleasure as if he was personally responsible for the death of his enemy. "Anybody I know? Do we get to take the credit?"

"General Balith," I murmur absentmindedly, trying to sift through the images from the vision.

"If it's not someone from the Underworld, we should immediately recruit them," he interjects, eyebrows raised in shock. "Balith was ancient, a real O.G. One of the best. Who managed to get the jump on him?"

My brows furrow. "I'm not sure. One minute he was standing in front of a human, and the next he was lying on the ground. Dead. Not a mark on him."

Vargas' face fills with outrage. The thought of a human

taking out someone so powerful is an anathema to him, even if it is an angel and his arch nemesis. "A human? I don't believe it. Are you sure?"

I flick him a dark look.

"Right," he states, shaking his head vigorously. "Sorry. I'm sure you know." Translucent fingers tap a rhythm on his chin. "Could it have been a witch? Nobody knew about Arden. Maybe there's another witch out there with significant power."

A smile graces my lips at the thought of Arden, Vargas' ward—although he thinks of her as his daughter. She's also bonded to my son, the First Vampire, Daire, and part of my family. As far as we know, Arden is the most powerful witch alive.

"It's a possibility; although, witches aren't the only humans with magic. Druids are human," I remind him absent-mindedly.

He snorts. "It's been a long time since Druids had significant power. I doubt they could kill an angel today."

My mind calculates the odds of a human, without power, killing an angel, and it's so astronomical, it's ludicrous.

Then, who? And not just one, but three. "Balith isn't the only angel to die recently. Two others have also met their end. Admittedly, he was the most powerful one of the three, which is why this concerns me."

Vargas' narrows his eyes. "Could another angel have taken them out? For power or position?"

"A possibility, but highly unlikely. Only three... two archangels possess the ability to kill another angel. Mercy and Michael," I reply, contemplating the odds. Technically, I'm not an archangel anymore.

I silently snort. The odds are higher than a human without power. Getting cast out of the kingdom of Heaven and losing everything is a pretty powerful deterrent. I doubt anybody, much less Mercy or Michael, would be stupid enough to follow in my footsteps.

"Besides, the aether showed me..." My voice trails off. His death. That's it. Not *how* he died. Another thought occurs based on recent events. "Him facing off with a human and dying. Besides their own magic, they could have used a magical artifact, protection spell, or perhaps called upon a powerful protector. All are possibilities. We need more intel."

Vargas nods in agreement.

I skim his translucent body. "Can anyone else see you?"

He thinks about it for a minute. "I don't think so. I've been to The Abbey several times to see Solandis and Arden, but they can't see or hear me." A sad smile graces his lips. "Arden's mates and the staff are often nearby, but none seem to know I'm there." He pauses. "Although, I think Valerian's dragon senses something because he'll glance around, but the feeling isn't enough to put him in defensive mode."

"Good," I reply with a nod of satisfaction. The Abbey is full of supernaturals from various races and the perfect testing ground. "Your inability to find a suitable body gives us a huge advantage. The angels will be all over the crime scene. Observe them. Find out what they know."

He laughs and rubs his hands together. "Brilliant. They can't see or hear me. This is going to be fun."

I chuckle. "Even if they know you're there, they can't kill you because you're already dead. But make sure you get the intel before you start fucking with them, got it?"

He nods his agreement.

"Before you go on this mission, I need you to do something for me. Lord Envidia and Lord Gula failed to deliver their inventory list. The deadline passed yesterday. I want you to bring them to me, so we can discuss the consequences of their actions," I snap, my voice filled with fury.

Vargas whistles, then disappears.

Minutes later, Envy falls to the floor in front of my desk.

Bewildered, he looks around, unsure of where he is until his gaze finds mine. Panic flashes across his face, and he scrambles up. Brushing off his pants and straightening his jacket, he opens his mouth to speak, but I hold up a finger and he slams it shut.

Vargas appears with the Gluttony and drops him to the floor beside Envy.

The lord scrambles up, power sparking in his hands, quickly spinning in an attempt to find his enemy.

Vargas laughs.

My lips twitch. "Thank you, Vargas."

Envy blanches at my words. "Commander Vargas?"

Vargas strikes terror in every Underworld citizen. His talent for fighting and battle is unmatched by anyone. A true warrior. As a Chaoticus, or Chaos demon, he holds the rank of High Demon, equivalent to a duke from the House of Sin, but he rarely uses the title, preferring instead to focus on his military rank. At one time, he was my Executioner, the individual I sent out to eliminate my enemies. His success rate cemented his fierce reputation.

Gluttony swivels to search for Vargas, but finding the room empty, he turns to face me. Power flickers in his hands, but instead of extinguishing it, the ball grows astronomically larger.

Understanding dawns. "Ah, I guess you've already been to visit Cormal and used the torque?" I stand up and lean over my desk until I'm inches from him. "How does it feel to have all that power? Pretty good, huh?"

Envy takes a few steps away from his friend.

I wave a hand, freezing him in place.

"I'll get to you in a minute, Envy. Excuse me, Lord Envidia,"

I assure him. "Gluttony's little show of power has all my attention right now."

Gluttony glares at me for calling him by his sin. "This is just the barest hint of the power I have access to now. Did you know that the torque exponentially increases the amount of power each time you use it? The first time, it increases your power tenfold, but the next time, it doubles. And again, the third time."

A tinge of sadness hits me. I really like Cormal. Too bad I'm going to have to kill him.

"Three draws, huh?" I ask, as if I'm impressed.

A broad smile appears. "I'm the most powerful demon in Underworld now."

I pull back a little, and his confidence grows. "The first one was free. What did the other two cost you?"

His smile dims. "My daughter and half my wealth. But it was absolutely worth it. And when I'm done here, I'm going to pay a little visit to Cormal to get my money back."

Cold rage rises in me. The fact that he gave up his daughter in exchange for power when I would give up all my power for one more day with mine infuriates me. I want to shred him to pieces, but first, I need him to pull all the power he gained from the torque, so I chuckle.

"What's so funny?" He snarls.

"Cormal has more power at his disposal than you could ever acquire from the torque. He's accumulated it over several lifetimes. Killing you would be no more effort than swatting a fly," I taunt, deliberately coming around to sit on the corner of my desk directly in front of him.

He takes a half a step back and pulls more power from the air. His hands start to shake, and his eyes turn red from the effort it takes to control the increased level.

I lift an unconcerned shoulder. "Maybe you should apologize and beg for my forgiveness now. I might extend some leniency." Or not. I let him see the amusement in my face.

One more.

Enraged, he pulls more power into himself. The shake in his hands cascades over his entire body until he suddenly morphs into his demon form—a purple, hairless demon with a large physique. Jagged teeth slam together, and the tendons in his neck pop out while he tries to wrangle the power under his control. After a few minutes of intense struggle, he finally manages it.

His head swivels slowly to his friend, Envy. "The torque is mine, do you understand? Mine!" He waits for him to respond, but nothing comes out of his mouth.

Oops, I forgot to unfreeze him.

Envy darts a frantic glance toward me, but I simply smile.

When Envy turns to face Gluttony again, he flashes a sad smile. A line of red appears across his throat moments before his head falls to the floor.

Who knew Envy would fall before Gluttony?

Vargas snarls and glares at me, frustration bleeding from every line on his face. His hands twitch, eager to step into the fight.

I tilt my head and raise an eyebrow.

As if I can't handle a demon lord, even one with this much power. Maybe Vargas needs a reminder of the power I wield.

"Your friend, huh? Such loyalty. And for what? This power trip? The torque has cost you everything. Your wealth, sanity, and your best friend," I state snarkily. One down, one to go. "And let's not forget, your daughter. You know, I might have been lenient if you hadn't traded your daughter."

Gluttony looks at me like I'm deranged. "Let's see, shall we?" He steps back and flings his power toward me.

Vargas steps between us in an attempt to shield me, but the power passes right through him.

I sigh and easily catch it. Flexing my fingers, I dig them into the very heart of glowing orb, absorbing the power bit by bit. "Not bad. Still, it doesn't come close to the power I held as an archangel, much less as the Ruler of the Underworld." I extinguish it. "Try again."

Bent over, he pushes his head up to look at me in shock. Lips blanched from the effort to contain the power open and close while he repeats the spell he spoke earlier. Lines appear between his brows.

I snap my fingers. "Did Cormal forget to tell you it was a one-time deal?" He rears back in disbelief. "Yes, the power can only be used once. You combined all three of your draws into one, didn't you? I guess it's my turn now."

He stumbles back, trying to get away from me, but Vargas grabs him from behind and holds him in place. Red eyes widen, and his head whips back and forth, trying to figure out why he can't escape.

"This is going to hurt like... Hell," I state, a brutal smile on my face. Not at the pun, but at the pleasure I'm going to get from taking everything he has left. Every drop of power. And his demon.

With an ancient spell written by the Devil, the last ruler of the Underworld, my lips form the words to extract his demon. Six times I repeat the spell. When the words die, his demon appears between us. It glowers at the Gluttony for a brief second, then disappears, back to the hellfire of its birth.

The remaining embers of Gluttony's powers are absorbed by mine.

The lord clutches his chest, tears streaming down his face. "What did you do?"

"You're human. Sucks, doesn't it? But don't worry. I'm not

going to kill you. Death would be too easy. Instead, I'm going to send you into the dregs of the Underworld. It shouldn't take long for someone to find you," I explain, watching with satisfaction as understanding and terror dawns on his face. A human amidst the worst this world has to offer.

I glance at Vargas, who eyes me with respect and a glint of satisfaction.

"Where do you want me to drop him?"

"The Slag," I reply, referring to a part of the city where Lesser Demons congregate to trade their unscrupulous services to Higher Demons for scraps of power.

A grimace flashes across Vargas' face. "Appropriate, but I hate that place."

My shoulder lifts in reply. "I'll send you the address for the other matter we discussed via our private channel." Telepathy. It's a rare trait, and one we didn't have before the bond, but it has come in handy numerous times, especially with his less than corporeal body.

I gesture to Envy's body on the floor to see if Vargas wants it for his own. "What about this one?"

Vargas' lip curls. "No balls." He disappears.

FIVE

LUCIFER

Fire cascades like a river down the sides of two, six-story black obsidian pillars. The stone gate guarding the entrance into the Underworld Market. Spells embodied on their surface during creation send a call to those outside its walls. With barely a thought, visitors find themselves eager to enter and spend their gold.

Full of wonder and danger, Underworld Market offers goods and services from across the worlds. If a customer wishes for an item, a stall appears ready to sell them what they need. Like markets since the beginning of time, it's a riot of color, rich smells, and a cacophony of sound, reminiscent of life itself.

Vendors hawk their wares, and customers haggle for the best prices. Spices, perfumes, and food fill the air, all designed to enhance the senses and attract customers. The main thoroughfare is packed with various races, young and old, friends and strangers. Petty thieves slip in and out of the crowd, relieving the unsuspecting of the coins and valuables in their pockets.

Unwilling to announce my presence to the masses, I'd dressed accordingly. In dark jeans and a hoodie, I slip quietly through the bodies. Normally my size would draw the eye, but in the Underworld, there are plenty of species much taller and more muscular than me. For the most part, the crowd ignores me. Several vendors eye me suspiciously, but their eyes dart away when they realize it's their ruler walking by.

A hand slips inside my coat pocket. As it slides away, I grab it. Rough leather rubs coarsely against my fingers. Common skin amongst most demons, but the small bones tell me it's likely a youngling or a female. Turning to face the thief, I watch their black eyes widen in fear. But only for a second.

A mutinous expression appears on the young demon's face, and he sneers in my direction. "Does *he* know you're here?"

Surprised at the audacity of such a young demon, I lightly cuff his ear. "Is that how you speak to your ruler? Do you not value your life?"

He shrugs nonchalantly. "Cormal takes care of his own. He's the one who gives me work and access to food and shelter. What have you ever done for me? If you want to take my life, go ahead. You won't get much power or satisfaction from my death." Eyes turned from black to dark red peer up at me with only a hint of fear in them.

Startled to hear the combination of vitriol and resignation in his voice, I hold out my hand. "Give me what you stole and take me to him."

His eyes meet mine, trying to read my intentions, but I simply stare him down. With a sigh, he hands me back my gold watch and the coins from my pocket.

I chuckle when I see the watch. Must be getting slower in my old age.

For some reason, my laugh generates the fear I originally expected. With a swallow, he jerks his head to the back of a nearby stall. "Follow me."

The vendor bows deeply as we go by, his face full of speculation and fear. Right before we pass through the curtain, I see him signal to another demon nearby who takes off running.

I try to think of my last visit here but can't recall, which tells me it's been way too long. It's obvious the people feel indebted and loyal to Cormal. Not just the criminals he rules or the customers he serves, but the people whose livelihood depends on the market. It's humbling to realize he provides for these people. An unspoken ruler.

Maybe I've been paying way too much time tending to the upper classes, settling disputes, pacifying council members, and creating alliances to guarantee their loyalty and keep the wars at a minimum. Stabilizing the top has paid off. With less internal conflict and wars, everyone has prospered. Yet, the wealth doesn't seem to have trickled down to everyone.

The boy exits the stall into another area filled with vendors and booths. The black market. Like all illegal markets, this one is hidden from the common crowd. Dark and full of shadows, these stalls offer the forbidden. Precious and rare merchandise locked in safes and disguised by magic. Vendors don't hawk their goods and services here. They wait like predators for customers to whisper requests in their ears.

The quality and quantity available are astounding. Need a bottle of hellfire? Or the voice of a siren? It's available for the right price. But you better have deep pockets. It will cost you. Gold, jewels, a body part, a rare artifact, magic, or a deed so dark your soul won't recover. All payment options are on the table.

Beyond the black market lie two more sections, the brothels and Cormal's criminal headquarters. My skin prickles from all the eyes watching us walk farther into this den of sin and services.

Unlike other parts of the world, the brothels here are held to Cormal's immaculate standards. Many apply, but only the best is hired. Best doesn't necessarily mean the most beautiful, although there is plenty of beauty here. Unique is prized higher than looks. Cormal is their boss, not their pimp. The talent is paid well and protected from those who think to harm them without permission. It's lucrative employment and big business for Cormal. He ensures it remains that way.

Turning away from the brothels, the boy stops and points to a nondescript blue door. "Cormal is in there." He holds out his hand.

Cheeky little shit. But I owe him one. Not for the unnecessary tour. It's obvious he took me the long way around to give Cormal plenty of warning. I owe him for the reprimand he unknowingly gave me.

"Thank you for the tour," I tell him, holding several gold coins above his hand. "Although I would appreciate a more direct route next time." His eyes flicker with greed, and I drop them in his palm. "If you ever pick pocket me again, I'll cut out your eyes. Hard to take what you can't see. Be sure to pass the message along to your friends."

He straightens, giving me a hard, assessing stare, then lifts a shoulder. "I'll pass it along." The door opens, and he salutes the large, hulking male in the doorway before leaving.

Seven feet tall and stacked with muscles, the massive male is a warrior. An air of lethality rolls off him in waves, a warning to all. Instead of red demon eyes, his are gold with black slits, and they watch my every move with a predatory glint. Defined muscles top a large barrel chest. But it's the golden skin and flowing reddish-brown hair that gives me my first clue to his species.

My eyebrows rise.

A Nemean Lion. Almost extinct. Warriors by nature, their hide renders most weapons useless, but their fighting prowess is their true talent. Some of the best and most fearless warriors from our world. And extremely loyal to those they choose to protect. Another point in Cormal's favor.

Without a word, I step up to the door, but when I attempt to pass through, the lion grabs my arm. While I might have extended leniency to the boy, I have none for him.

I grab him by the throat, lift him up off the floor, and repeatedly slam his head against the doorframe until he lets go of me. When his head lolls to the side, I drop my arm, dragging his barely conscious body along behind me as I enter Cormal's den of iniquity.

Expecting moody and dark, I'm surprised to see light exploding everywhere. From high above, artificial sun floods the glass skylight and streams down into the space. It flows over the focal point, Cormal's desk, and into the lounge where I'm standing. It's an obscene use of magic, but an interesting insight into the mysterious man in front of me.

Cormal laughs when he sees the lion. "I told him not to mess with you, but he's too stubborn for his own good." Pride gleams in Cormal's eyes. He moves around his desk to greet me.

Angry at the whole charade, I lift the lion up and slam his head on a nearby table. "Assaulting the ruler of the Underworld is treason, and there's nothing I tolerate less." With a swivel of my wrist, I place my sword upon the lion's golden neck.

Cormal freezes. "If you want someone's head, take mine." His stance and worried expression tell me the offer is sincere.

"I plan to do that, too."

Worry changes to unease but with a calculated glint. "I assume this is about Lord Gula?" Cormal asks, his eyes flicking from me to the lion and back again. "The price he paid for the additional two jolts was astronomical, I assure you."

"Yes, I heard. His daughter and half his wealth," I snarl. "Where's the girl?" The anger I felt earlier returns with a vengeance, and the room pulses with my power.

Cormal rears back. "I gave her a choice. Return home or work for me. Smart girl decided to do both. She returned to the House of Sin, but as a spy working for me. Why?"

Damn. Another mark in his favor.

I ease up on the lion's neck, but not before deliberately marking him with my sigil. Permanently. The lines of the pentagram with a V in the center is a distinct pattern, and it fills the entire side of his neck. He roars loudly and clamps a hand over it.

"When you look in the mirror, my mark will stare back. Nothing you do will remove it. Both punishment and reminder, you'll think about your actions and my leniency every day," I state softly, releasing him.

Gratitude flashes across Cormal's face. "Thank you. Loyalty is his only fault, and the one I value the most. Orlo, leave us."

The lion heaves his massive body up and snarls at Cormal before prowling out of the room.

Cormal lifts a decanter and I shake my head. With a shrug, he pours himself a bourbon. "You set the terms for the torque, and I made sure a high price was extracted for each use. Where is Gluttony now? I assume he fucked up, and that's the reason you're here now."

"He thought he'd accumulated enough power to ignore my orders and attack me," I state softly, chuckling at the look of incredulity on Cormal's face. "If he's still alive, you'll find him in The Slag. Look for a desperate human."

The tumbler in Cormal's hand drops to the table with a thud. Bourbon splashes everywhere. "And the envy demon, Lord Envidia?"

I shrug. "Killed by his friend, Gluttony. I staked his body out on the House of Envy's lawn to serve as a warning."

"How did you do it?" he asks hoarsely, fingers tight around the glass in front of him.

"The Devil created a spell to separate a demon and his magic from its host, leaving only the original species behind. Gluttony was originally human. Now he is again," I explain with a nonchalant shrug, but my eyes sharply assess the impact of my words on the individual in front of me.

Cormal took the darkest of paths to gain his immortality. From human to... whatever he is now. That kind of sacrifice doesn't come without a powerful reason. Now, he has an astronomical amount of power and wealth at his fingertips and rules over his domain with a tight grip. Losing that immortality, and consequently, all he's gained, is his biggest fear. I'm not entirely sure why.

I continue with my subtle threat. "The Devil only used it on demons because he wanted to absorb their powers, but I assure you, it works on any species." My warning is subtle, but powerful.

Cormal exhales heavily. "What do you want from me?"

"I came to kill you, but for several reasons, I've changed my mind," I muse, surprising myself. "The torque is mine, but you may retain possession of it for now. It's off the market and unavailable to everyone else. Have you used your one shot?" When he shakes his head, I nod. "If you do, it returns immediately to me."

His chin lifts in anger, but he agrees to the condition. "Anything else?"

My hand lifts and I raise one finger. "I want you to come to the palace and share your knowledge of these people with me. It's obvious I need to change things, but I've been out of touch with the masses for a while. Underworld Market is a microcosm of the rest of the kingdom. The individuals here respect you and believe that you have their best interests at heart. Although for a price." I chuckle. "I'm giving you a chance to prove your loyalty and advocate for the people. All of them, not just your little fiefdom."

He eyes me suspiciously, a touch of disbelief in the twist of his mouth, but eventually he holds out his hand to shake mine. "I'll be there."

CHAPTER

SIX

<u>LUCIFER</u>

My study is an embodiment of the Underworld, dark and oppressive, full of secrets and hidden dangers. Old couches, chairs, and rugs constructed from the hides of enemies are scattered throughout the room, relics inherited from my predecessor and initially kept for continuity. Yet, somehow, never changed throughout the eons I've been Underworld's ruler.

A massive fireplace, large enough to roast a demon or two, roars continuously along one wall. A source of heat and light in the gloomy room. Shelves cover most of the other walls, but only one wall contains books. The rest are filled with trophies and not the kind given for achievements. Like everything else in the room, they serve a deadlier purpose. Another, albeit useful, gift from the previous ruler.

It's grim. My personal stamp is almost non-existent. I did

add a large window beside the desk to bring in a bit of light, but it's nothing like Cormal's magical sun, which I now have to replicate.

I run my hand across the top of the rich-looking surface of my desk. Built by my own two hands, the scarred acacia wood with its knicks and deep gouges reminds me of the time I spent with the humans, and the simple tables where we broke bread. A small tribute to the friends I met along my journey.

Time is a weird thing for those of us who live forever. Minutes and days don't even register. Years and centuries feel the same. It's only when centuries gather dust that the passage of years becomes noticeable.

Only once have I ever felt the passing of time.

Betrayed and cast out of Heaven, I roamed for nearly a century, every second ticking by with excruciating slowness.

Angels don't experience physicality in Heaven like humans do on Earth or like angels do when they can't return to sanctuary. Constantly bombarded by the unfamiliar, my body felt... everything. Hunger, exhaustion, extreme temperatures, pain, and so many others. My senses were bombarded day and night.

I struggled to function, much less find a place in my new world. The act of eating was disgusting. Finding clothing and shelter a nightly chore. But the worst was the weakness I felt in my bones. I hadn't been stripped of all my powers, but I was greatly diminished. A shadow of my former self. Weak.

Repentant and filled with sorrow, I continued to serve, hoping he would look down and see me, love me, save me. Every day, I rose and searched for people to help. His people. The ones he created and loved like his children.

But the world was a dark place. Full of fear and mistrust. Tension was high, especially surrounding the offspring of the fallen. The Nephilim.

Still, I trudged on, finding souls of light in the darkest of places. Those who still worshipped their creator. We bonded together, held candlelight vigils, and offered friendship and forgiveness to those who sinned against him.

But when I could no longer hear his voice, it extracted a powerful toll, both mentally and spiritually. Resentment and bitterness crept into my heart like thieves, stealing the peace and love I'd held onto for so long. At night, the two emotions would swarm and settle like locusts, covering me until I could barely breathe.

Inevitably, the sun would rise, and I'd claw my way back into the light to start a new day. Day in and day out, this continued, until the day the waters started to rise.

Wailing and cursing filled the air. Humans bolted to mountains and ships, but it was futile. The few supernaturals here, including the Nephilim, scrambled to find portals and bolt holes to other worlds.

Not many humans were brave enough to follow. Most of them stayed, believing the rain would stop. I knew better.

Before the creation of everything, the Earth was covered in water. I watched the land rise and waters recede. I watched the creation of light and life. I marveled at the wonder of it.

Its destruction broke something inside me. I watched the same waters rise and cover every bit of the Earth, extinguishing the lives of everyone I knew. Good and bad. Humans and Nephilim dead. Everyone but Noah, his family, and a few animals. Anger tore through me, ripping me apart at the devastation and the loss of those souls.

The Earth fell silent.

My tears ran with the rain the day I lost all hope of returning to grace. The desire to love and devote myself was gone, washed away with the sins of the world.

With nowhere to go, I came here to find a new life.

Underworld offered no refuge. An archangel in Hell is already a target, but I was Satan's killer. The angel they'd chosen to replace the Devil. With his death, they were stuck with a vicious ruler who cared little for his people. They instantly declared me "public enemy number one."

And with that title, the warrior in me returned with a roar. A savage, take-no-prisoners soldier, I relished every opponent who died by my hand. The feelings of weakness and uselessness I experienced while walking the Earth blew away like cobwebs caught by a stiff wind. The only thing I knew was pain and death. It was glorious.

And it paid off. Annihilating my enemies gave me status, wealth, and the comforts I'd been denied since I was cast out. But more than anything, I gained power.

When the Devil asked for my fealty, I spit in his face. I would never vow to uphold the tenets of evil, nor would I give my vow to those who did. It was a line I refused to cross. We battled in a legendary fight to the death. It took 665 days to vanquish my opponent. The next day, I crowned myself ruler of the Underworld.

Many thought they could take me. They were wrong. The crown clenched in my fist would never go to someone else. This world was mine.

The Underworld Army swore fealty to me, but at best, it was reluctantly upheld. Until Vargas, a respected general, stood in front of his men and loudly declared his loyalty. After him, others followed. Once I had followers, my power grew exponentially.

When I held a majority of the people's favor, I turned from fighting to ruling. Underworld was a mess. Internal squabbling and civil unrest plagued the kingdom. The different species were divided, all with separate rulers and kingdoms of their own, and I realized the only way we were going to collectively become powerful was by uniting into one kingdom. Mine.

I chuckle. Easier said than done. It took over a thousand years for us to conquer our enemies, both internal and external, and find peace. And another thousand to build us into the powerhouse we are today. Underworld. The one word guaranteed to make our enemies quake in fear.

Brutal, yet organized. Underworld operates on the tenets of free will, not as a proponent of evil or champion for the greater good, and for the most part, it thrives.

I grimace at the black leathery hides on the floor. But maybe it's time to make a few changes.

<u>LUCIFER</u>

The History of the Druids is resoundingly boring and astonishingly inaccurate. The leather tome in my hand offers little evidence of their power or magic. Instead, it's entirely focused on the high rank they held in society as scholars and learned men and their abilities to commune with nature or mediate between humans and gods.

I snort. As if the gods listen to humans.

It also says the Druids didn't exist before the second century BCE, but I knew of them long before that time. I toss it in the trash and reach for another book.

Vargas shimmers into sight, his dark eyes shining with glee.

Leaning back, I stretch my shoulders, easing cramped muscles. My mouth twitches. "Had a bit of fun, did you?"

"Highlight of my current non-existence," he jokes. "None

of the angels could see me, but a few of the old ones could sense something sentient was nearby. If I stepped close, they would move away or whisper so low I couldn't hear them."

Sounds like a party. "How many showed up?"

"A couple platoons were stationed around the alley, and roughly twenty-five high-ranking angels came and went during the investigation," he informs me. "It's a good thing I'm in this current state. Nobody else would have been able to get near them." Satisfaction and pride shine in his eyes.

A whistle escapes me. Almost a hundred angels outside of heaven congregating in one place? "It's been a while since we've seen a force that big on Earth, but Balith was well respected and a general. Did they determine his cause of death?"

Vargas scowls. "No. There isn't a mark on him. Nothing. It's as if he lay down and died like a dog. They have a lot of theories, similar to the ones we discussed, but nothing concrete." He paces back and forth. "Frankly, the idea of something that powerful running around killing immortals sets me on edge. Maybe I should have Ishkova run the men through some training exercises."

Before I can reply, he stops in front of my desk. "You said Balith was following someone? A woman?"

"I caught a glimpse of her in the aether," I confirm, reluctant to give him a description. Disturbed by the thought, I shove her green eyes out of my head. "He was definitely following a woman. Why?"

"None of the higher ups seem to know why he was here," he reveals. "He wasn't on assignment."

My back straightens. "Every move they make is dictated to them. Not one of those generals would do anything that wasn't sanctioned by someone above. Killing a human only comes from the highest levels. It must have been a secret assignment.

But who would dare?" A brief flash of hope passes through me, but I quickly tamp it down.

He raises a shoulder. "They found traces of a human female beside Balith's body. Some were quick to dismiss her, but others thought she could be relevant. I tried to find out more but couldn't hear without getting closer and spooking the elders."

"She's absolutely relevant," I confirm. "Now, we have to find her before they do. Go back and put them under surveillance. Try to get a name or something."

"They're gone," he reveals, a strange look on his face. "It was really fucking eerie, too. One minute, we're all standing in this dank, dirty alley together. The next minute, they all look up and vanish, taking Balith with them."

Satisfaction flares in me. "They were recalled. Someone at the top is pulling strings and trying to keep this quiet. This is the best news I've heard all day. It means something big is going on." My mind immediately starts working the angles, trying to figure out what my next move would be if I were trying to keep this quiet.

"If it were me, I'd handle it myself," I conclude out loud.

Vargas blinks, but then a slow smile spreads across his face as he catches onto my train of thought. "We need to slip a spy into every corner of that city. Even if they can't see them, a high-ranking angel will be felt the second they land. We can use the vibrations to pinpoint their location and, hopefully, find the human."

I summon General Ishkova and give him the orders to disperse our spies.

"Don't engage, but if you can get to the human before they do, that would give us significant leverage," I tell him.

With a nod, he vanishes.

I look over at Vargas, and my smile dies. He's frowning

down at his translucent body. "Good work, Vargas. Nobody else would have been able to get the intel today. Let Ishkova take the lead now. You need to find a body. I have a feeling we're going to need you corporeal sooner rather than later."

He flashes a wry half smile, then disappears.

When he's gone, I close my eyes and listen to the whispers of the dark. The shadows are restless. Change is here. My blood pumps with excitement. It's been a while since I felt this invigorated.

UNABLE TO SETTLE, I shove aside the remaining books and wait quietly in the lingering firelight. Here, in the capital of Underworld, the palace is shrouded in darkness. Perpetual night. The seat of my power and the place where most of my worshippers live.

But the majority of my power doesn't come from the denizens of this world. My predecessor chose to rely on the power he gleaned from his worshippers and sin. I wanted more. While I certainly benefit from worshippers and sin, the bulk of my power comes from free will. Millions of acts, small and large, feed my source of power. Choose the donut over the carrot? A lie over the truth? Hate over forgiveness? Thank you. Those grains of sand add up. An unending supply of power at my disposal for eternity.

A vibration in the air is the signal I'd been unconsciously waiting to feel. Inhaling sharply, I focus on Ishkova and follow the path to his side. When I appear, he doesn't even blink. Nor does he turn his eyes my way. Instead, they're fixed on something in front of him. Hate, fear, and a twinge of wonder shine from their depths.

I follow his line of sight and the world falls away.

A tall, familiar man in a navy-blue pinstripe suit stands in front of the gorgeous red-haired woman from the alley. Her head is tilted sweetly to the side as she listens to the words coming out of his mouth.

I snort. He's intentionally made himself visible to her. For what purpose, I'm not sure.

With jet black hair and the usual blue eyes, humans often mistake him as one of their own. Charming. Approachable. His deceptively reassuring aura never fails to lull even the most hardened of souls into believing he has their best interests at heart. Something he takes great pride in telling all the angels under him.

Utterly lethal, he's anything but human. One of the original seven archangels, and preferred messenger to the one he serves, he's Gabriel. Modern day Christians believe him to be nothing but a messenger. I scoff. He's The Messenger, but he's so much more, too.

One of the original four Watchers, he's second only to Michael in terms of hierarchy, and he's one of two who has the right to wield The Power. Fanatically dedicated to defeating evil, his legions of angels follow his every word and command. But most of the power he wields is not his. It belongs to the one he serves.

The blood coursing through my veins turns molten with rage. Once I called him brother, friend, and warrior. Now, I call him one name—The Betrayer.

She must have good instincts because she steps back, putting space between her and Gabriel. Or maybe she sees the same fanatical glint in his eyes that I do.

He unsheathes his sword.

Between one breath and the next, I appear between him and her. My sword meets his in a clash of power, deflecting it away from its target. The resounding ring of the two striking repeatedly is music to my ears. For several minutes, we battle against each other, neither gaining nor losing ground. Even though he wields a godlike power, so do I. My own.

Over a thousand lifetimes, I've waited to face him again. When I pictured our meeting, it was on the battlefield. On Judgement Day. A fight to the death. His death.

Instead, the moment is here, now, way ahead of schedule. I sway with the impact this thought has on me. The chance to annihilate my biggest opponent is within my grasp, The burning need to rid the world of this sham of a protector is overwhelming.

A thin line of blood appears across his cheek, and his eyes widen in understanding.

I can't help but laugh. So close. He thought he was fighting Lucifer, the archangel he knew thousands of years ago, not Lucifer, Ruler of the Underworld.

"Wow, how the mighty have fallen," I sneer, deliberately poking the beast I sense beneath his urbane exterior. Once, he'd been significantly higher in rank and power than me. I'd worshipped and feared him in equal measure. Not anymore.

"Don't you have better things to do than interfere in earthly matters?" he asks, his mouth twisted in disdain.

Stepping back, I hold my arms wide and laugh. "Everything here concerns me. These people are mine. They feed my power. Let me repeat that phrase. *My power.* I don't have to borrow it like a servant. It's mine to wield." I smirk. "Gain any of your own power yet or still abusing the power you *borrow* from your lord?"

He steps forward to strike while my arms are out, but I bring them together with a clap of power and push him back.

A glow begins to emanate from beneath his suit, a sign of his control slipping. "I remain a humble servant." A snide smile appears. "In Heaven. You remember that place, don't you? Or has evil wiped all the memories away?"

Touché.

A few shadows slip from my control and slither on the ground under my feet. "Those who are stuck in the past are doomed to repeat it. Evil," I repeat with a snort. "Get with the times. The world isn't only a construct of good and evil, and my power doesn't rely solely on sins like murder and mayhem. No, most of my power comes from something more divine."

His brows come together in a fierce frown at the use of the word divine, as if he's the only one who has the right to use it.

"The one thing given to us all—free will," I say with a mock shiver of pleasure. "When humans decide to act without the constraint of necessity or fate, they use free will, and I benefit. Why? Because I choose to do so. Free will is empowering and creates a certain energy and excitement, as if they are doing something naughty, and I feed off it. But I have to admit, it's even more delicious if it comes from someone powerful, like you or... General Balith. Oh, sorry, was that too soon? I heard he passed recently."

Golden power spills out, and the suit disappears, leaving only the Archangel Gabriel in all his winged glory. The gleaming sword in his hand swivels in preparation for his strike.

Unconcerned, I silently contemplate ending this charade. My mind plays out numerous scenarios, trying to figure out if there's an option that doesn't have catastrophic repercussions. But I can't find a single one.

If I kill Gabriel, a favored archangel, before Armageddon, the retaliation will be brutal. Humans could be wiped from the

Earth. Again. Their cries haunt me to this day, and I refuse to stand by and watch that happen again. Not under my reign.

If death isn't the answer, then what? Forgiveness? I hiss. Never.

A curtain flutters behind him, startling me out of my deliberation. In my eagerness to confront him, I'd lost sight of the original reason we were here.

I was right. Someone high ranking had sent Balith, and two other angels, to kill a human. Gabriel. He's the one who's behind all the secret assignments and subterfuge. But why? Who is this female, and why is she such a threat?

I gesture to the sword in his hand. "You know that won't kill me. Might hurt a bit... if you can land a blow. While you've been doling out assignments from above, some of us have been fighting for a living."

He steps forward with a taunting grin on his face. "Let's find out, shall we?"

"Oh, did you suddenly gain the power to kill an angel? Because regardless of what I have become, at the core, I'm still an angel," I remind him, striking a blow to his ego and following it with a right cross across his cheek. The satisfying crunch is music to my ears.

The power to kill an angel will never be offered to him. An angel is either born with the power to kill another or not. In addition, those born with the power are eternal, not immortal, which means he can be killed. I cannot. If this body is destroyed, I can simply find another, but my power and spirit live on. And if I needed proof, all I have to do is look at Vargas.

Angry, he strikes, power whipping across the divide.

Curious about its strength, I deliberately step into it. Pure power slams into me. Racing along my core, it searches for a weakness to exploit, a path to my destruction, but it finds nothing. My body sways. The damage to my body and power is extensive, but not enough to take me down. It finally dissipates. The wells of my power replenish themselves quickly, healing me in the process.

An uneasy expression slides across his face. I guess he never thought the power I gained ruling the Underworld would match the power of a god.

He widens his stance and raises his sword, readying himself to meet my counterattack. I laugh when my power shoots up from the ground, wrapping him in shadows and sin, the latter feeding off the light in his soul.

He grunts. Seconds go by. A golden fist suddenly punches through the dark barrier, once, twice, then again and again until he's free. Whirling toward me, his muscles tense as he prepares to launch himself at me.

Before this can become a battle to the death, I hold up a hand. "Stop. We're even. In more ways than one. You can't kill me, and unfortunately, I can't kill you either. If I did, it could bring about Armageddon, which is something I'm not willing to chance. At least not today."

Something dark twists the lines of his face, and he shudders. "Me either."

The stiffness of his reply tells me he watched the flood too.

He tilts his head toward the street. "Maybe you should leave and let me finish my business."

The tinge of desperation in his voice makes me pause. He's gone to great lengths to rid the world of this human but can't seem to get the job done. Why? And if he continues to fail, will it drive him over the edge?

"What business is that?" I ask politely.

A muscle ticks in his jaw. He stares at me for a long minute, contemplating his next move. It's a stalemate, though, and he knows it. With one last glare, he disappears in a flash of white wings and brilliant light.

When Gabriel falls from his lofty pedestal, I'll cut off his wings and drag him to the Underworld to fight for his life. Until then, I need to make sure he remains dedicated to achieving his mission. Unsuccessfully, of course.

I turn around, but she's long gone. Time to look for a pair of memorable green eyes and gorgeous red hair.

CHAPTER

EIGHT

<u>EVREN</u>

This world is truly remarkable and so are its people. The air is saturated with emotions that seep into my bones until I can't help but feel their highs and lows. With a contented sigh, I push my red hair over my shoulder and soak up all the feelings.

Humans excel in emotional intelligence. Their ability to identify, assess, express, and control emotions for oneself and others is remarkable. In this single area, humans reign supreme over all other races.

Unfortunately, emotions are not a defense against the supernatural races and the magic they wield. Humans are outmatched in power and strength. The only reason they haven't died out is their astonishing ability to procreate. Sheer numbers. Normally, I'd count this as an advantage, but not in the war that's coming. It only makes them cannon fodder or a fleeting snack, easily consumed along the path of destruction.

During our travels, my mother and I met a prophetic seer who told us humans would need us to help them evolve and survive. They had magic but needed to find a way to cultivate it. Thinking this a simple task, my mother returned to Earth two thousand years ago to help humans evolve. But she never returned. I looked for her but found no trace. At first, I hadn't worried. She would often become distracted by theories and disappear for long periods to observe or conduct experiments. Absolutely sure I would find her in another world, I left here and searched far and wide.

Nothing. With hope dwindling, I went back to the seer. He showed me the few visions he could glean from the aether. My mother coming here, her giving a warrior a torque, a black beast, and a dark-haired angel. Her path becomes blank at that point.

Desperate to know the truth, I returned to the place of my birth to search for clues about her disappearance, along with any information I could find on the warrior and angel. Not knowing where to start, I focused on her quest to help humans evolve. Magical humans don't appear every day. Through my research, I discovered two human races with powers—witches and Druids. Using deductive reasoning, I concluded Druids fit the best because their source of power is unknown.

If history is captured in some form, verbal or written, it's accessible, especially to those like me who can pay in both magic and power. So, I put the word out. In exchange for conclusive information or evidence, I offered a one-of-a-kind amulet as payment.

Oval in shape, with a quartz in its center, the spell engraved on the back makes the wearer invisible to their enemies. They can hide forever as long as they wear the amulet. I cast a wide net and waited like a spider in its web.

Not long after, a sorceress came forward. In one gloved fist, she carried a torque and in the other, a tome. She refused to leave the torque because she'd stolen it from some powerful Duke but offered to let me study it for a couple of hours. The book she handed over freely.

When I read the spell on the torque, joy filled me. It was my mother's spell. Not only was it written in our language, Viridian, but her symbol, a circle overlapping a triangle, engraved at the end like a signature offered incontrovertible proof. After copying the spell, I returned the torque to the sorceress and handed her the amulet. She immediately disappeared.

It was an amplifying spell. The best I'd ever seen. But it didn't give me the answer I sought. The torque didn't give power to humans, it only increased power. So the Druids must have had power inside them for the torque to work. Was it a latent power triggered by something and enhanced by the torque?

I turned to the book for the answers. Inside its dry, brittle pages, were generations and generations of names dating back to the tenth century BCE and a warrior named Brennus. His name is listed first. A painted image to the left of the name depicts a massive, bearded warrior with sword in one hand, a brown shield in the other, and a gold torque around his neck.

Brennus had sixteen children. No wives were listed in the book. Every single one of the children was listed, but four names had lines scratched through them. Under all but the four, more names were scribbled. Although the handwriting varies wildly, this pattern continues throughout the book.

Marveling at the sheer number of names, I realized my mother succeeded in her task. Somehow, she found their unused power. With the torque, humans were able to amplify their power into something useable and powerful and pass it to their children and their children's children. They became a new race of humans with magic—Druids.

A few centuries ago, the number of names started dwindling in count. Fewer babies were born, and even fewer lived. Now, Druids are almost extinct. But why?

Since the book came into my possession, I've been spending all my free time trying to figure out the mystery of the Druids' power. If I can determine what makes Druids different from other humans, maybe I can help them find their magic and increase their numbers. Or maybe I can replicate the magic in all humans to help them evolve.

So far, it's been an exercise in futility.

Fortunately, experiments are something I excel at, and the work has the added benefit of taking my mind off the mystery of my mother's disappearance. A timer dings telling me to run another batch of blood.

HOURS LATER, I wipe my brow and straighten my aching back. The latest batch of test tubes is ready to go. Each vial contains the blood of a Druid. With methodical precision, I load them into the centrifuge and turn it on.

While I wait for the machine to do its job and separate the components of the blood, I think back on the last week. Three times I've had to raise my dagger to defend my life against angels. It would have been four tonight, but a supernatural stepped in and saved me.

I left him to fight the battle. None of the angels have been the one I seek. The only one who might know something about my mother's disappearance. It's selfish, but I need to limit my exposure so I can keep searching for her.

Do the angels not realize they can't kill me? Instead, they play games and waste time while my questions go unanswered. If they would only talk to me, I could find the angel I need. I've tried, but they're soldiers following orders.

The whirring of the machine slows and finally stops. I remove each vial and set it in the tray for tomorrow's tests, then store it in the refrigerator.

Placing my hands palm down on the cold stainless steel, I lean over to read the results in front of me for the millionth time. They remain unchanged. Every batch has produced the same results, and I'm still no closer to the answer. There are only a few tests to conduct, but this is the last batch of blood I have available.

The reports show there is no difference between Druids and humans without power. Their blood is identical. It doesn't make sense. There has to be a variable I'm overlooking. One group has power. One does not. There must be something, maybe an obscure strand of DNA I keep missing?

My mother wouldn't have had access to the most basic of labs back in the tenth century BCE. How did she know which humans had the ability to become Druids?

EVREN

I slowly set down the test results. "Are you here to kill me?" I lift my chin, waiting for the shadows to answer my question. My heart pounds with the feeling of impending death. It's so strong, I can't help but wonder if this is the angel I've been waiting for.

Unbelievable power ripples across the room in warning before settling behind me. His power tastes and feels angelic. My heart beats with anticipation.

"Maybe I'm here to save you," a husky voice murmurs in my ear.

I can't help the shiver that cascades down my spine. Intrigued, I keep my back to him and reply, "An angel from heaven sent to save me?" The smell of a bonfire on a cold winter's night teases my senses. It's delicious and musky and makes me take a tiny step closer to him.

His harsh laugh makes my stomach tighten. "More like an archangel from Hell, but we can't always pick our saviors, can we?"

Disappointed, I turn to tell him to get lost, but the words never make it out of my mouth. The exact opposite of the dark angel I seek, this magnificently tall warrior with white-blond hair is stunning.

He looks like an angel, with his perfectly symmetrical features, strong jaw, aquiline nose, and high cheekbones. Features carved by a master sculptor with perfect intent.

Yet, there's something unique about him.

A crease appears between his arched brows, marring the perfection. I skip over it and focus on the piercing turquoise blue eyes that glow with an inner light. Similar to the angels I'd killed the last few days, they have a luminescent quality to them, but where the other angels' eyes were blank, fierce emotions shine from his.

He waits for me to say something, but I'm not done studying him.

His differences intrigue me. Instead of the blinding white aura of most angels, his is a void. The absence of color or aura. It does nothing to indicate what or who he was once upon a time. Both his power and physical body screams angel, but more. Angel plus what?

My eyes drift down the tight-fitting black t-shirt to the equally tight black jeans. Muscles bulge in every conceivable spot, indicating a warrior of the highest caliber. This is only emphasized by the small scars crisscrossing his forearms and hands. Barely perceptible to the human eye, they tell of innumerable battles against sharp weapons.

Beyond all the physical, the power he exudes easily eclipses the highest angel. God-like power is his to command.

I pick up his large hand, and he stiffens. "May I?"

Blue eyes harden with suspicion.

I wait for him to decide if I'm friend or foe.

Curiosity softens his eyes a fraction, and he reluctantly nods.

Warmth travels from his hand to mine, and I turn his palm up to study it. Calluses. Numerous and in the right position for weapons like swords. I glide my thumb across them. Tough, with a slight rough edge. Holding his hand up to the light, I study his scars. Very interesting. Mortals scar, so do some immortals, but angels heal the minute they return to Heaven.

"Are you going to tell me my future?" he asks, a hint of laughter in his voice.

My eyes flick to his. "If I was, I'm not now. What are you?"

"A little of this and that. Do you question all your saviors or just the wicked ones?" he jokingly answers.

Non-answers drive me crazy. So does polite chit chat. "Can I have a sample of your blood?" I blurt out, eager to look at its composition under a microscope.

A seductive grin flashes across his face. "That's a first. Usually, a woman only wants my blood if I've failed to contact them again. I've never had one want it upfront." Sharp blue eyes observe me keenly. "Why do you want it? For a spell?"

I give him an exasperated look. "To study it, of course. I can't quite figure out what you are, but your blood would tell me your genetic make-up." Or at least it should. The recent Druid results have shown me nothing.

"My origin is angel. Wouldn't my genes tell you the same?" he states, but I hear a flicker of interest in his tone.

"You're an angel, that's true, but you seem different than them," I inform him, utterly fascinated by this male standing in front of me. "Are there others like you?"

He shrugs nonchalantly. "Looks like we're both interested

in answers. Why don't you answer my questions and I'll answer yours?"

The scientist in me is screaming for answers. Why can't he just give me his blood? It's not like I'm asking for his firstborn. My mind latches onto the idea. Does he have children? His blood mixing with other races could produce interesting results. I contemplate asking him, but he's already moving on to something else. Pushing him at this point would probably have a detrimental effect.

He arches a brow.

Right. An irritated sigh escapes. "What's your first question?"

He shifts his stance, coming in closer to my body. A large finger swipes a piece of hair and tucks it behind one of my ears. "Why do the angels want to kill you?" His voice is low and dark as if he's trying to entice me into telling him my secrets.

My body clenches from the seductive edge of it. "I'm not sure. You'll have to ask them." My answer is true, but there's a husky tone to the words that I'm not used to hearing. I clear my throat and refocus on the conversation.

He opens his mouth, but I place a finger across his pouty lips. "My turn, right?" He doesn't answer, but he does close his mouth. "Who are you?"

He tenses and enough seconds pass that I wonder if he's going to answer. "Lucifer." Blue eyes stare steadily at me, as if waiting for my reaction.

That makes complete sense. The rebellious angel. The keeper of Hell. So much speculation surrounds him, but with all the stories, it's hard to tell fact from fiction. I deal in facts.

"Evren. It's nice to meet you." I squeeze the hand I'm still holding, then release it.

The look of suspicion is back. Is introducing myself not the polite thing to do?

"How did you kill those angels?" he bluntly asks.

I raise my eyebrows. He's making the huge assumption that I killed them. I mean, I did, but it's a leap to think a human killed an angel. "I stabbed them with a knife." All true, although the knife alone wouldn't kill them.

His brows come together in confusion. "A knife? There was no evidence of a stabbing. Is it spelled? I'd like to examine it."

My mouth twitches with amusement. "As a scientist, I thought I had a lot of questions. One question. One answer. It's my turn."

Eyes narrowed; I ask the one question that's bothering me the most. "Why do you want to save me from the angels?" Lucifer isn't exactly known for his benevolent acts of kindness. There has to be a more self-serving reason.

"I'm guessing it isn't enough to want to save a beautiful woman such as yourself?" he murmurs, a flirty smile on his lips that never reaches his eyes.

When I don't respond, he sighs and mutters something about losing his touch. "The angels want you dead. More importantly, Gabriel wants you dead. He wants it badly enough that he's hiding his actions from those above him." He pauses. "I'll do whatever it takes to prevent him from killing you. Why? Because he hates failure. Will do almost anything to avoid it. I can't help but think if he repeatedly fails, it will push him over the edge, and he'll fall right into my hands."

Harsh. There's not an ounce of forgiveness in his bones for his enemies; only hate blazes from his piercing blue eyes. I like it and admire it. Unfortunately, his need to keep the angels from me is the exact opposite of what I need to happen. I'm searching for one angel, so them coming to kill me actually saves me time.

"I see. That answer doesn't work for me," I inform him, much to his shock. "As you know, I'm quite capable of taking care of myself. I don't need a savior, especially not one with your agenda. So, thank you... but no thank you."

He tilts his head as if examining my words, then smiles so broadly, dimples appear.

"I'm not asking for your permission, but I find it oddly endearing that you think you can dictate my actions," he replies, his voice full of amusement.

Leaning down, he inhales deeply. "You smell human, but more. Not witch. Druid? Or Nephilim? Maybe the daughter of one? It's hard to tell. I'm looking forward to spending more time together. Unfortunately, I have to leave, but I'll leave my guards here to protect you. If you need me, call out. They will know, and I'll appear."

With those final words, I blink, and he disappears. Closing my eyes, I cast a net to search for power, but nothing comes back. He's gone. For now.

Bemused, I shake my head. I guess if the angels want to kill me, they'll have to go through him. The idea of him protecting me is truly absurd, but instead of laughter, a weird bubbly sensation fills me. I scoff. It's not personal. He's not trying to save me, only thwart them.

So why can't you stop thinking about it? My inner voice whispers.

Determined to focus, I dismiss the thoughts and turn my attention back to the lab. Where was I? That's right. Blood and specimens. Stepping over to the computer, I create an ad and infuse it with magic to make sure it finds the right specimens... Druids and dying humans.

CHAPTER

TEN

LUCIFER

The conversation with Evren was intriguing but not the least bit informative. I snort. That's an understatement. But for some reason, I don't even care. For the first time in a long while, both my body and brain are in sync... and fascinated... with her. Why though? She wasn't even flirting.

What intel did I get? She kills angels with a knife. That's it. Obviously, there must be something special about the weapon, yet she never said what. I meant to circle back to the knife on the next question, but her questions derailed my train of thought. Not to mention the smell of her.

What is she? Her incredible scent still lingers in my nose. I inhale deeply, then shake it off. Human, but with a tinge of power. Whatever she is, she's bold. A scientist asking to

64

examine my blood. I'm half tempted to let her just to see what she finds.

Striding into my study, I see Cormal is waiting for me. I was tempted to postpone the meeting, but it would only prove him right. He's already too much of a smug bastard, with more than his fair share of power. I don't want to feed his ego by acting how he expects. Besides, both Vargas and Ishkova, along with a platoon of demons, are watching over Evren right now. They'll alert me if Gabriel shows up.

Cormal's studying one of the Druid books on my desk.

"Care to comment on the accuracy of them?" I ask, dropping into the chair behind my desk.

The book drops to the desk with a thud. "Is this why you asked me here? For a lesson in the history of a forgotten race?" Blue eyes stare blankly into mine.

I retrieve the tome from the trash and show it to him. "This one was utter rubbish. Fabricated nonsense. If you think they're all nonsense, tell me now." I wave a hand at the papers on my desk. "I could use the time for something more important."

He reads the title and laughs. "That one is a waste, but some are likely to have the truth. Or at least a version of it. Druids are secretive by nature."

I toss the book back into the bin. "I'm making my way through each of them. Hopefully, the truth is in there somewhere."

A wry twist of his mouth tells me what he thinks. "Not sure why you're so interested in Druids. It's a waste of time, if you ask me, but I know you have plenty to spare."

Irritated, I gesture to his glass. "Don't drink my good bourbon and think you can insult me. Just because I like you, doesn't mean I won't kill you. Understood?"

He chuckles. "Sorry, bad habit. Now, what do you want to talk about?"

Idly, I pick up the pen on my desk and twirl it in my fingers. "Underworld is stable. We're not constantly at war with our enemies. And because of Arden and our recent assistance with the disposal of the light Fae Queen, Underworld now has alliances with other races. Internal strife is also at an all-time low. We're in a good place. Except for the masses. Peace goes a long way, but it doesn't feed and house the people, give them purpose, or generate much loyalty. Am I right?"

Surprised by my answer, he answers truthfully. "They have to fight every day for the smallest of comforts. The world hasn't changed much with you in power. Less fear of the world collapsing around them, but overall, it's the same."

That's exactly what I think, too. "What if we gave them jobs that improved Underworld as a whole?" The image of Cormal's skylight flashes in my mind. It's incredibly dark and dismal around here, and while I'm sure the gothic theme is preferred by most of the population, we're now a world of mixed races.

"Merfolk, water demons, ogres, nymphs, hellhounds and other creatures like your Nemean Lion, and so many others..." I begin, listing a few of our more interesting citizens. "They all have different needs. What if the masses were given jobs to build habitats for these various groups? Lakes, parks, forests, training courses... whatever they need to feel comfortable. Personally, I'd like to see your fabricated sunlight in some of these areas. Not everyone shares a love of the dark. Although that would mean you'd have to share the secret of its design."

For the first time since I've known him, Cormal looks stunned. "Who would pay the workers? You?"

"Underworld," I reply. There's plenty of money in the coffers, especially when you're not spending it on war. It's another reason I was so infuriated with myself when I saw the people in the market. The boy pickpocketing for payment. He deserves a choice. Pickpocket, work for the Underworld, or...

I lean forward. "Also, what do you think of a university of some type? A place where Underworld citizens could get specialized education. Or send their children. Magical and practical. An engineer who builds magnificent feats like the Underworld Market. Or a doctor who heals all races. They can choose their own path."

I pause, waiting for Cormal to digest the information and decide if he truly wants the best for the people who count on him for their livelihood or if he only cares about his empire.

Cormal downs the rest of the bourbon in his glass and holds it out for more. "This is going to take more than one glass."

Satisfied I picked the right man to assist me, I wave a hand and the decanter appears. "Let's get to work."

Two hours later, we've got an outline of the initial plan to build the habitats. The university is going to take more thought as well as some guidance from others whose expertise is in education, but we've made a lot of progress in a short amount of time.

Cormal stands. "We'll need a pretty large team to manage it all. I'll send you a few supervisors who I think will be the most qualified for this project. You can interview them, see if they'll work, and add the best to your staff." He clears his throat. "Orlo is one of them. He's incredibly smart and deserves a chance to be more than he is today."

I lift a shoulder. "If the Nemean Lion wants the job, he'll need to interview well. The competition will be stiff. It's entirely up to him, though. I won't stand in his way."

Cormal tilts his head. "I must admit, you constantly surprise me, and it's quite fucking uncomfortable. Why can't you be the predictable, power-hungry bastard like the Devil?" With those words, he disappears.

I scowl.

Damn it.

I forgot to get the security upgraded.

VARGAS SENDS me an image of an angel, and I immediately stop adding notes to the plan and follow his signal. When I come out of the brick beside him, he jumps and glares at me.

I chuckle. "Now you know what it's like to be around you these days." My eyes dart to the street. "Where is he?"

Vargas motions to a corner diagonally across from us. "There. He's waiting for her to come out of the coffee shop next door." He points to a storefront.

She steps out, and the angel steps toward her. With a wave of my hand, I stop the traffic and move to intercept him. Focused on my target, I miss the warning signs and leave my back open. Power strikes hard, and pain explodes between my shoulder blades. I swivel around to face my opponent. Gabriel stands behind me. He readies another hit, but I know it's only a diversion. Spinning, I start running toward Evren.

"Evren!" I shout, pointing at the angel coming toward her. Another hit slams into me, and I stumble, but at least I have a shield up now. I keep moving.

Evren turns to look, but I can tell by the way her head is swiveling, she can't see the angel striding toward her.

Another blast hits me. This one is stronger than the previous one and burns through the flimsy shield I raised a minute ago.

Fuck, that hurt.

The angel is a foot from Evren. I'm too late. With a burst of speed, he grabs her shoulder, and they disappear from the sidewalk.

I turn toward Gabriel to fire off my own shot, but he's gone, too.

Damn it. He's gone after her.

I pull out my phone and bring up an app.

The world is high tech now. As a ruler, I decided a long time ago to use every tool and weapon at my disposal. Technology is certainly a tool I enjoy.

The tracker I planted behind her ear shows me she's about thirty miles from here, halfway up a mountain. I send the location to Vargas via our private telepathic channel and shimmer out.

Vargas and I both appear at the same time. It's a cave. We peer around the corner. Evren is standing in the middle of the opening with the one angel holding her arms from behind, and Gabriel standing directly in front of her. He's made himself visible to her again.

"I deserve to know why you want to kill me. I haven't broken any laws. At least, I don't think I have, but I don't really know your laws. Have I broken a law?" she asks, frowning up at Gabriel.

My mouth twitches. She's full of questions, even when she's facing death.

"Do you think we don't know about your experiments?" Gabriel snarls at her.

Evren shrugs. "You'll have to be more specific. I'm conducting several experiments." Her head is tilted to the side while her green eyes are fixed on Gabriel with a puzzled expression... and not an ounce of fear.

Impressive.

"You're trying to revive the Druids," he spits out. His anger makes the cave shake. "Wait. What other experiments are you conducting here? Are they on humans or supernaturals?"

"Right now, I'm trying to find out how the Druids got their magic, and why they're almost extinct," she admits. "But your theory is sound. If I figure out the secret to their magic, I will try to help them. This world is going to need Druids. Humans must evolve to survive. Giving them their own power will create a human force that can help protect other humans. It's not as if the angels or other supernaturals will put them first."

Gabriel shakes his head, disbelief creasing his brow. Whether it's because she isn't scared of him or because of her frank answer, I can't tell. Maybe both.

Regardless, I refuse to let him kill her. Carefully taking aim, I hit the angel holding Evren with a massive bolt of power, and he disintegrates.

Gabriel roars in anguish.

Evren doesn't flinch. Her eyes are on the sword pointed at her heart.

I fire at him, but he's placed a shield around them both. I move closer to Evren and ready my next hit. If I can hit him hard enough to bring his shield down, I can grab her and disappear.

Gabriel raises his sword.

I fire rapidly into his shield.

A small gold knife appears in Evren's hand.

He takes a step back and stares at her in horror.

The shield drops, and I immediately grab her and disappear.

ELEVEN

LUCIFER

Unwilling to chance Gabriel finding us, I take her to one of two places in this world where I know she can't be detected. When we arrive, the lake is sparkling under the noon sun. Bees and insects buzz along the water's edge, singing their song of nature. The rolling green hills we're standing on lead to a white two-story stone cottage, where herbal plants and flowers grow wildly in its yard.

She looks around uneasily. "Where are we? Why can't I feel anyone else here?"

"There's nobody here but us," I answer, my reply simple, although I suspect she means something more.

Her eyes sweep the landscape. "We didn't go through a portal to Fae or Elven lands, so I'm guessing we're still on

Earth," she speculates, giving me a suspicious look. "Where are we?"

I shrug nonchalantly, but my stomach tightens in knots. This was a bad idea. There are only a couple of places I can hide her from the angels, and this is one of them. I didn't want to potentially endanger those at The Abbey, so I chose here. A place full of gut-wrenching, personal memories, and I bring a stranger. A woman.

But the only other place she would be safe from Gabriel is another world. Humans can't survive in the Underworld and taking her to another's land requires advanced warning and diplomatic maneuvering.

She shoves a swath of her luxurious red hair behind her ear, exposing the slim column of her neck.

The urge to lean down and skim her delicious neck is strong, but I force my eyes to return to hers.

Green eyes examine me closely. "Why is Gabriel so worried about Druids?"

"I was hoping you might know. Aren't you a Druid?" I interject, trying to figure out what the hell has Gabriel so twisted up in knots.

"I'm not a Druid. A prophetic seer told my family humans must evolve to survive. So, a long time ago, my... ancestor helped Druids find their power and gave them a way to amplify it," she explains. "But now their race is slowly dying out, and I'm trying to help them by finding the source of their magic. But it's about more than just the Druids. I want to find a way to help humans evolve. They need power in this world of super-naturals, or they'll be crushed beneath their ambitions."

"Didn't your ancestor keep any records?" I ask, still caught on her ability to kill angels and Gabriel's look of horror when he saw her knife. Does he know she killed the others? Or does it go deeper than that... Does he know who she is? Why are the Druids almost extinct? Has Gabriel been hunting them?

Cormal said their insular ways made their numbers dwindle. Perhaps a bit of both? After all, if Gabriel actively hunted them to near extinction, it isn't something he would have been able to keep quiet. Picking off a few key people here and there, though, would barely be noticed, and if they were the last of their line, it would result in fewer Druids in the future.

She stares at the lake. "She disappeared shortly after." For the first time, her voice is full of emotion and not intellectual reasoning. Interesting.

"Let's see if I've got all this straight. Your ancestor is responsible for giving Druids their power and using the torque to amplify it. Gabriel wants to kill you before you're able to help Druids replenish their numbers. For some reason, he sees them as a threat. I think he suspects you killed the other angels. You claim you're not a Druid, but you haven't really told me what you are."

"I never mentioned a torque," she interjects, with a suspicious glint in her eye.

I raise an eyebrow at her singular focus. "A torque recently found its way into my court. A source told me it was passed down from Druid to Druid and used to amplify powers. I can attest that it amplifies anyone's power, not just the Druids. It has a spell written in Viridian on it."

Her breath catches. "You know Viridian?"

"Of course, it was the language we first spoke as angels, until humans were created, and new languages were introduced," I reply. "Why? Do you know Viridian?" It's my turn to sound incredulous.

"Yes, my mother taught it to me," she says slowly, as if afraid of what she's revealing. "Viridian was spoken here a long time ago." One shoulder lifts in a dismissive shrug. "She's taught me many languages, both ancient and modern."

It's a perfectly logical explanation, and I can't detect a lie in anything she said, but something doesn't feel right.

"You can kill angels, too," she replies almost defensively. "I didn't know it was possible for one angel to kill another." Her head tilts to one side while she waits for me to explain.

"Three angels were born with the ability to kill other angels—myself, Michael, and Mercy. Gabriel doesn't have that power, and it's always been one he's coveted. Not because he's evil, but because he's a fanatic who will do anything to serve 'the greater good.' In his mind, he needs the power to serve justice to those angels who deviate from the path." I grimace when the distasteful words come out of my mouth. "I'm supremely grateful he doesn't have it."

She gives me a speculative look. "Maybe there's a tie between you and Druids that you aren't aware of... did you reproduce during your time with the humans?"

Words escape me for a second, and I simply stare at her. Laughter bursts out of me. "I can assure you, I don't have any bastard children who went on to give birth to Druids. My children weren't born until a few hundred years later."

Interest flashes across her face and she opens her mouth to speak.

I hold up a hand to stop her. "My daughter was a witch and human, like my wife. My son... his birth created a new race—vampires. Although he's still one-of-a-kind compared to the others." None of the others have magnificent wings, nor can they heal. Attributes from me and his mother. If anything, her interest seems stronger. "No, you may not have his blood or DNA or anything to study. Keep to your Druids."

She blinks. "Your wife?"

"Both she and my daughter passed several centuries back,"

I state, my voice gruff with emotions. The fact that we're talking about all of this here makes it worse. "We should get going. Find a more permanent place to hide you."

Without a word, she walks off in the direction of the cottage.

I grab her arm and pull her around to face me. "You can't go in there."

A knowing look shines from her eyes. "This was your home, wasn't it?"

Unable to voice the words, I nod.

She looks around with new eyes. "It's a bubble, isn't it? Protected and hidden from the world. A place for her to live, because she... they couldn't stay with you in the Underworld." She turns in a full circle, taking it all in with a breathtaking smile on her face. "It's beautiful and peaceful. A true utopia. Thank you for bringing me here when I'm sure it's the last thing you wanted to do."

It was literally the last thing I wanted to do. This place rocks me to my core, bombarding me with sharp memories, good and bad, but I'm thankful to have them. At least the happy memories ease the devastation of Danica's death. I squint. It didn't hit as hard today, though. Maybe, after fifteen hundred years, the pain is dulling.

My eyes trace the delicate features of the beautiful woman beside me. They're perfect, but in some way, they almost seem too delicate for her personality. She's unlike anyone I've ever known, man or woman. Analytical and strong minded. Impatient and dismissive. The constructs of polite chitchat and flirting seem to be beyond her understanding. She hides her emotions well, except when she's talking about work. Then she becomes a passionate warrior, battling even the great Gabriel for what she thinks is right.

"There's one other place I can take you. Supernaturals of all races are accepted and protected there. Not all of them like humans, but they wouldn't jeopardize their sanctuary to try to kill you." I stumble a bit trying to explain The Abbey without giving too much away. "But it's also where my son and his family lives, and I'm not sure if it's a good idea." I'm reluctant to introduce her until I know who she is and if she's safe for my family.

The hurt in her eyes tells me she caught the underlying meaning, and she takes a small step back.

"Thank you for the offer, but I can't accept. I need to return to my lab and finish my experiments," she says stiffly, with a negative shake of her head. "Besides, I'll be fine. I think Gabriel knows I can kill him. That will be enough of a deterrent for now. If it isn't, I'll figure out another solution. I've been on my own for a long, long time."

The thought of her being alone makes me scowl. "Nice try. You're not getting rid of me, nor am I abandoning you. Gabriel's dangerous. You're under my protection and will remain so until I decide differently."

<u>LUCIFER</u>

She converted an old sewing machine factory on the north side of the city into her lab. But instead of the dirty, abandoned building I expected, it's pristine, not a speck of dirt anywhere, and filled with stainless steel counters and state-of-the-art equipment. Moments after we arrive, a sea of humans appear in the yard, wearing confused looks on their faces, as if they're waiting for something but not sure what or even how they got here.

Evren immediately grabs a white coat off the hook and rushes outside to organize them into two lines.

Following, I lean down to whisper in her ear. "What are they doing here?" The delicious smell I'm quickly becoming addicted to drifts up to me.

She bites the inside of her cheek and turns to regard me with a speculative look. The same one I'm getting used to seeing on her face when she has something to say and isn't sure if I'm going to like it. I cross my arms and wait.

"Some are here to give blood, and some are here to receive it," she replies nervously with a wave of her hand at the two lines. "Can you make yourself useful or leave? You're making them nervous."

Ordering me around again. Does she not realize who I am? I look at her incredulously, but when I see worried eyes continuously dart in my direction, I sigh and step to the corner of the room to watch.

Evren grabs a nearby cart filled with medical supplies and waves the first line of individuals into the building. She motions for the group to file into each of the chairs along the wall and instructs them to roll up their sleeves and prop their elbows on the small table in front of them.

With a speed that tells me she's done this many times, she quickly moves from one to the next, filling her vials with their blood. Once the vials are full, she motions for five people to leave. I notice they're all women and children. She reclines the remaining men and sets up a bag to extract more blood from them, then heads outside.

Her eyes dart to mine to see if I'm still here. When she sees me watching, she immediately turns to focus on something else.

With a clipboard in hand, she walks to each person in line and asks them how long they've been given to live. She explains that the experiment is in the early stages and may not prolong their life. It could shorten it if their bodies react negatively to the medicine. A few stomp off in anger, along with a couple more who look resigned to dying, clearly unwilling to take the chance she's offering.

Five people remain. A woman and child, a young man in his twenties, a middle-aged woman, and an elderly man.

She brings each individual to a curtained off bed and leaves them to dress in the gown lying on the end. Except for the woman with the little girl. She pulls her aside.

"You should take your daughter to her favorite places and let her enjoy them one last time. Be together," she urges gently, smiling down at the blond-haired little girl with the thin face and deep brown eyes.

"She's my little sister, and we've already done all of her favorite things. She's not afraid of death. We lost our parents a few years ago, and we're well acquainted with it," the young woman replies, with a side glance in my direction. "If this doesn't work, she's ready to go and be with them. If there's a microscopic chance it does work, we'll take it."

The little girl at her side smiles at Evren. "I'd love to stay here with my sister, grow up, be a ballerina, and marry a handsome prince." She squeezes her sister's hand. "I'd also love to see my parents again. I miss them so much." Her little hand then reaches out for Evren's and clasps it in her own. "Either way, I'll be okay."

She tugs Evren down to her level. "I worry about my sister, though. Can you promise to look after her if something happens to me? Becca will be all alone."

Evren looks at her solemnly and nods. "I will." She glances at the clipboard in her hand. "Aurora. You're a brave little girl with an awesome sister, you know that?"

She giggles and shakes her head. "Yes. Thank you." With everything resolved to her satisfaction, Aurora pulls her sister over to the bed and closes the curtain.

Evren stares after them, her lip pulled between her teeth.

"Are you giving them Druid blood in the hopes it will heal them or give them magic?" I ask, my eyes darting from the men donating blood to the dying patients. Gabriel is already infuriated with her interference with the Druids. If he knew about this additional experiment, he'd go off the deep end. Changing the order of things like life and death is crossing a line he won't be able to ignore. Uneasy myself, I stare at the closed curtains.

"My hope is to cure them, but if they evolve and develop magic or pass the ability on to their children, I wouldn't be disappointed," she returns, nervously eyeing me. "If you want to leave, I completely understand. We just met, and this is beyond your duties as a savior."

My jaw clenches, and I pull her closer. "Listen carefully." I wait until her focus is entirely on me. "I will not abandon you. Period. There is no disclaimer. No out clause. Is that clear enough for you?"

She nods, but the look in her eyes says she's not quite convinced. Proof. It's the only thing she'll believe.

I sigh. "Go, do your thing. I'll protect us." My eyes linger on the little girl being tucked into bed. She reminds me so much of Danica at her age. Smart, fearless. If the experiment doesn't work, she will die. Here. In an abandoned factory.

I head outside and make a few phone calls.

An hour later, Ishkova arrives with the Druid books from my desk, along with a handful of artifacts the scholars found with Viridian spells on them. This is all of the Druid information we have on file. They're still waiting to hear back from other libraries. I don't hold out much hope it will happen quickly. The Dark Fae King is notoriously difficult when anyone asks to look at his library, much less borrow a book, but he likes me. Sort of.

She mentioned her temporary living quarters were upstairs, so I take everything up for us to read later.

The upstairs loft shocks me. Sparse is an understatement. A tiny kitchen lies along one wall. There's one comfortable-looking chair with a small table beside it. A large desk with a computer, laptop, and a large monitor. A bathroom and another room, which I assume is the bedroom, although I don't go in there.

Frowning, I place the items on the kitchen counter.

This isn't going to work. It's cold and drafty up here, and barely livable. Not wanting to alert Gabriel to our location, I keep my magic low key. A couch, a king-sized bed with all the bedding, a fireplace, and a kitchen table with chairs appear in the space one-by-one. Each arrival uses the most minimal of magic, easily attributed to a witch with moderate powers, not the Ruler of the Underworld.

For the pièce de résistance, I add rugs throughout the space and heavy drapes along the windows. It's not much, but it will be enough for now. Satisfied, I transfer the books and artifacts from the counter to the kitchen table and head back to the lab.

When I get downstairs, the men giving blood are gone, and Evren's closing the curtains on the bed closest to the door. I arch a brow, and she shakes her head. The elderly man didn't make it through the first phase of her experiment.

My gut tightens, and I can't help but look over at the little girl. Her cheeks are flushed, and her heart is beating a little fast, but she's holding in there. My hand trembles a bit at the thought of seeing her die. Her sister glances over at me, her eyes filled with worry, but looks away quickly as if I scare her.

Evren's pacing back and forth outside. Her mouth is moving along with her fingers, as if she's mentally retracing her steps.

Instead of interrupting, I lean against the building and watch her. I expected her to be upset at the old man's death or to feel defeated, but it's almost as if it adds fuel to the fire that burns inside her. She needs to help people. It's ingrained in her.

The young woman comes running out. "Something's wrong with my sister. She can't breathe. Help her! Please,

please, help her." Sobs escape, but she shoves them back and rubs furious hands across her face to wipe her tears away.

So young to have to be that strong. I pick up the phone. "I need you now."

I rush to Aurora's bed and stand at the foot while I watch Evren working on the young girl. Her little face is now bone white, and her breathing is labored. She's dying.

"Fight, little one. Fight to stay here with Becca. She needs you, more than she will ever say," Evren tells the girl. She smooths her damp hair back from her face while she listens to her beating heart.

It's almost too late. Her heart beats slowly now, as if each contraction takes great effort. A slim hand lands on the crook of my arm, and I turn to find Arden behind me.

"Evren, the experiment didn't work, but we can still save the girl. Let Arden help," I say softly, reaching over to grasp her hand.

At first, she doesn't respond, but a second later, her hand grips mine and she takes a step backward. "Can she really save her?"

"Maybe, but Aurora doesn't have much time," I reply, slowly pulling her away from the side of the bed to the foot, where I'm standing. "Let's give her some room." I wrap an arm around her from behind and pull her against me.

She immediately grips my forearm with both hands. Her nails dig into me, but I move in closer to lend her my strength. The sweet scent of her body drifts up, and I automatically inhale, filling my senses.

I motion for Becca to move closer to Evren. She swallows her fear of me and does it, but her eyes remain fixed on Arden and her sister.

Arden takes a deep breath and places her hands over the little girl's body. A golden glow appears, and she guides it over

Aurora's heart and lungs. Seconds turn into minutes before she finally takes a breath.

"She was on the verge of leaving us, but she's stable for now," Arden says softly, relief in her voice. Little beads of sweat dot her brow. "I'll come back in a few hours to do another treatment."

I look around for her escort but find no one. "Who came with you?"

Even at 5'11", Arden has to stretch up to reach my cheek. She presses a kiss lightly on one side, then whispers in my ear, "Who's the gorgeous redhead?" Her Elven green eyes are dancing with mischief, and I can't help but chuckle.

"You're avoiding the question," I reply with a mock frown.

"So are you," she retorts. "I'll be back."

"Do they know you're gone?" I call out, although I already know the answer.

"They do now," she says with a grin as she walks out the door.

A warrior and powerful witch, Arden can certainly take care of herself. Still, I wouldn't want to face the five males who are undoubtedly standing by the portal, waiting for her return.

I look down to find Evren staring up at me with an analytical look on her face. Her deep green eyes are quickly noting all the details I usually try to keep hidden.

Leaning over, I whisper in her ear, "One day, I'd like to see you look at me without speculating on my motives or trying to analyze my every move." I grin. "Do you realize you have the tiniest freckles scattered across your nose?"

Her eyes flick away, but seconds later, they're locked with mine again. "And if I looked at you, what would I see?"

"Me," my reply is simple but honest.

"Maybe one day." She waves a hand at the door. "Who was the witch? You seemed close."

Movement catches my eye. "I'll explain later. Look at Aurora."

Evren turns her head to watch Aurora's eyes flutter open. Her breath catches, and her hand squeezes mine tightly. Seconds later, she's rushing over to examine her patient.

THIRTEEN

<u>EVREN</u>

When evening comes, two patients are left. The middle-aged woman had a sudden heart attack and died. The young man is holding steady and even seems to be improving. He's the most promising patient I've had since I started this experiment. Leaning over, I draw some fresh blood.

Aurora is also holding steady, but I can't count her as a success because the transfusion didn't save her; Arden did.

The thought of the gorgeous blond witch makes me frown. I'm grateful she's healing Aurora. I am. I'm also a tiny bit resentful that I can't use my powers to save her, but it's a childish thought I'm choosing to ignore.

What is she to him? She must mean something. Lucifer is extremely comfortable around her, and the emotion that shines out of his eyes… is love. I can feel it. He mentioned being married, but never said anything about whether he has someone now. Are they together?

It's not like we know each other that well, really. My original analysis pegged him as a lone wolf, but maybe I missed a detail. I'm not usually wrong, well almost never. Am I wrong? Why is this bugging me so much? An analysis is subjective. Besides, I need to concentrate on finding answers for my patients not on figuring out Lucifer.

Cracking my neck, I slip in to check on Aurora and find Arden conducting another healing session on her. When I see Arden tense and reach a hand to the dagger at her side, I realize she's more than a witch. Her reflexes are too quick and instinctive. She's a warrior.

She glances at me, then returns to healing Aurora.

With her attention diverted, I take a second to study her. Somewhere around 5'10" or 5'11", athletic build, with long blond hair and bright green eyes. Too bright. The color suggests Elven in her blood. A hybrid? Maybe. It would explain her immortal status since most witches are human.

A second later, she rests her hands on the bed and hangs her head. "With a few more treatments, I'll be able to get rid of the cancer completely. It's a tricky disease, though. Healing her now won't prevent it from returning."

I tentatively reach out and lay a hand on Arden's shoulder. "Thank you. She came here looking for a microscopic chance, and you gave that to her. And to Becca."

Arden looks over at the young woman asleep in the chair across from her and nods. "I'm glad. It's sad. They only have each other in this world." She links her arm in mine. "Come on, let's go tell Lucifer the good news. He'll be incredibly relieved to hear Aurora will make it."

I tilt my head. "Why does he care so much about Aurora?"

It's puzzled me ever since Arden arrived, but I was so grateful, I pushed it aside.

"My guess is she reminds him of Danica. Something about her. Maybe her coloring or her personality. He loved his daughter very much," she replies with a thoughtful look.

"He said something at the cottage about his wife and daughter passing away," I admit to her. "I didn't realize she had been young when she died."

Arden stops walking and turns to me in disbelief. "He took you to the cottage? The one by the lake?"

She's been there, too? He acted like he never brought anyone there. A twinge of disappointment hits me. "It wasn't a romantic rendezvous. I needed a temporary place to hide. We didn't stay long." Why am I trying to reassure her?

Arden eyes me with a puzzled look on her face before suddenly laughing. "Lucifer and I are not together. We're family. I'll let him explain, though. He can be a bit touchy on the subject."

She hesitates for a second. "For a long, long time, he grieved for his wife and daughter. To escape it, he concentrated on making the Underworld a safe place for his people. This is the first spark I've seen in him. Keep up whatever you're doing."

Dismay fills me. What am I doing? Lying to him. Hiding who I am. Unable to say anything reassuring in return, I paste a smile on my face.

Her phone rings, and she pulls it out and looks at the screen. "Oops, got to go. Promised I'd be back by now. Give Lucifer the update on Aurora, and I'll return later."

They're family. The thought brings a real smile to my face. The tingling at the back of my neck warns me I'm being watched. I scan the space and find Lucifer's intense blue eyes on me. He's standing by the front door talking to one of his demons, but his attention is on me.

Flustered, I turn away and walk over to my lab to find something to do. The vials of blood I drew earlier are waiting on the counter for my analysis. Relieved to have something to occupy my mind, I snatch them up and start running tests.

Hours later, the results are in. The cancer markers are considerably lower, a promising indication that the experiment is working. John, the young man, might have a chance.

My primary goal is to get rid of the cancer, but I'm also looking for some sign of magic. I run new tests to check for any other changes to the blood. Nothing shows up. Some of my earlier excitement deflates a little.

Reaching up, I rub circles at the base of my neck to alleviate some of the tension.

Strong hands come down on top of mine and I freeze.

"Let me."

I hesitate for a brief second, but when he doesn't move, I remove my hand and drop my head forward. Fingers dig into the knots in my shoulder, and a small moan of relief escapes.

"Thanks, I needed this."

"You need to rest," he replies firmly. His hands move across to massage my shoulders. "Relax. All you have done since we arrived is work. Stop thinking for a few minutes."

Ignoring the words, I update him on the latest. "It appears to be working. The cancer is receding. Whether we can get it in full remission, I don't know, but this is the first positive results I've seen since I started these experiments."

His hands pause, and he leans down to murmur in my ear. "Stop thinking. For a few minutes. Breathe." Fingers press down on the sides of my spine. "This would be easier if you were lying down."

The words tumble through my brain, and I can't help but

imagine myself on a bed with him leaning over me. Strong hands working their way slowly down my bare back to the base of my spine. The massage changing in tone to something more sensual.

His power crackles over my skin like static electricity, driving me from a relaxed state to the edge of desire. I jump up and rotate my shoulders. "Feels so much better. Thank you. I'm going to go upstairs and relax for a bit. Get away from the lab."

My mother and the experiments. That's it. There isn't time for anything else. Or anyone else.

Focus, Evren.

Blue eyes crease with amusement, and he grabs my hand. "Come meet General Ishkova first, then I'll go up with you."

He drags me over to the blue-haired demon I noticed earlier. "Evren, this is General Ishkova, my third-in-command." The man dips his chin in respect. "He and his men are going to stand watch tonight. Hopefully, knowing it's safe, you can get some rest."

I stare at the light green eyes assessing me with an unblinking stare and swallow. I'm not sure if he approves of this assignment, but it is nice to know we have back-up.

"Nice to meet you, General Ishkova, and thank you." I glance at Lucifer. "I'm going to go upstairs. Meet you up there?"

Lucifer studies me for a second. "I'll be there in a couple of minutes. It couldn't hurt for me to walk the perimeter."

Relieved to have a few minutes to myself, I nod and bolt up the stairs. Except when I get there, I stop abruptly and blink. Then blink again. The normally bare room has been transformed into something... cozy. A fire blazes in the previously non-existent fireplace with furniture grouped around it. Rugs line the cold concrete floors and drapes flank the drafty windows. In the far corner sits a massive bed fit for a ruler, piled high with luxurious-looking pillows and plush blankets. A good place for a massage. I quickly shift my gaze away.

It feels like the home I had when I was a child, when my father was still alive. It was him, my mother, and me, and it was full of cozy moments like this one. I haven't felt this way in ages, like someone gave me a warm hug. When he died, my mother turned her focus to science, and I followed in her footsteps.

With a sigh, I run a hand over the soft, furry throw on the back of a chair. The urge to tell him who I am is strong, but it's too early and dangerous. Soon though.

A pile of books catches my eye, and I move over to the new dining table to grab the one on top. It's the hierarchy of the Druids. Fascinated, I flip through the pages to see if there's anything new to note but find I know most of the information.

The air around me stirs with power and something dark and sensuous.

"Those are from my personal library. When the torque came into my court, I ordered the scholars to find everything we had on Druids. I have also sent requests to other libraries to borrow any books they might have on them, too," he explains, before reaching over my shoulder to push the books aside. His breath blows on my hair, and I shiver at his nearness.

He motions to a small pile of metal items on the table. "In addition, I asked them to find all the artifacts with Viridian engraved on them. This is it."

The heat from his body surrounds me, and for a second, the image from earlier flashes in my mind. My feet shuffle the tiniest bit closer to him, wanting to feel him wrapped around me. I pull in a deep breath. It's so very tempting, but we... I have more important things to do. To prevent myself from giving in, I exhale, turn, and face him.

"Thank you. This means a lot. I put out additional requests

for information, but few have come forward, and what little they brought didn't amount to much. There doesn't seem to be a lot of information available, maybe because the Druids led a mostly secretive existence," I tell him, my voice husky.

His eyes darken a shade. "My sources say they were a pretty insular group. Only married other Druids," he informs me.

If they only married other Druids, it means there was more than one line of succession with Druid power. The chances of several families evolving at the same time are astronomical. My mother must have used power or magic to make this happen. How did she choose the families? How many were chosen? I look over at the pile of books. There has to be some-thing in there. I wonder if other families have lineage books like Brennus'?

"I seem to recall at least one family's book," he replies. The amused tone to his voice tells me I spoke the last question out loud. "Who's Brennus?"

"I thought he was the first Druid, but now, I'm not sure. If there were other families, we need more information. Is there something that connects them? If they share a commonality, all my experiments will need to be adjusted, but I'd be closer to the answer," I say excitedly, already starting to think about the possibilities.

He studies me closely. "Why is this so important to you? Is it a legacy you're trying to fulfill? The science? Or something else?"

His questions make me pause. I could have come here and searched for clues on my mother's whereabouts, but instead I made a choice to get involved. "I wish I could stand on the sidelines of life, but I can't. I'm not built that way. I can help them. I may not know how yet, but I know, with every ounce of my being, I can change their lives for the better. Humans deserve a chance."

"I hope so, but I've learned that some things can't be prevented," he replies with a distant look in his eye.

"You helped Aurora," I point out to him.

He stills. "How's she doing?"

"Aurora's doing well. She needs a few more treatments, but Arden thinks she will be able to eliminate the cancer... at least for now," I tell him.

He dips his chin in a brief nod.

"Why did you save her?" I ask, curious to see what he'll say.

Hooded eyes study me for a second. "She should have a future. A chance to grow up, dream big, and find love. Out of everyone, children deserve it the most."

His vague reply doesn't fool me.

"Arden thinks Aurora reminds you of Danica. Is that true?" I tentatively ask, not wanting to intrude on something that seems so personal, but unable to stop myself from asking the question.

His lips curl in disdain, but his eyes shine with memories. "Trying to analyze me like you do everything else?"

Ignoring his reply, I arch a brow and stare at him. The look on his face reminds me of the sadness I sensed when we were at the cottage.

The emotion disappears as if it was never here. He waves a hand toward the room. "What did you think of the changes?"

"It's cozy," I tell him coolly, disappointed in the change in subject. I look around the room and sigh. I can't really be upset he isn't opening up. I'm not exactly sharing all my secrets either. "It's really nice. Thank you." I place my hand on his arm and squeeze. When I find my thumb rubbing the muscles in his forearm, I immediately pull it back to my side.

The hard lines of his face soften. "Good. We have a lot of work to do. I want to know how many Druids are left and why Gabriel fears their resurrection. His sole objective is upholding the greater good. What possible power could the Druids have that would put that at risk?"

I nod in agreement. "I'm not tired, so we can start right away."

He gestures to the bed. "Are you sure? I don't really need sleep, but I brought a bed for you."

Worried now, I can't help but bite my lip. "I have a bed. Didn't you see it in my room?"

He shakes his head. "I didn't go into your bedroom."

Relief pours through me. "I'm going to change into something more comfortable." Without waiting for a reply, I head toward my bedroom.

Slowly twisting the knob, I crack open the door. When only darkness slips through the small opening, I release the breath I'd been holding and enter the room. Thankfully, I remembered to close the portal this morning.

FOURTEEN

<u>EVREN</u>

When I come back to the room, Lucifer's wearing a pair of loose pants and a long sleeve t-shirt. In black, of course. Does the man own anything in any other color? Black might be the perfect foil for his white-blond hair and golden skin, but it would be nice to see him in some other color. Maybe a shade of blue, like his eyes.

He looks up from one end of the couch where he's reading and cocks an eyebrow when he sees me. He takes a sip from the mug in his hand. "I made some coffee, although I'll warn you, it's strong."

I nod. "Thanks. I've never developed a taste for it. Plus, it makes me bounce off the walls, which is never a good thing." I wander over to the dining table and grab the slim book I spotted earlier.

Heading back, I debate between the chair and the other end of the couch. The couch it is, not because it's next to him. Absolutely not. It's closer to the fireplace, and it's cold here at night. I don't know why I didn't think to get a fireplace. Or furniture. I grimace. Oh, wait. As usual, the science always comes first. Basic comfort is at the bottom of my list.

Lucifer shifts restlessly on the couch, and I find myself unconsciously leaning closer. Immediately straightening, I flip open the cover of the small leather-bound book.

The History of Druids by Tadg, Druid bard. 940 (BCE)

Inside the book is an official-looking document stating the addition of BCE. Contents transferred from the original scroll to parchment in 337 CE. Bound in leather 1620 CE.

I lean over and point to the document. "Look. This book was transferred from a scroll. Did you do that for all the scrolls in your library?"

He peers over my shoulder. "We did. Some of them were almost illegible due to age and handling. They are now kept in a sealed vault to protect them."

Fascinating. "Is Underworld a scholarly place?"

He hesitantly answers. "No, not yet. I'm working to change it, though."

"That's wonderful. I'd love to see your library. It must be incredible and filled with forgotten history." I murmur with a wistful smile.

His face is sad when he replies. "I wish I could give you a tour. Out of everyone I know, you are one of the few who would appreciate it. But unfortunately, Underworld isn't viable for humans."

My mouth turns down. I can't help but picture all the treasures I could find in there. *Like this one.* I rub a hand over the book. Bards were the truthsayers and historical record-keepers back then. This might provide the most accurate and interesting account of Druid history than the books I've read so far.

Most of them have been extremely dry, not to mention the fact... I snort... they were full of propaganda. All of the books portray Druids as learned men and scholars, not a race with power. There's not one mention of magic. How did the Druids keep it a secret for so long?

I flip the page and dive in.

Druid history has been passed in song from one bard to another for four hundred years, but there are fewer bards now. Druids with power want more than to wander the Earth telling the tales of our origin. They want wealth and dynasties. And, of course, more power. If there comes a day when there are no bards, will we lose the knowledge of our history? In order to preserve the words I learned from my bard father, I'm committing the ultimate act of betrayal and writing it down, not for spite, but to ensure future generations know of our origin.

Brennus, legendary warrior and uniter of kings, became the first of us to receive the gift of magic, along with the golden torque. According to the songs sung by my father, a divine being with red hair appeared to Brennus in a dream. She offered to bestow magic upon him. Like the Fae and Elven, the demons from below, and the wolves from the north, he too could wield power, if he so wished.

Brennus asked her why she chose him.

She explained, "The first must be a warrior. Not only a human of considerable strength, but a person who can exhibit bravery, self-discipline, and wisdom in equal measure. A true leader for a new race."

Brennus agreed, and the goddess put him asleep. When he woke, his blood was on fire. Fevers and chills wracked his body, along with the pain of a thousand cuts. Death stalked him. He begged for mercy, but she gave him none. His breathing became labored, and a heaviness entered his chest. Still, she refused to heal him or ease his pain.

For six days and nights, he fought death. On the seventh night, she sliced open his arm and watched his blood spill onto the floor. The light faded, and everything went dark. He thought his life had ended.

When he woke a second time, there was no pain. Instead, his blood buzzed with life and power. With magic. And the strength he had before this day was nothing compared to the strength he could call upon now.

When he thirsted, a cup of water appeared. When he was cold, fire would flare high in the fireplace. And this was only the beginning. She explained his magic came from the mind. With thought and will came power and results. But power of the mind is a two-edged sword. Anger can just as easily coalesce into thought and will and bring down a friend or enemy. Self-discipline and wisdom are necessary to control the mind and wield the magic.

Not only did she give Brennus magic, but she also presented him with a second gift... a golden torque with a spell written on it. She explained her words would not only allow him to amplify his own powers, but to perform impressive feats of magic beyond the single power of one Druid.

Confused, he asked, "But am I not the first and only Druid?"

She smiled. "Today, you are one. Tomorrow, I will bestow this gift on nine others across the Earth. From ten shall come two hundred. From those children, almost a thousand more. And so forth. You will be their leader."

Stunned at the thought of leading all Druids, he bowed humbly before her. "Thank you. We shall honor your gift and honor you. Our temples will be named after you and statues erected in your image. Every year, on this day, we will celebrate you."

"You must not mention me, nor can you build anything in my honor. The magic is a secret gift, one I'm only sharing with ten

humans. You'll pass it along to your children, and your children's children. That is how you will honor me, understand?"

The book goes on to give an account of the nine families who were given the same gift—Amenemhet, Akakios, Domitia, Minako, Chen, Floriana, Kawisenhawe, Zoya, and Retha. Men across the globe, who became Druids and pledged their allegiance to Brennus. Each of those men sired many children, almost the two hundred she predicted, and the Druid powers passed to all of them. He ends the book with one last paragraph.

Brennus is long gone, but the Druid legacy lives on with each new child born. Our powers are a blessing, our blood a secret, and every day, we whisper our thanks to the divine goddess who gave them to us. Let this account live as the official history of the Druids.

The book falls to my lap. Words run in circles in my mind while I try to decipher what she did to change them. Over and over, I come to the same conclusion, yet I push away the answer, determined to find another, one that doesn't make me sick to my stomach.

I spear my fingers through my hair, separate the strands into chunks, and start braiding it while I think about the answer.

Shit.

She didn't help humans find their powers; she gave them hers. A long exhale leaves my lungs. Occam's Razor. The simplest explanation that will account for a circumstance or event is most likely the correct explanation.

It's obvious her first attempt was disastrous. Brennus almost died from the transfusion. When she realized he was going to die, she bled him out, then tried a second time with a new variation. My guess is she diluted the blood using some natural herb or a common spice like turmeric, ginger, or ginseng.

The reason Druids have power is because of their Viridian blood. The reason Druids have dwindled in numbers is due to a number of factors... insular marriages, blood diluted with each new generation born, and possibly death by Gabriel and his band of merry angels. To replenish their numbers, they need a new infusion of Viridian blood.

I sigh.

"Is everything okay?" a voice filled with gravel asks beside me.

I blink and take a moment to erase the shock from my expression. Turning to meet his intense blue eyes, I nod. "This journal gives details on the ten individuals who received the gift of magic. I'm going to look them up and see if there are any progeny alive today."

"Did it say anything as to why Gabriel might want to destroy them?"

My hand clenches the book for a second, but I slowly extend it to him. "No, not really. It's an account of how the ten dynasties were started and their magic. Their power lies in the mind. Their foundation is thought and will. With those two things, they can create and destroy equally."

His fingers grip mine and the book for a long minute. "Interesting magic. I'll keep reading through the other books to see if I can find the answer." He releases me.

I'm not lying. The book doesn't say why the angels, or why Gabriel, don't want the Druids resurrected. I only know because I know her. And her blood. My mother. The one with the power to kill angels. The same blood she passed to the Druids.

If she weren't eternal, I'd think she was dead, killed by the angels for this great blasphemy. But she is.

So where is she?

FIFTEEN

LUCIFER

Truth rings in her voice, but the tightness of her eyes tells me she's hiding something. Or rather... hiding something new and serious. She's been a closed book since I arrived, but this is different. My eyes slide to the slim book clenched tightly in her hand. The answer lies in its pages.

With a sigh, she slides it onto my lap. "You should read it."

Trust builds in the smallest of gestures. "Thank you." I thread my fingers in hers. "I—"

Vargas appears in front of me, a similar look of panic on his face. "Gabriel took Ishkova."

"Are you fucking kidding me?" I roar, startling Evren. "Not you. I'm not yelling at you." I pull my hand from hers and wave a hand in front of us. "My second-in-command, Vargas, is sort of here. Long story, but he's temporarily without a body, which is why you can't see him."

Turning back to Vargas, I start firing orders at him. "I'll give you a note to take to Ishkova's second. What's his name?" My mind sees an image of the hydra, but I can't remember his name.

"Moge," Vargas replies.

I snap my fingers. "Right, take a note to Moge. Make sure he grabs our top men. I want them to surround The Abbey and protect Evren while I go after Gabriel. Can you—?"

Fingers tap on my shoulder. "Excuse me? I'm not going anywhere," Evren pertly informs me. "I have work to do. Patients to take care of here. Families to find. I'll be fine."

My face hardens. While she might be able to kill an angel, she's still human, with a human's vulnerabilities and weaknesses. "Gabriel took Ishkova, who is thousands of years old with ferocious fighting skills and the ability to beat almost any angel in battle. He's one of the best warriors I know and my third-in-command for a reason. You think he went quietly? I know you can kill angels, but how well can you fight? If Gabriel sends a full platoon to get you, can you fight your way through thirty angels?"

She crosses her arms and glares up at me. "Stop yelling. Offer me a reasonable alternative, and I'll consider it."

I scowl. "This isn't a negotiation. You're going to The Abbey. It's a sanctuary protected by a primal source. Gabriel can't cross the threshold, nor can any of his angels. If you want to keep your patients safe, you'll take them there."

She sucks in a breath. "You think he'd kill my patients?"

I give her a firm nod. "At this point, I don't think he's operating on sound logic. He's desperate." I smother the tinge of satisfaction the latter statement generates. "So, what's it going to be?"

"We're going to The Abbey, of course," she replies, throwing both hands in the air. "I'll get everyone ready to go.

At least Aurora will be able to finish her treatments. I assume The Abbey is where Arden lives?"

She blinks innocent green eyes at me, but I see the knowledge in their depths.

The reminder of how close she will be to my family makes me uneasy, but there's not much choice. An incredibly powerful spell protects the cottage and surrounding land, but spells can be broken. The Abbey is protected by a primal source. If I have to choose the safest option, it's definitely not going to be the cottage.

"What did Arden tell you?" I ask gruffly.

"Not much. She said you were family. At the lake, you mentioned your son and his family live at The Abbey. I simply put the two together," she explains with a smirk. "I wouldn't worry about Arden. She moves like a warrior, and like you said, I can kill, but I can't really fight. She could probably take me out in less than five seconds." With those final words, she walks out of the room.

Vargas roars with laughter. "She's good. I like her."

"You like anybody who compliments your daughter and her fighting skills," I say exasperatedly. After all, he's the reason she's so good at it.

His dark eyes study me. "True. But it's also nice to see someone stand up to you."

It is actually, but I don't admit that to Vargas. "Let's get back to the plan. While you're taking the note to Moge, I'll transport everyone here to The Abbey. Then I want you to focus on finding Ishkova. When you have his location, send me the coordinates. Got it?"

When he nods, I wave a hand over a piece of paper and a note to Moge appears. Sometimes electronics don't work well in Underworld. The old-fashioned method is often the best, and surprisingly, the fastest due to portals, although Vargas has an even faster route now.

I hand it to him. "Thanks."

He disappears, and I head downstairs.

"Aurora and Becca are ready to go," Evren says when she sees me. "You can take them now."

"We're all going together," I state firmly.

She looks puzzled but keeps moving, aware our time is short.

I dial Daire. "I need your assistance and the protection of The Abbey." Given Arden's been here several times already, I don't bother to give him my location. I hang up and cross the room to help Evren get her other patient ready to go.

The young man sways when she pulls him into a sitting position. "He can't sit up, much less stand. Can we take him in the bed?"

"Yes," I tell her. "Are you ready to go? Is there anything you need to take with you? I don't want you to return until I'm sure it's safe."

Something odd flashes in her eyes but disappears quickly. "I'll grab my laptop and a few other items." She runs to her desk and grabs a backpack.

Seconds later, Daire walks into the lab, followed by Arden, Valerian, and Fallon. "What happened?"

A familiar flash of regret runs through me. Danica taught me a valuable lesson, and in my effort to keep my remaining child safe, I ordered Daire not to show emotions or affection to me in public. When he follows those orders, I can't help but wish things were different.

"Gabriel took Ishkova," I tell him. "Sorry for the short notice, but I need a place angels can't enter."

Daire's blue eyes take in the four humans in the room. He swivels back to me with an eyebrow cocked in question. He knows I've avoided humans like the plague since his mother died. Not because I hate them, but their vulnerability is something I can't afford.

I ignore it and turn to Evren. "Ready to go?"

She eyes the four supernaturals in front of me and shuffles closer to my side. "Introduce me. I don't like strangers."

My eyebrow rises at her demanding tone.

Valerian chokes, trying to stifle his laughter, but he's used to people being scared of his massive size. "I'm Valerian. Dragon shifter. You'll be safe with us. I promise."

I snort at the understated description of himself but appreciate the ease with which he introduced his supernatural status.

Aurora's and Becca's eyes widen with understanding, but they don't say anything.

Evren, of course, is as cool as ever. "Evren. Aurora, Becca, and that's John in the bed. Human."

Daire's eyes narrow on Evren, but I subtly shake my head. She's human... plus. I still think she's Druid. She even smells like them, although she insists she isn't one.

"Fallon, elf," the dark-haired warrior announces.

"Daire, vampire," my son says, following Fallon's description with a similar version. "Is everybody ready to go?"

Evren nods slowly, but her eyes are swiveling between Daire and me.

"The Abbey is a sanctuary where all races are welcome, supernatural and human, although only supernaturals live there at the moment. I promise, you'll be safe," Arden says with her usual wide, confident smile. "I'll carry Aurora."

Evren holds out her hand for Becca, but I motion to Fallon and grab her extended hand in my own. "You're coming with me. Fallon will get Becca. Valerian will help John, and Daire will protect our rear flank." I can tell she's nervous about going to an unknown place.

She gives a strained laugh but grips my hand tightly. "I'm trusting you, not only with my life but theirs too. Don't make me regret it." Her green eyes search mine for reassurance.

I inhale sharply, drowning in their dark depths. It's the first time she's looked at me with something other than speculation or suspicion. *Damn it.*

Tearing my eyes away, I squeeze her hand. "I won't."

SIXTEEN

<u>EVREN</u>

Within seconds of arriving at The Abbey, Lucifer leaves me with a barely muttered goodbye. Wondering what to do, I look around and find a pair of violet eyes assessing me from the corner. Tall, lean, fastidious-looking in a sharply creased suit and tie, he's handsome and obviously Fae. There's an icy coolness about him.

He steps forward. "Evren? I'm Theron. Welcome to The Abbey." He motions for Becca to step closer, then waves an elegant hand behind us. "Let me give you both a tour before I show you to your rooms."

When I turn around, I'm shocked to see a large dance floor flanked by two levels of tables and chairs and a large bar on the far side. Everything is glittery and gold and quiet right now.

"He brought me to a bar?" I ask, trying to smother the laugh threatening to erupt.

Theron stiffens. "The Abbey is a sanctuary where paranormals from all races can congregate. We shelter or help individuals when they need it, even if they're hiding from their own." He turns to me. "Nobody crosses that threshold without our permission. The Abbey is protected by a primal source that recognizes no authority but its own."

Nerves slither down my spine as I wonder if it will let me stay.

Theron explains the hours for the club, then leads us into the kitchen, where a large, fierce man is yelling orders right and left while the staff scurries to do his bidding. His build and demeanor scream predatory shifter, but his staff seems to be a mix of paranormals. A witch, a few shifters, and a vampire.

I pretend to listen when Theron explains where to find food and encourages us to help ourselves. The chef scowls when Theron waves a hand toward one of his immaculate stoves but says nothing. That alone tells me a lot about the power dynamics here.

Becca is wringing her hands, so I reach out and take one of hers into mine. She gives me a tremulous smile. "Do you think we could find Aurora now?"

Theron glances sharply at her, then flicks his eyes to our joined hands. "Of course. Follow me."

With purposeful strides, he leads us over to an elevator on the far wall.

"How big is this place?" I ask with a frown.

"It depends on the day. The Abbey flexes to fit our needs," he replies, his eyes darting in my direction. "After you." The doors open at that very moment, making me wonder exactly what I'm getting into here.

Becca pulls me into the elevator, and Theron follows.

Without a single word or push of a button, the doors close and it begins to move.

I'm instantly and utterly captivated. The merging of technology with magic is seamless and so incredibly functional for a sanctuary that is constantly "flexing" to meet the needs of its inhabitants.

My hand reaches out and glides down the wall nearest to me. "Who designed this incredible feat of steel wrapped in magic?"

His violet eyes show a spark of something natural. Pride. "I designed it. Why?"

The elevator shifts and we're suddenly moving horizontally, not vertically. It truly does utilize magic to defy the laws of physics. "It's incredible. I'd love to hear how you were able to merge technology and magic in such a way that the original element is almost unrecognizable. The elevator uses magic to serve its original purpose of transporting individuals to a different location, but in a way that eclipses its design."

One side of his mouth lifts almost imperceptibly. "I'd be happy to explain it, but I'm not sure a human would understand the complexities of it." Violet eyes turn to me with a challenge in their depths.

It's obvious he knows something is off about me but can't quite place his finger on what it is that's bugging him. I smirk.

"I'm a scientist. We're universally cursed with the need to break down the complexities of life." Although I'm dying to know how he did it, I have enough on my plate right now, so I let it go.

The doors open and we step out into a hallway. He motions to a door on the right. "This is Becca and Aurora's room. John's is next door, and yours is farther down the hall. Arden figured you would want to stay together."

When he opens the door, Becca drops my hand and runs

over to Aurora. Her little face is flushed with health, while Arden, who's standing by the bed, looks a bit tired.

"Another treatment?" I inquire lightly.

Arden flashes a broad smile. "The cancer is gone. It may come back later, but if it does, we'll do more treatments." She pops Aurora on the nose. "How do you feel about that, poppet?"

Aurora looks at Becca. "It means we get to stay together. I can go back to school, and Becca can find someone to marry. Right, Becca?" Her beautiful brown eyes meet her sister's.

With tears flowing down her face, Becca chokes out a laugh and smooths Aurora's hair back from her forehead. "Only the best for us." The words are all she can get out, but the beaming smile on her face tells us how happy she is right now.

An ache builds in the back of my throat. Her emotions are bleeding into me, and the urge to cry along with her is building fast. I swivel around to Theron.

"While they're celebrating, why don't you show me my room?"

He nods shortly and flicks an assessing glance at Arden. "Maybe you should go lie down for a bit."

She narrows her eyes in return. "Stop fussing. I'm a little tired, that's all. I'll go with you, though, to give them some privacy." Her hand reaches out and pats Aurora's.

Theron leads us a short distance down the hall to another door. He opens it and ushers us into the room.

This one is smaller, with a few basic necessities—a bed, chair, and dresser. My bag of clothes is sitting on a nearby stand. I'd hoped for a desk but can easily make do with the bed and chair.

"Have you shown her the lab?" Arden asks, her eyes studying the man standing beside me. She heaves an exasperated sigh when he gives her a look. "Come on. Lucifer told us you would need a lab." Pulling me out of the room and down the hall to the very end, she opens the last door with a flourish. "Ta da!"

I step into the room to find stainless steel counters, beakers, several centrifuges, microscopes, a couple of PCR machines to amplify and target DNA, and a UV-lightbox. It's a state-of-the-art geneticist lab. Everything in my old lab has been replicated here.

My palm skims the cold surface of the table. "Thank you. This has everything I need to continue my experiments. I don't know how long I'll be here, but I'm happy to pay for everything." My mind immediately starts rearranging the room to suit the experiments I'm running now.

Arden leans her head on Theron's shoulder. "We didn't buy it. Lucifer gave us a list and a chest of gold." She looks at Theron. "Someone really should teach him how to use a more current money system."

"I believe Daire has tried, but Lucifer refuses to use money. He says gold is universally accepted, and it's a waste of time to learn a system that will be obsolete in another thousand years," Theron replies dryly.

Arden thinks about it for a second, then gives a resigned shrug. "I can see you're dying to get started, so we'll leave you alone. Let us know if you need anything. The elevator will take you to the main floor with just a thought."

I wave a hand bye and immediately get to work. It takes me almost an hour to get everything in place, but when I do, I know I'm ready. Excitement thrums in my veins. I know exactly what I'm going to do first. Replicate my mother's experiment. The best way to prove my theory is to test it. Unfortunately, John's blood won't work, because I've already given him Druid blood.

I need new test subjects. Healthy humans. Based on the

bard's account, my mother picked someone physically strong and healthy in order to give them a better chance of surviving the transfusion. One might be too small of a sample for me, though. Five is a better option.

Biting my cheek, I sit down at my computer and craft an ad to place in the paper. With a magical plea creatively woven in its words, it should draw my subjects to me. I wonder how Theron and the others will feel about housing more humans.

SEVENTEEN

<u>EVREN</u>

The elevator doors close behind me, but nothing happens. What did Arden say about using the elevator? It moves with a single thought.

"Bottom floor," I both think and say the words.

The elevator pauses for a long second, but then moves swiftly down.

For some reason, I'm incredibly nervous about telling them I've invited five more humans to the sanctuary. Well, invited is a bit of a stretch, but it's not like I can tell them I put out a spell to call for specimens. Who might die. Or change into something… magical.

I deliberately bump my head on the back wall of the elevator a couple of times. This was so much easier when I was in my own lab without anyone else around to question me.

The doors open, but when I step out, I'm not in the place I

expected. There's a cave in front of me, not a dance floor. My brain tries to figure out what I did wrong, and I realize I used the words "bottom floor" and not "main floor."

Shit.

"Main floor," I say, but nothing happens.

Something pulses in the darkness of the cave.

"Main floor," I repeat, visualizing the dance floor and bar in case it needs a picture to help it along.

A beautiful woman with long blond hair and the darkest of eyes steps into my line of vision. "Hello, Evren of Viridian. Granddaughter of Creatus, daughter of Viridis and man. I was wondering when you might visit me. I'm Theia, daughter of Gaea and granddaughter of Chaos. Welcome."

Main floor.

"The elevator will not go until I wish it," she says, with a tinkling laugh. "Walk with me. Tell me why you are here, and I may decide to let you stay."

With a long sigh, I step out of the elevator and walk over to her. "Forgive me." I dip my head in respect. "I'm not trying to be disrespectful, just hidden from the creator above. And to be honest, I didn't expect to see another goddess here. My mother told me he banned all gods and goddesses from Earth ages ago." My eyes slide to her curiously.

She gives a delicate shrug. "He cannot banish what was here before him. Since the primordial gods and goddesses rarely intervene in the affairs of this world or the humans who live in it, he leaves us be. Besides, with few worshippers, most of us are but residue compared to our previously powerful selves." Her eyes are twinkling when they meet mine. "There are a few exceptions, of course. The sanctuary and protection I provide is necessary for the survival of all. For those who find themselves here, I see a different path for them than the fates envisioned. If I didn't save them, terrible things could come to pass."

I stop walking. "Lucifer brought me here. I didn't come on my own. What does that mean for me?" I doubt I'm a danger to anyone, despite what they may think. Well, except those who attack me first. Maybe I should return to the warehouse so I can be closer to my portal. The humans I brought with me will be safe at The Abbey.

She lightly lays a cool hand on my arm. "I'm not sure. It's strange. Your path is hidden from me. Maybe because you're not in your true form."

My eyes drift down to the body below me. "This is my true human form, the one I used from birth until I was around a hundred years old. It's also pretty close to my Viridian form."

She tilts her head. "You're not a demi-goddess?"

I think about it for a second. "Viridian blood is dominant. While the two exist inside me, my inherent genetics are those of my mother, the goddess. The human part of me is more or less a shell I can wear when I wish to, but I don't have the usual frailties or needs that exists in their genetic code, like eating or sleeping."

Her eyes change from dark to white for a few seconds, then return to their original color. She shakes her head and removes the hand on my arm. "I thought touching you might help, but I still can't see a clear path. I will say this: a goddess' will is more powerful than fate. Be careful of the choices you make here. There is a delicate balance to it all, and one wrong move can lead to its destruction." She smiles. "But you found your way to sanctuary, and I trust in the ancient magic that brought you here."

She takes a step back, and her body starts to fade. "Sanctuary welcomes and protects you. Come back and see me again."

Between one blink and the next, she's gone.

Her words echo in my head. Maybe I should hold off on any new experiments. After all, time is on my side.

Decision made; I realize I need to get upstairs to release the humans from my spell. I move toward the elevator but stop when an auburn-haired man with a massive collection of runes tattooed on his body appears.

"Sorry, I didn't see you standing there."

He flashes a sinfully charming smile. "I know. I felt it would be rude to interrupt your conversation with yourself."

I wonder how much he heard.

I decide to ignore the possible repercussions for now. "I seem to have requested the wrong floor. Can you help me find the one with the bar?"

"Truth, interesting," he remarks, a rune flaring on his arm. "The floor with the bar is called the Main Floor. I'll escort you up there." He offers me his elbow. "Out of curiosity, what floor did you request?"

"Bottom floor. Why?" We get in the steel box, the silver doors close, and it begins to move.

Instead of answering, he leans in and inhales deeply. "You smell of Lucifer and human. Along with an underlying current of magic that is oddly familiar." His head tilts while he thinks about it. He straightens suddenly. "Cormal. You smell like Cormal."

The doors open, but my attention is solely focused on the warlock at my side.

I tense. "Who's Cormal?"

"I'm Cormal," a clipped voice answers from outside the elevator.

My head swivels toward the front where I find a stunning petite Fae female with platinum silver hair and turquoise eyes and a tall, dark-haired male with bright blue eyes who's staring at me with a strange look on his face.

"Viridis?" he murmurs in an incredulous tone.

Panic and confusion hit me simultaneously. "Evren," I reply, desperate to ask if he knows what happened to my mother but unwilling to chance it. "Viridis was my mother."

The Fae looks swiftly from him to me and back. Her eyes narrow. "Are we getting into the elevator or not?"

A sardonic smile slides across his face. "Jealousy is a beautiful expression, especially on your face."

She rolls her eyes and gets into the elevator. "You wish. I got over you a long time ago. I'm looking for a Fae Prince Charming, not Mr. Wrong-and-Full-of-Secrets."

He gets in and stares down at her. "Prince Charming won't save you. When will you learn to save yourself?" The underlying current between these two is enough to set my teeth on edge. Their words are innocuous, but their tones are full of recrimination, anger, and a whole lot of sexual tension.

Their emotions are affecting my ability to think clearly. Thankfully, the elevators open, and we spill out onto the main floor.

The warlock looks deep in thought but flashes me another killer smile. "I'm Astor, by the way. Let me know if you need anything while you're here."

I flash him a dismissive smile. "Thanks."

He slowly saunters away, and I hold my breath until he's gone.

"Don't say a word," Cormal hisses in my ear. "The walls have ears." He eyes the silver-haired Fae who is now glaring at him from across the room. "Meet me outside in ten minutes."

I weigh the consequences of learning more about my mother with the very real threat of Gabriel and his minions. "Angels are breathing down my neck."

"Not surprised," he retorts. "Ten minutes." Without another word, he stalks over to the bar, completely ignoring the beautiful Fae.

Furious, she flicks a glance at me, then sidles up next to a pair of twins on the dance floor.

I can't help but look back and forth between her and Cormal.

"Have a run in with Cormal and Meri?" Arden murmurs beside me. "Those two are a flashfire waiting to happen. Are you okay?" Her startling green eyes widen. "I just realized we're about the same height. Do you know how rare it is to find another 5'11" female? Almost impossible."

A tattooed arm comes around her. "What's impossible?" Brown eyes lock on me over her shoulder.

"We're the same height," Arden tells him. "I'm so used to towering over other women. I can't believe I didn't notice when we met."

I silently curse myself. Probably because I'd grown a couple of inches in the last hour. Being in Theia's presence brought out a little bit of the goddess in me. Now I'll have to remember to keep this height.

He hums. "You're usually very observant, gorgeous." The smile he gives her is filled with seductive sweetness, like the richest dark chocolate in the world. "Would you like to join us on the top level?" He looks at me and points to the second level.

I follow his eyes and see Daire, Valerian, Theron, and Fallon seated at a large booth, watching our every move.

"Sorry, I'm feeling a bit tired. I'll grab a glass of water and go to bed."

As I walk away, I hear him whisper "lie" in Arden's ear.

EIGHTEEN

LUCIFER

Vargas sends the coordinates to my mind, and I can't help but roll my eyes. Gabriel is holding Ishkova on the mountains of Ararat. The same mountains where humans believe Noah's ark landed after the great flood. It could be, but I don't know. By the time the flood receded, I was fighting my way through the ranks of the Underworld and didn't give a damn about the few survivors.

As a meeting place, it's a subtle, but effective, reminder of what can happen to the people here. Gabriel loves symbolism more than most angels. It bleeds into all the messages he carries to the people.

When I land beside him, Gabriel doesn't look the least bit surprised.

He waves a hand toward the snow-capped mountain in

front of us. "It's a good place to meet, don't you think? The greatest symbol of benevolence and faith. A glorious spot designated as the great reset. Or the rebirth of the human race." An ugly tone enters his voice, and his eyes dart to mine. "I hate it, don't you?"

Startled to hear the word hate come out of his mouth, I turn from the mountain to him. "I hate all the reminders. I'm surprised to hear those words come out of your mouth, though."

He continues to stare at the mountain. "It was literally my job to know the people, bring them messages, and build their faith. I knew every single soul. Good and bad. I knew their children and their children's children. Every generation since the first humans walked the Earth. They knew me. When the flood happened, whose name do you think they cried out when they received no answers to their prayers?" He pauses. "Even now. I hear them calling to me."

"How many did you save?"

He shakes his head. "None. I'm a servant, not a god. It's not up to me who lives and dies." He finally turns to face me and not the mountain. "Did you save any?"

I cross my arms. "I saved any who were brave enough to go through a portal to find a new life." The corners of my mouth turn down. "Very few were willing. They believed the water would stop and they would be saved."

"The same thing could happen again. If evil rises up and takes over the world, do you honestly think the end won't come for them all? It's why I fight every day to make sure things stay in balance." Gabriel's voice rises with each word. "Evolution needs to happen naturally. It can't be forced."

I tilt my head and give him a droll look. "Are we moving from your sad story to Evren now?"

His head rears back. "How well do you know her and what

she's doing? Druids can't be entrusted with humanity's survival."

I paste a blank expression on my face. "Tell me why, and I'll consider helping you."

His fist clenches. "I can't. You aren't to be trusted with humanity, either."

"This is going nowhere. Give me Ishkova and do what you think you have to do. But I warn you, Evren's under my protection, and I'll protect her from anyone you send after her, including yourself. I was lenient once, but I won't be again." I emphasize every word, so he knows I'm serious.

Gabriel starts pacing back and forth, his desperation apparent with every step. "We believe there is a purpose for everything under Heaven, right? If so, then the decision is already made. The race is on the decline. Let it stay that way. If they aren't surviving, there's a reason. It's the foundation of everything we believe in."

I snort at the use of the word "we." "You don't know me. Not anymore. You lost that privilege long ago. Where is Ishkova?"

He whirls around and throws up his arms. "You're picking the wrong side again."

Furious, I stalk toward him and grab his shirt in my fist. "I didn't pick a side the last time. I was given an order by you. Because I trusted you, I lost everything. My entire world. My family. The grace and love I'd been given."

He scoffs. "I might have suggested it would be good to have him gone, but I didn't order you. You took it upon yourself to kill Satan. You knew you could, so you did it. Our savior. Getting rid of the great evil. All you could think about was the glory you would get for saving us all."

The ground rumbles under our feet. My anger increases along with my voice. "You betrayed me! I thought I had his blessing, but you manipulated the situation until it suited your outcome. You were my commander, my brother, and my friend. I looked up to you. Trusted you. Look at where that got me. I'll never believe another word that comes out of your mouth. The only thing I live for is the day you fall. Then, you'll be mine."

He laughs hysterically. "You seem to have come out of it fine." He throws his hands up in the air. "Look at all the power you have now. Practically a god yourself. Back then, you were an angel rising through the ranks, a lowly foot soldier."

"Ishkova," I grit out.

He waves a hand and Ishkova appears beside me.

Beaten badly, and straining at his bonds, his usually light green eyes are red with fury. He narrows them on Gabriel.

"Humans don't belong to her," Gabriel calls out.

I help Ishkova to his feet. "They don't belong to anybody. Stay away from Evren."

With those words, I vanish, taking Ishkova down to the Underworld with me. Vargas is waiting in my office when we arrive.

Once we get the bindings off of him, blue scales coat the surface of his skin. He's close to changing into his true form. A wyvern.

The window behind my desk rattles with the fury that is rolling off him in waves. "I'm going to pluck every single feather from that bastard's wings before I kill him." He raises his fist to pound it on my desk, but I stop him with a raise of my eyebrow.

With his strength, he could put a dent in it; then I would really be pissed. Strangely, I'm not as angry as I thought I'd be.

"You can't kill him," I inform him. "At least not until he falls from grace." I pause to let him curse Gabriel and all his angel minions. "Can I finish?"

He looks down with a contrite expression on his face and nods.

"Did he say what his plans were for Evren?" I ask him.

"He wants her dead. When he took me, he expected you to leave her at the warehouse, and he was furious to find everyone gone when he arrived at her place. He destroyed her lab," he reveals. His body flickers for a second, then changes to his more human-like form.

"Anything else?"

He hangs his head. "Sorry, I couldn't hear much over the beatings. It sounded like he said 'abbey', but I can't be certain."

I glance at Vargas behind him, and he disappears immediately.

"Go rest. I've got Moge watching Evren and the others," I order him.

He strides to the door but pauses for a second. "Thank you. The Devil would have let me rot in my enemies' hands forever or until they killed me. I won't forget this." Without waiting for my reply, he leaves.

The second he's gone, I create a portal to take me to the street in front of The Abbey and arrive in time to see Evren meet up with Cormal. Outside the protection of its walls. What is she doing? Do they know each other? I start to walk toward them, but a golden light catches the corner of my eye.

I turn to find Gabriel's fanatical gleam focused entirely on Evren. With a quick shift, I move in front of him, completely obscuring the sight of her. Frustrated, he takes off. I turn around only to find Cormal and Evren gone. *Damn it.* It looks like I'm going to really have to kill Cormal.

EVREN

There's a line to get into The Abbey when I step outside. Before anyone can register what I'm doing, I whisper a spell to release the humans from the compulsion I placed in the ad. Several large men step out of the line and walk away with a dazed expression on their faces.

A hand cups my elbow, and I quickly turn to face the possible threat only to find Cormal. "You startled me."

His eyes dart around the street. "There's too much power out here. Can't you feel it? We need to move. Now."

I look around but fail to see or feel anything. This form prevents me from accessing my powers and puts me at a huge disadvantage. The only defense I have is the gold dagger I infused with my blood. Angels aren't the only thing it can kill.

Cormal points to a shadow on the wall. "There."

I look at him like he's crazy. "The shadow?"

"Portal," he corrects, his tone abrupt. "Let's go."

I know it seems stupid to go with someone I just met, especially someone who seems to be as powerful as him, but he knew her. My mother. He knew her real name and what she looked like, enough to mistake me for her. With a nod, I follow him through the shadow.

When we emerge, we're in some kind of market. My body starts seizing up, and the breath rushes from my lungs. I frantically grab Cormal's arm and dig my fingers in to alert him.

"Shit. I didn't realize," he stutters. Quickly pivoting, he pulls me back through the shadow.

We land in a cave deep in the mountainside. I fall to my knees, and he immediately places an oxygen mask over my mouth. I guess he conjured it when we got here.

Breathing deeply, I glare up at him. As the oxygen hits my blood, my muscles slowly unlock, giving me back control of them again.

I pull the mask away from my face. "What the hell?"

He looks uncomfortable. "Underworld doesn't tolerate humans in its domain. I thought you were a goddess." Blue eyes look me up and down. "I'm confused. Was Viridis your mother or not?"

"I can take either form. Goddess or human, after my father," I say wearily. "If I'd known where we were going, I'd have informed you of my limitations. Maybe share your plans with me next time."

He looks relieved. "This cave was designed by your mother to provide Druids with a protected place. She knew we would need a bolt hole when the angels realized we could kill them." A harsh chuckle escapes. "It didn't do us any good. In our arrogance, we thought ourselves invincible and never used it."

I tilt my head to study him. "You're a Druid?"

"Sort of. A long time ago, I was human, but sometimes

events force you to become something else. I exchanged my Druid powers and mortality for something more powerful," he admits, eyes flashing to black.

With care, I set down the mask and stand up to face him. While I can't feel his power, the hairs on my neck are standing up. "I only want to know what happened to my mother."

His eyes return to their original blue color. "I'd never hurt Viridis' daughter. You can relax."

Puzzled, I walk around the cave to get a better look. "Are there any sconces in here?"

With a whoosh, he lights the ones on the walls without moving a single finger.

"Thank you," I murmur, my attention completely focused on the words written on the walls. "This spell hides you from your enemies. I recently wrote a similar one for an amulet." I point to the spell written around the entrance to the cave. "That one provided for my mother's protection."

Farther back in the cave, I see an altar and another spell written around its base. "This is a containment spell for something called the brùid," I inform him, circling the stone to read all the words. "I thought brùid was a Gaelic term for beast."

"It is," he says grimly, stepping away from the altar. "Brennus had four children from a previous wife when he was changed by your mother. He thought if he gave them his blood, he could change them into Druids. It didn't work out that way. One died immediately. The other three were seemingly fine. Until the night they changed into dark beasts, full of nothing but hunger and attacked the village."

"Your mother used her powers to trap them. Then, she called for a portal and swept them up inside, away from this world," he says, thrusting his hands into his pockets.

Shocked, I reared back. It's the same experiment I've been

conducting, and yet all of my subjects have died. Except for one. John.

"How long did it take for them to change into these beasts?" My voice is strained with worry when I finally manage to spit out the question.

"A week," he informs me.

I count backward. It's been three days since I gave John the first transfusion. I sigh with relief. I've still got time to get him into a cell of some sort.

"Unfortunately, the moment your mother used her goddess powers to open the portal, the angels came to Earth to search for her. It wasn't exactly populous back then, and it didn't take them long to find her. She was in the village with Brennus when they descended. As a warrior, he immediately went into fighting mode.

"She tried to stop him, but instinct had taken over, and seconds later, an angel lay dead on the ground. Killed by a human. The angels with him immediately stopped fighting and disappeared," Cormal explains, his voice full of memories.

"It sounds like you were there," I state softly, puzzled by his tone.

"I was, and I wasn't. Brennus was my father, and I was one of the four he tried to change," he admits gruffly. "Your mother should have left as soon as the fight ended, but instead, she went into the portal and captured one of the beasts. She needed to know why the blood changed us the way it did."

"Knowledge is like air to Viridians. We must have it to survive, I think," I joke, but it's a sad kind of humor.

He nods vigorously, as if he understands exactly what I'm saying. "She captured me. Her experiments went on for days. Finally, she drained my entire body of blood and slowly replaced it with a mixture of her blood and Brennus'. The purity of her blood overrode the impurities in my human blood. It worked. Mostly."

He flashes me a wry expression. "There were a few side effects. Determined to fix all of us, she returned to the portal to get another beast. When the portal opened, there were a hell of a lot more than two beasts on the other side. They had replicated or procreated. And fast, too. She managed to wrangle one of them to this side. It was my sister. She saved her, although she was also a bit different from your typical Druid."

"She quickly sent word to all the other families, but it was too late. Three of them had done the same thing Brennus had done. They managed to kill most of the beasts, but a few escaped.

"Brennus begged her to save his last child, but when she opened the portal again, there were at least a hundred and she couldn't tell which one to grab. She told him she needed to help the other families capture the beasts before they killed more people, but that she would come back and figure out a solution. She never returned." He finishes the story with a sigh.

My mind is trying to wrap itself around the possibilities. "She's eternal. It's impossible to kill her. But she never returned to me, either. I searched for two thousand years and never found her. It's why I'm back here. Someone must know what happened to her."

"We aren't sure what happened to her. We thought the angels or beasts had gotten to her, but if she's eternal, I'm not sure what to tell you," he admits slowly.

I can tell his brain is working furiously to put the pieces together.

"The seer saw a dark angel speaking to her, but I haven't found him yet. Maybe he'll know," I inform him, straightening my arms to stretch them over my head.

"Could he be holding her somewhere?"

I shrug. "I'm not sure. I know Gabriel's pretty pissed off about the Druids."

"Your mother created a race of humans that can kill angels. Trust me, the angels are livid, and they've taken out a lot of Druids over the years to reduce our chances of survival. Add that to our insular ways, and it's the perfect recipe for extinction," he says, agreeing with me.

"Thanks for telling me all this. I need to return and get John into a holding cell," I tell him.

He grabs my arm. "Who's John?" His eyes are wild with anger and concern.

"I've been experimenting with Druids and humans, trying to find the source of their powers. I didn't realize until yesterday that my mother created Druids by giving them her powers through a blood transfusion," I explain, looking at him in confusion. "Why?"

"It took us a week to change the first time, but it happens faster now." Fierce emotion burns in his eyes. "Shit... Meri. We need to go," he snarls, immediately dragging us both through the portal.

When we arrive, the street is eerily quiet. He rushes straight into The Abbey, and I follow. We both come to an abrupt stop when we get inside the doors.

Valerian is lying on the floor, deep claw marks across his body, with shredded pieces of skin hanging off his torso and one of his legs. Arden's leaning over him, her healing hands hovering over the worst of his injuries. A sword lying by her side.

Astor's leaning against the wall, hands trembling, the strain on his ashen face evidence of the amount of magic he must have used.

Daire's checking the fallen bodies and marking the dead ones with an X.

I swallow hard at the number of bodies that already have a red mark on their body, yet he can't have been doing it for long.

Theron's walking around releasing people from the ice encasing them.

My eyes move to the far side of the room.

Lucifer is standing there, chest heaving, with a black, shaggy-looking beast at his feet. Dead. His bright blue eyes are blazing with fury. "Care to explain what the fuck is going on and where you've been?" His tone is soft and dangerous. Anger coats his every word.

<u>EVREN</u>

Cormal curses. "Where's Meri?" He spins around and around, his eyes scanning the room. When he doesn't see her, he rushes to the nearest platinum blond lying on the floor. One hand flips over the body while the other swipes the hair away from her face. When it's clear it's not her, he moves to the next one. And the next.

Arden calls out. "She left right after you did." Her green eyes flash sympathetically at him.

He stops immediately. "Thank the goddess." Hands drop to his side, and his shoulders sag in relief.

Lucifer strides over and fists his shirt. "Where have you two been?"

I step forward. "Cormal knew my ancestor. He even thought I was her earlier tonight. You can ask Astor. When I realized who he meant, I asked him to tell me what he knew of the Druids. He took me to the village where Brennus lived."

Lucifer shakes Cormal hard. "She's here because she needs protection. Did you not think about the possible consequences when you were taking your little trip?"

Cormal looks around at the bodies on the floor. "It's a good thing we weren't here. If we had been, John would have gone for her first. The beasts eat anything, but they crave her blood."

"I'm not Druid," I remind him, breathlessly inserting Druid instead of Viridian with the wild hope he understands my hint.

He dips his chin. "When your ancestor went near the beasts, they would go into a frenzy. Her blood called to them. Drove them mad. I assume yours would do the same," he reveals, much to my horror.

"Why?" Lucifer rasps out. "Why hers?"

Cormal flashes me an apologetic look. "Her blood has special properties in it. When combined with healthy, strong human blood, it creates Druids."

Lucifer whips around. "Did you know this?"

I lift my chin. "When I read the journal yesterday, I suspected it was true, but I couldn't be sure until I ran some tests."

"You mean experiments," he retorts, lip curling in disgust. "Look at what your experiments have done to the supernaturals in this club." Instead of the soft tone of repressed anger, his voice is now roaring with rage. "They're all dead because of your need to experiment. Gabriel was right. You're messing with things you don't understand. Why is it up to you to see to the survival of humans? Who appointed you god?"

My mouth tightens, but I say nothing. There's nothing I can say.

Cormal steps forward. "Is this the only human who has received Druid blood?"

I shake my head. "No, but all the others died. It might have been because the Druid blood was weak or because the humans were already dying of disease."

Arden jumps up. "Aurora. Did you give Aurora Druid blood?"

Dismay hits me. After Arden healed her, I'd completely forgotten about her being a part of the original experiment. Instead of answering, I run for the elevator. Lucifer is close behind me, followed by Cormal.

Lucifer throws a look over his shoulder. "Stay here."

Daire flips him off and follows us straight into the elevator. "This is my Abbey." His curt voice reminds his father.

The three men draw large swords out of thin air at the same time. I pull out my small gold dagger. Daire rolls his eyes, and Lucifer gives me an indulgent nod. Frustrated, I glance at Cormal, but his eyes are locked on the dagger in my hand, a small smile on his lips.

The door opens to a blood-soaked hallway. My heart sinks. Body parts are everywhere, red smears on the floor and walls lead down the hall toward Becca and Aurora's room.

I dash out of the elevator. Lucifer tries to grab my arm to push me behind him, but I slip past. This is my responsibility. I did this. In seconds, I'm at their door, the horror of the scene stopping me in my tracks.

A woman the size and build of Becca lies beside the bed, her body bathed in so much blood, it's hard to tell the color of her hair or clothes.

The bed itself is empty, but the sheets are shredded and soaked with blood.

In the corner, a small beast is hunched over another body, gnawing on one of its body parts. It sniffs. Then sniffs again. It drops the leg with a thud and turns to the door, drool streaming out of its mouth.

"It smells your blood," Cormal murmurs from behind me. "Do not underestimate it because of its size. It's faster than most supernaturals, stronger too. Their hides are tough and impervious to most weapons. Your best shot is between the eyes. Use your dagger."

Lucifer jerks his head toward him and mutters something about misdirection and a serious talk. Daire simply readies himself and his weapon.

The beast suddenly leaps straight at me.

"Daire," Lucifer calls out, moving to intercept it in mid-leap.

Strong arms band around me, and a second later, the world blurs. When we stop, we're near the body by the bed. I don't think I've ever moved that fast in my life. I look over my shoulder to find Daire standing like a sentinel behind me, his eyes locked on Lucifer and the beast.

I bend down and sweep the blood-soaked hair away from the woman's face. Becca's blank brown eyes stare back at me. The last time I'd seen them, they'd been crying tears of happiness. Now, they'll never cry again. I sweep a hand over to close them.

A thunderous boom sounds. I look up to see Lucifer and the beast crashing into each other mid-air, then falling to the floor, both of them shaking their heads.

The beast is the first to recover. It rears up like a bear on its hind legs, towering over Lucifer. It drops heavily, intent on pinning its prey to the ground, but instead it's stopped by a sword piercing its belly.

Enraged, the beast howls and swats at the sword.

Lucifer pulls it out and stabs it again in the chest.

"The head," I yell, darting a glance at Cormal for confirmation.

He hasn't moved an inch from the door. It's almost as if

he's frozen in place. His blue eyes have a ring of black around them, and he's staring at the beast as if it's a nightmare come to haunt him.

Lucifer grunts, and my gaze swings back to him. Claws have flayed open one of his thighs. Furious, he becomes a whirlwind, feet flying in a warrior's dance, trying to move fast enough to avoid the claws and reach its head.

But the faster he moves, the less the beast does. Instead, it waits for its prey to make its move. When Lucifer moves in to strike, a large fist comes in and clocks him on the side of the head.

Lucifer stumbles back, a dazed look on his face.

The beast takes the opportunity to start running toward the door and Cormal. Lucifer shakes off the hit and follows.

It sniffs the air, then looks directly at me. Swerving at the last minute, it leaps and lands a foot away. Daire tries to move us to a safer place, but I shake him off, turn my left side toward the beast and step closer.

Lucifer roars in fury.

The beast goes into a frenzy, claws digging deeply into my left arm, shredding the skin, until there's nothing but muscle, bone, and blood left. A long tongue unrolls from its mouth to roughly lick a line from my wrist to my shoulder. When the first drop of my blood hits its tongue, it begins to hum.

Pure agony shoots down my side, but I shove it into a tiny box in my mind. Whipping my right arm around, I drive the gold dagger into the top of its head. The beast staggers, going down on one knee, and drops my arm. Black eyes look up at me, comprehension dawning in its depths. It unleashes a loud snarl, then falls silently the rest of the way to the ground.

I drop down on one knee beside it and smooth the rough hair back from its face. "I'm sorry. So, so sorry, Aurora. Go, rest in peace with your parents and Becca. They're waiting for you."

The heaviness in my chest expands, and I drop my head onto the beast's chest. The image of a beautiful little girl with sparkling brown eyes fills my mind. Did she know this was happening, or did she turn between one moment and the next? Goddess, I hope she wasn't aware of anything, but especially what she did to her beloved sister.

The smell of a bonfire wraps around me like a warm blanket as Lucifer bends down and gently picks me up.

I bury my face in his chest, not wanting to see the condemnation in his intense blue eyes. He brought me to The Abbey and entrusted me with his family, and look what happened. I almost destroyed everything, including them. Their friends and staff are gone. People who had put their trust in them and the sanctuary.

He walks out of the room and into the elevator. "Someday, you're really going to have to show me what's so special about that little dagger of yours. I almost had a heart attack when I saw you step forward with that tiny thing in your hand." His hand grasps mine and guides it to his chest.

"My heart's still beating fast. Do you feel it?"

The rapid thump beneath my hand tells me he's not simply placating me. I press my face harder into his warm chest. "I'm sorry. So sorry." With those words, I pass out from the pain wracking my body.

CHAPTER
TWENTY-ONE

LUCIFER

My heart stopped when she stepped into the beast's arms. At first, I thought guilt was driving her to sacrifice herself. It didn't occur to me what she was doing until her dagger punctured its tough skull and it fell to its knees in front of her. One thrust. That was it.

The guilt... it came after the beast was dead. When she could acknowledge it was Aurora inside and not some random monster. The same sweet little girl who had been so happy to have her cancer gone and a plan for the future. Her head dropped and hands trembled as she sent her off in peace.

After she passed out and Arden healed us both, I slid the dagger from Evren's side and carried it into the light to examine it further. To my surprise, there was a Viridian spell engraved on the blade.

Once is a coincidence, but twice? Seeing the language

engraved on another gold piece tells me it's all connected, but the pieces are jagged, and don't quite fit. Something is missing. But what? For me, it all started the night the torque entered my hall, but where is the beginning? In the past with Evren's ancestor or in the present with Evren herself?

The beasts are nothing new. They've lived on the other side of a portal for eons. None of us knew where they originated, but everyone in the Underworld knew them as dangerous and tough-to-kill monsters. When I took the throne, I established a patrol to alert us if one slipped into our world so we could immediately hunt them down.

Now I know their origins—humans who were given Druid blood. It's astounding to think those beasts were once innocent mortals walking this Earth. When they change, they retain none of their human form or intelligence. The only common trait with their human origins seems to be their ability to reproduce rapidly. One of my enemies opened the portal during a recent battle in the Underworld, and there were thousands and thousands of the ravenous beasts straining to get to our side and feed.

When Evren doesn't immediately wake, I use the rest of the day to engrave the spell onto the blades of my sword and two of my favorite daggers. I must have stabbed the beast seven times, and it barely noticed. She killed it with one hit. Next time, she won't have to sacrifice her body, because I'll be there to put it down first.

I consider sending the spell to others, but if it also contains the power to kill angels, I can't take the chance. It's not an issue for me, because I already have that power, but our world is a delicate balance. If others were to gain the power, it could tip the scales too far.

When she wakes two days later, it's almost as if her body is nothing but a shell. She doesn't eat or sleep. The only times she moves is when Arden comes into the room to heal her. I know the pain must be intense, but unlike most, she doesn't cry or scream. She locks her jaw and sits there, stone-faced, until it's done.

Her eyes are the window to her soul, though. In their bewitching green depths is a maelstrom of emotions swirling around. Loads of guilt, sorrow, and anger… and loads of heavy thinking.

She says nothing. Not a word. To me or Arden.

Needing her to know she's not alone, I ease myself onto the bed and gather her in my arms. I talk to her about life in the Underworld. It's so different compared to here. It's unique and marvelous, but since she's human, she won't ever get to see it. Still, I want to share it with her, and I can tell she's listening when the creases at the corner of her eyes flex in response to something I say.

Not wanting the guilt to overwhelm her, I don't talk to her about the ones who were killed that night. We burned them all, including the beasts and Becca, in a funeral pyre. Then Arden, Astor, and I worked together to cleanse The Abbey. We didn't want to take the chance that a single drop of blood could cause another beast to rise. Arden and Astor created a spell to isolate the hellfire I laid down. Once it was all gone, they rebuilt those areas.

Cormal left as soon as Meri returned. There was a haunted look in his eyes and a tinge of madness in his face. Seeing the beast did something to him. Resurrected a part of his past he'd worked hard to forget is my best guess, but you never know with him. It worries me.

While I stayed at The Abbey, he conducted the interviews for the staff and got everything kicked off for our project in the Underworld. Orlo, the Nemean Lion, was hired as one of the supervisors, but Cormal sent me videos of the interviews, and I agreed that he was the best candidate for the job.

Excited about the project, I tell Evren about our plan to help improve the Underworld for all our races, not just the demons.

I explain the different habitats we're building to help the non-demon races feel more at home. "When I came into power, only demons lived in the capital. Once I started reuniting the outlying kingdoms, other races came to live in our dark city. They left their natural habitats and their families to live in a harsh environment. Instead of returning home, they stayed and built new lives. This will finally give them a piece of their home. Something to rejuvenate them and their powers."

She shifts closer to me, and I silently groan at the feel of her body lined up against mine. With every breath, she settles in closer until I don't know where I end and she begins.

Needing a distraction, I pull out the sketches Cormal sent over. "I'm most excited about the school we're building. This is a rough sketch of the campus and the buildings." One sketch depicts all the buildings and layout of the campus. "It will be a school for all ages at first. If it proves successful, we'll build another based on what we see is needed." I excitedly show her the sketch of each building, already proud of it, even though we haven't broken ground yet.

Her body leans into mine, and her green eyes glow with intensity as she stares at me, questions swirling in their depths. "The Underworld doesn't currently have schools or education for its citizens? How do they learn? What jobs do they do?"

Thrilled to hear her voice again, it takes me a second to respond. "Most of the demons have been operating within their own mini hierarchy for years. The high demon or duke assigns tasks according to their sin, capability, race, or power. But outside of this structure, there is nothing."

She frowns. "So not everybody has a purpose?"

It's a good way to think about it. Everyone should have a purpose. Whether it's convincing humans to sin, providing goods and services to the people, or whatever they choose.

"No, they don't," I answer. "For the first two thousand years of my reign, I battled anyone who was a threat to my throne." I can't help but wince when the words come out of my mouth. "The next two thousand years, I made peace a priority, along with a strong army and a good defense. Our allies see us as a dominating force, and we're valued for our ability to fight. To keep our alliances, I'll continue to make that a priority. But I know we can be more."

I *want* more for my people. "Underworld is lost to the ancient ways. When I went to war against the light Fae for Arden, I saw sophisticated, orderly cities with commerce, advanced magic, and educated citizens. I want my people to have the same advantages, not through an ally, but through our own resources."

Her gaze is locked on me as if she finds every word of this fascinating.

My brow furrows and I shift uncomfortably. "It's more than that, though. Angels serve. They don't make decisions or choices on their own. I loved serving, but it's nothing compared to the power of choosing your own path. As a ruler, I want my people to have choices."

She nods. "Everyone in my family is a… scientist. I truly love it, but it would have been nice to have a choice." A wry smile graces her lips. "Is this the first school?"

My shoulder lifts. "I wasn't sure what to do at first. The task felt overwhelming. It took me a while to realize I don't have to do it all at once, nor do I have to do it alone. And if there is an expert in the field, I'll bring them in to help," I say with a wry smile. It took me a while to admit I couldn't do it all.

There's a knock on the door. I hand her the sketches and get up to answer.

Daire motions me into the hallway.

"I'll return in a second, Evren," I inform her, and step out.

"Have you found somewhere else for her to go?" Daire asks, his face set in a frown. "Arden said she's pretty much healed, and with what has happened, she can't stay here."

My head rears back. I hadn't thought about it, but I can see the issue with her staying. "The only other place is the cottage. It's not quite as secure, but we can go there."

Daire's icy blue eyes look shocked. "You would take her to our home?"

Exasperated, I blow out a loud breath. "She's human, Daire. I can't exactly take her to the Underworld. And it would take a lot of negotiation for me to find her a safe place with the Fae or Elven," I remind him. "Is there a hurry?"

He throws his hands up. "I don't understand why you continue to protect her or be with her after everything she's done."

Straightening my shoulders, I return his hard look with one of my own. "It was a simple mistake. She didn't know that would happen. Nobody did. There's not a hell of a lot written about the Druids. Nothing about their blood turning humans into beasts. Trust me. I've read almost all the books on the subject."

"Her mistake cost thirty-seven supernaturals and three humans their lives," he spits back at me. "We're a sanctuary. Right now, we can't guarantee anyone their safety. She needs to leave."

My patience is running dangerously thin, but I try to view

it from his perspective. "We'll leave after the next healing session." I reach out to clasp his shoulder, but he jerks it away.

"Why do you have to go with her? I don't understand this hold she has on you," he snarls in return.

I scoff. "There is no hold. I promised I would protect her from Gabriel. There is something about her that is driving him to the edge of insanity. For thousands of years, I've been dreaming and hoping he would fuck up and fall from grace. My gut says this is it. And when it happens, I'll be there to drag his ass to the Underworld to pay for what he did to me. That is why I'll stick with her to the end." The words have a hollow ring to them that I ignore. It's all about revenge. That's it. "When he's no longer a threat, she can go her own way and I'll go mine." Patience gone, I slide a hand through the air. "Discussion over."

His icy blue eyes study me intently for a second, then he stalks off, leaving me to wonder if the massacre is the only reason he's upset.

The bed is empty. I spin around to head back in the hall when the sound of the shower penetrates my panic. I stop. My heart slows to its normal beat. I'll wait. Once she's out of the shower and resting, I'll head to the cottage.

I pick up my papers from earlier and put them on the nightstand. It was nice to share my plans with someone outside of the Underworld. It's not a place many visit, so they can't begin to understand how different it is to every other world.

With a wave of my hand, I replace the sheets and blankets on the bed with fresh ones. I wonder if Evren has a favorite flower? With barely a thought, I bring in a vase full of a variety of flowers. Bright and interesting like her.

A loud sob breaks the silence, and I move to the bathroom door. "Evren, are you okay?"

She doesn't reply. I stand there indecisively for ten seconds. *Fuck it.*

The bathroom is full of steam, but I can clearly see her crouched down on the floor of the shower, crying. I sit down beside her, wrap a towel around her body, and gather her in my arms.

"Let me go," she cries, barely able to get the words out.

"I won't," I tell her, uncertain whether I mean now or at all, but knowing I mean the words.

My response makes her cry harder. "Why are you doing this? It's my fault all those people are dead. Forty people." Her sobs continue. "Forty lives cut short. I don't know what to do with the guilt."

I stroke a hand down her back. "You find a way to live with it and learn from it. Whatever you do, you can't let it consume you," I reply. "If you do, it will break you. Trust me. Guilt can change you into something you don't recognize in the mirror. It took me forever to find myself again."

She tilts her head to look at me with her sad green eyes. "How did you do it?"

I give her a wry smile. "I channeled all my energy into the Underworld. You have to find your own way. But I'll be here to help and protect you while you figure it out." My finger reaches out to catch the tear lingering on the edge of her lashes. I close my fist to capture it.

She nods and her head drops onto my chest. I shut off the shower and stand with her in my arms. With little thought, I dress her in clothes similar to what she's been wearing and carry her into the bedroom.

When I lay her down, her eyes are closed, and her breathing even. The freckles across her nose stand out against the paleness of her skin. I can't help but lightly rub a finger across this very human characteristic. Not wanting to disturb her much-needed sleep, I decide to leave and stock the cottage with some food and other necessities in preparation for our move. Maybe Arden will be willing to help. I grab the sketches and leave her resting.

Daire's right. The cottage isn't a long-term solution. If Gabriel continues to stalk her, I'll need to find a new world for her. I consider the options. Elven would be the best. Arden's father might consider it, given his daughter is half human. He's also one of the few allies I have that likes me and might be open to my visiting. It's worth running the idea past her first to see if she thinks he would be open to it.

TWENTY-TWO

<u>EVREN</u>

When I'm absolutely sure he's gone, I open my eyes. My thoughts are swirling in my brain. I don't know what to think. One minute, I'm a pawn, and the next, he's holding me in the shower while I cry. Are we friends? Or is he my temporary protector? Tears trickle down my face, but I scrub them away. No more tears. I need to get out of here.

The world spins when I stand, but it settles after a few seconds. Thankfully, Arden brought my things down from my room and the lab a couple of days ago, so all I have to do is add a jacket and shoes, then find a portal. I slip my feet into some tennis shoes, then bend to carefully slide the backpack with my computer, along with the duffle, onto my right shoulder. The left one is still a bit sore.

That's it. I'm ready to go.

A piece of paper catches my eye, and I bend down to pick it up. It's one of the sketches for the campus. Without thinking, I tuck it into my pocket.

There's one last thing. Closing my eyes, I place my right hand on my heart and left hand on the wall. "Theia, please accept my apology for the pain and suffering I caused the people in this sanctuary. It was never my intent to put anyone in danger, especially those under your roof. Thank you for the protection you extended to me. I'll never forget it. I hope by leaving, you can offer sanctuary to those who need it most without any concerns my presence might cause."

The walls pulse with a return message, but I can't understand the words. It's probably better that I don't know. She warned me about the will of a goddess being more powerful than fate. My choices certainly proved that correct. If I hadn't intervened, John and Aurora would have died a human death, and Becca, while grieving, would still be alive.

Making my way to the elevator, I take it down to the main floor. It's utterly silent without the staff and patrons. Everything is immaculate again, but all I see are the bodies still lying on the floor.

What did Daire say? Thirty-seven supernaturals and three humans. Forty people. Gone because of me and my experiments. No, my arrogance. Why did I think it was up to me to change the future of mankind? To save it? I totally ignored the fact that humans have adapted and saved themselves many times since their creation.

A few tears fall, and I let them coat my face in sorrow. Not for me, but for them. Lives cut short because of my actions. My hand automatically reaches up and makes the sign of blessings to help the ones who died find the peace they deserve.

Hearing a noise near the kitchen, I stride quickly to the

portal. It opens when I get close, and with one last look, I step in and return to the warehouse. It spits me out on the top floor, but instead of the neat, orderly bedroom I expect to see, there is only rubble. Tripping over a rock, I set everything down and make my way through the debris to the stairs.

When my feet hit the last step, I stop. There's nothing left. Not a single machine or beaker. It's all been destroyed. Even the massive steel fridge with all the specimens is flattened as if a giant stepped on it. Nothing is salvageable. The old me would be furious. Right now, I'm glad. The thought of running another experiment sickens me.

"Bravo. Look at you. Creating beasts and killing innocents. Your talents know no bounds," a dark voice full of hatred spews from the corner. He starts clapping, and the sound echoes loudly in the cavernous room.

Gabriel unfolds his tall body from the only piece of furniture in the room and starts toward me. His stride is graceful, but his demeanor is threatening. A dark-haired predator sheathed in an expensive blue suit.

"I told you to stop, but you didn't listen. You thought you could play god and revive a dying race or create new, improved humans. What is that saying about the best laid plans…" He looks at me, but I shrug, not knowing the answer to his question.

I take a cautious step back. The look in his bright blue eyes has surpassed fanatical. Crazy lives inside him now. Slowly reaching down, I feel for my dagger. My fingers slide along the seam of my jeans, but there's nothing there. Panic sets in. Where is it? An image of it sitting on the bed flashes in my mind. It's at The Abbey.

I take another couple of steps back up the stairs. If I can reach the portal before him, I have a chance to get out of this without playing my last card.

A dangerous glint enters his eye. "Where's that beautiful golden dagger you like to wave in my face? Forget it somewhere?" The thick muscles in his legs bulge as he shifts into a slight squat.

Knowing he's going to launch himself at me, I spin and run up the stairs, letting a little of the goddess slip into my form to lend speed to my legs. I make it to the top step, but a hand grabs my ankle and jerks me to a halt. This is it. With no other recourse, I reluctantly begin the change.

He eyes me warily. "Faster than I expected. That's good. Especially where you're going." He jerks my head to the side and plunges a needle into my neck. Damn, I didn't have enough time.

TWENTY-THREE

<u>LUCIFER</u>

Arden finishes stocking the cabinets and gives me a puzzled look. "The fact that you've never seen her eat is strange. I can't go a day without coffee or chocolate. And those are just the basics."

An uneasy feeling settles on my shoulders. "I don't eat," I inform her with a shrug. "Although, I have to admit, I enjoy a good cup of coffee or a glass of bourbon." Had she really not eaten or drank? Wait, wasn't she in a coffee shop right before the angel grabbed her off the street? The moment plays in slow motion, and I exhale in relief when I see the name of the shop. Definitely coffee. But later, she refused to drink coffee at the warehouse because it made her bounce off the walls.

"Yeah, but you're... you. You were originally an archangel and probably weren't designed to eat food," she replies haltingly, her eyes narrowed in thought.

I scoff. "Designed, really?"

Pink splashes across her cheeks. "Or created. Whatever. I doubt you were born like me," she says defensively.

"True," I admit, having never really thought about it. I simply *was*. "I'd like to return and see if she's awake."

Arden closes the cabinet and dusts her hands together. "All done. Let's go."

The minute we step into The Abbey, I see Vargas. He's pacing back and forth in front of the portal. "Vargas? What's happened?"

Vargas' eyes widen until they're as big as saucers.

A hand grips my arm and swings me around. "Did you say Vargas?" Arden asks hoarsely. "Can you see his spirit? Talk to him?" Tears fill her bright green eyes. "Can we talk to him?"

We. She's referring to Solandis and herself. Vargas is vigorously shaking his head.

I turn until I can grip her hands in mine. "Arden, I promise. After I find Evren, I'll sit down and discuss this with you. But right now, you have to promise me you'll say nothing to Solandis or anyone outside of the cadre. Promise me." I can't ask her to keep it from everyone, but if there's anyone who knows how to keep a secret, it's the cadre.

The hope in her eyes flares higher. "I promise. If you see him, tell him I love him. And my training is going to shit. They all take it way too easy on me." Her eyes dart around the room as if she can catch a glimpse, but she can't see him.

"Thank you," I tell her, then lean in close. "And you just told him yourself."

A broad smile sweeps over her face.

"I'll be back later," I promise her.

Vargas sends me coordinates, and I step outside the sanctuary doors and shimmer directly to them. When I get there, I draw my sword, but there's nothing to see. Literally nothing but a desert in front of me.

Vargas appears beside me. "Gabriel took Evren."

Enraged, I look around but see nothing. "The last time I saw Evren, she was sleeping. Gabriel couldn't have come in and got her, which means she left, didn't she?" I'd left Vargas to watch over her while I was gone.

"She returned to the warehouse," he pauses. "Gabriel was waiting for her. He injected her with something to make her unconscious, then brought her here."

"Then where the hell is she?" I grit out, barely able to keep my voice down.

"When I left to get you, she was lying on the ground, about twenty feet away," Vargas says bewildered. "Do you think he sensed me?"

A bright light appears in the sky about a mile north of us. "Let's go." I disappear, then reappear in the area where I spotted the light. Blazing bright white light is shining everywhere. I throw up my arm to shield my eyes. Squinting under the line of my forearm, I see the outline of a portal and black beasts pouring through the opening.

"No!" I shout, amplifying my voice until it's almost thunderous. "They'll devour everyone in its path. Close the fucking portal." Darkness begins to slowly eclipse the light, but it's not fast enough. I rush over to fight back the beasts while they get the portal closed. It takes us several minutes, but it finally shuts.

Gabriel drops to his knees, his chest heaving, as he tries to catch his breath.

Enraged, I walk over and punch him in the face repeatedly. The crunch of his bones is the most satisfying sound I've heard in a while. "What the fuck are you doing? One of those things took out thirty-seven supernaturals at the club a few days ago. You just let in at least a few dozen." The sickening realization of what he's done hits me hard. The club was nothing. This will be a massacre.

His wings snap out, shoving me backward. "Get off me. You're lying. They only go after Druids." The words are delusional, and since he won't meet my eyes, he knows they're nothing but lies. In his world—angels first, humans second, and that's it.

Fists clenched, I step into his line of sight. "Look at me. Those beasts are ravenous, and they'll eat anything in their way... supernatural, Druid, demon, or human." My eyes slide down his body. "I'm sure if they got a taste of angel, they'd really go into a frenzy. Get a couple of platoons down here now. We're going to need them."

He staggers to his feet. "As long as she's first, I don't care."

My brows draw together in confusion. I look at him, but he's not looking at me. When I see the glint in his eye, I immediately spin around to look for Evren and almost fall to my knees in horror.

She's tied to a pole in the middle of the desert with her head hanging down. Strands of red hair are blowing in the wind like a matador waving a red cape. Instead of a bull, there are thirty beasts heading straight toward her.

I immediately start running, but I know there's no way I'll make it before they do. I shimmer over and grab her. When I try to leave, nothing happens. I try again. Nothing.

Her body is wrapped in some kind of silver chains. I grasp them in my hands and exert all my power. They don't budge. I examine them closer. Prometheus' chains.

Fuck, they're unbreakable.

The beasts are bearing down on us.

I need fucking options. Back-up can't get here fast enough. Even with my tremendous power, I can't kill all of them before they reach us. Not unless I suddenly gain the power to replicate myself. A harsh, desperate laugh escapes.

"Evren!" I yell, not knowing why. My hands spear through her red hair and I pull her to me. She doesn't stir. Maybe it's best if they attack when she's unconscious.

The beasts are close, maybe a hundred feet away.

Images of her and me flash through my mind. Most of my memories are full of her studying me as if I'm the devil about to lead her astray. I blink.

The torque. That's the option. A one-shot deal, Cormal told me. I start digging into my pocket for the talisman and spell he gave me. I'd kept it on me since the incident just in case the power needed to be recalled.

The thunderous hooves stop, and the beasts lift their noses high in the air. They snort and huff, their nostrils flutter wildly. They smell her. Their bodies begin to vibrate, and a frenzy starts amongst them. Several of them rip into each other, unwilling to share with their monster brethren.

I hold up the talisman and shout the words. A familiar, almost translucent, cloud streams up from the ground. It moves swiftly to find me, then invades my body, filling every cell with more power. This time, I don't try to contain it, but let it flow and expand inside until every ounce is mine to use.

The beasts are ten feet away.

My body flexes, and my back bows. The power streams out of me and sweeps across the desert, destroying everything in its path. It's a tsunami rolling over them, leaving no option for escape. I wipe every single beast charging toward us from existence.

When the last one is gone, I raise a hand and lay hellfire over the same path to kill any leftover residue or drop of blood. Every blade of grass and vegetation burns, and the sand turns to glass. What remains is nothing but blackened, scorched earth.

I take several deep breaths as I try to figure out how to get the chains off.

She's awake and staring at the fire in front of her. "Thank you. I shouldn't have hesitated earlier. Waited too long." Her words are a jumble, but I'm barely listening.

"You don't happen to know how to get these chains off, do you?"

She looks down and laughs. "Prometheus' chains. How fitting. Mankind's champion. The one who brought them fire and knowledge." There's a bitter edge to her words. "They can't be broken." She thinks for a second. "Ask them to release me."

I grasp them in my hands. "Will you release her?"

The shackles fall to the ground and immediately disappear.

She sighs and closes her eyes as if she can't bear to look at me.

I stand and grip her head in my two hands. "Open your eyes, Evren." I need to see them. To know what she's feeling. Her lids lift, and she stares solemnly up at me.

"Why did you leave?" I ask her softly.

She shakes her head. "I want to find my mother and go home. I can't do this anymore. You'll have to get your revenge some other way."

My brows draw together. "Your mother?"

She tries to look away, but I refuse to let her. "Tell me."

"I heard you talking to Daire. He's right. You need to move on from me, and all of this, before it destroys you. Let it go. Let karma and the fates punish Gabriel," she urges me, her voice soft, but I hear the pain in it.

I shift closer to her. "Stop trying to push me away. I

promised to fucking protect you. Promised, Evren. When you're safe, I'll go."

She opens her mouth to speak, but I'm tired of listening. I lean down and capture her lips, silencing the words on her tongue. Soft and warm, the feel of them against mine tempts me beyond the simple kiss I intended to place on them. I tilt her head up and back, kissing her deeper and longer, needing to imprint myself on her. My body tightens with desire and fear.

She tastes like forever. But I know firsthand, humans don't last forever. They break... and die. I can't go through that again. I need to stop, but my lips cling to hers, mingling our two breaths. Her heart is pounding against my chest, and mine matches its every beat.

Her heart beats. She's alive, I reassure myself.

Still, my lips move against hers, needing more of this complex woman.

A furious roar sounds behind me, and I turn quickly, sword in hand, to stand in front of Evren. But for once, Gabriel's not focused on her. All his attention is on the angel standing in front of him.

"Did you happen to bring my dagger?" Evren asks quietly.

Hearing she left without her knife infuriates me, and I step to her side so I can look down at her and watch Gabriel at the same time. "I ran out of The Abbey as soon as I heard you were taken," I reply, shaking my head. "By the way, I'm still pissed that you left. I told you to stay put. Did you not believe me when I said he was dangerous?" I wave a hand at the scorched earth in front of me. "Does this not prove to you that he's losing his mind?"

My voice rises with each question, and Gabriel shifts his attention from the angel to us. Indecision wars on his face.

I rein in my anger and pluck my dagger from my belt. "Here. It has the same spell as yours engraved on it."

She pulls it from my hand and flips it over to read the spell. The sharp edge slices into her hand, smearing blood on the blade, but she barely flinches. "Thanks. I feel a lot better with a weapon in my hand."

"Damn it, Evren. Be careful," I tell her, my voice gruff. I reach down and rip off a piece of my shirt and press it to the cut. "This will have to do for now."

Her hand brushes against my side, bumping the hilt of my sword, as she pulls me close.

Gabriel leaves the angel and heads straight toward us.

I knew it.

The thought of helping him makes me grind my teeth. "I'm guessing you need some help to clean up the fucking mess you've made?" A part of me is tempted to say no, but we don't have time to fuck around with games. Human lives are at stake. Those beasts can obliterate a city and its residents in minutes. "Let's go."

He stops and stares at me.

"You can grovel later. If we don't hurry, they'll mow down everyone in their path and move on to the next city," I say impatiently. "We'll follow you."

He stalks off toward the angel waiting across the field.

My arm goes around Evren, and I draw her close. Her subtle scent wraps around me, and I inhale deeply. With a snap, the wings I keep confined spring free, and my back flexes in anticipation.

Evren's eyes immediately focus on my wings.

I expect to see her usual analytical gaze, but instead her face is full of awe.

She fits her body to mine and throws her arms around my neck. "They're magnificent, almost a pearl white. I knew you used to be an angel, but it didn't occur to me to ask if you still had your wings." Her finger reaches behind my head and strokes one of them. "Soft too."

The caress reverberates through my body, and my cock hardens. Swallowing hard, I force myself to ignore it and keep my eyes fixed on Gabriel. "Vargas, have a platoon of our men ready nearby." I wave a hand over the scroll Cormal wrote the spell on to send a new message to Ishkova.

Vargas gives a quick dip of his chin and disappears.

"You don't trust Gabriel?" Evren asks sarcastically.

"I trust very few people in this world," I murmur, gathering her tightly to me.

Gabriel points at the sky. The signal. My wings flap once, and I shoot up into the air to follow him, Evren gripped in my arms.

She clings to me. "It's faster than... I imagined it would be." The breathless tone to her voice tells me she finds this exciting and possibly a little terrifying.

Gabriel banks, coming down on the outside of a small town, where a platoon of angels is waiting for him. The ground trembles when he lands as he purposely makes a show of it.

We softly land a short distance away.

The angels move restlessly, shooting Gabriel questioning glances, before returning their gaze to me.

Gabriel controls them with one sharp glance. "They're here to help. Aim for the beast's head. It's the only vulnerable spot on them. Don't underestimate their strength or ability to move quickly. They might look dumb, but they're supremely adept at fighting. Pair up. Go."

Without a backward glance, Gabriel and his men take off.

Evren is frowning. "How many times has he fought these beasts?"

"They occasionally manage to slip through the portals, so

we've all had to fight them. Although, it sounds like Gabriel's had more experience than most," I admit, unsure of what this means right now. "Ready?"

She looks down at my hand. "Are you asking to be my partner?"

I laugh. "Are you flirting? As if I'd let anyone else be your partner. I told you... you're stuck with me."

<u>LUCIFER</u>

The trail of beasts splits off in multiple directions close to the city. The largest path leads into a suburban neighborhood sure to be full of people, so that's the one we take. Entering slowly, we walk down the center of the street, giving ourselves room to maneuver if one of the beasts come charging out of the house.

My jaw clenches to see the large number of bodies lying everywhere. Anyone on the street when they came through didn't have a chance. I glance over at Evren and find her staring at a woman on the sidewalk.

A beast stumbles out of a house with its coat on fire. We rush over, and I slide my sword between its eyes. When it lies dead on the ground, we peek into the house. A witch stands there with a fireball in her hands.

"Aim for the head. Pass it along." At the very least, we can give these people hope and a fighting chance.

Hands trembling, she nods and picks up her cell.

A scream pierces the air, and we rush outside. A little girl is crying on the sidewalk, a bloody heap lying at her feet. A beast is in the street, circling with a wolf.

Evren cocks her arm back and lets the dagger fly. It hits dead center between the eyes. The beast falls to the ground immediately.

I blink at her, then hold out a hand for the dagger. It flies into my hand, and I toss it to her. "Good shot, but you left yourself defenseless. Don't do it again."

Eyes narrow in anger, as she competently twirls the hilt. "Don't give me orders. I wasn't defenseless. I knew my partner would have my back." She palms the dagger and stalks off.

My lips twitch at the fiery tone of her voice as well as the reprimand, but the sight of her long legs striding away in anger makes it all worth it.

The wolf's tongue lolls out the side of its mouth as he, too, watches her walk away.

"Hmm. I could use a new rug for my office," I tell him, running a hand down his coat. "Interested in dying for a good cause?"

The wolf immediately backs away, hackles raised.

"Aim for the head," I tell him with a chuckle. With only a few strides, I eliminate the distance between Evren and me and grin down at her.

But her eyes aren't on me. They're on the bodies littering the street and sidewalks, and the trail of body parts leading away from them and farther into the city. She's chewing the inside of her cheek and guilt is rolling off her in waves.

I lean down and pull her chin up until her eyes meet mine.

"Gabriel did this, not you. Don't let his deeds make you feel guilty."

She blinks. "You don't understand…"

Gabriel's minion lands in front of us, and I push Evren behind me.

"We're overrun. Hurry up," he orders, then shoots into the sky.

My jaw clenches, but I grab Evren close and follow the little asshole.

When we catch up to him, he's hovering over a little downtown area where a swarm of beasts are circling ten angels. The warriors are picking them off one by one, but for some reason, they aren't making much progress.

"Are you going to help them?" the angel hisses from beside me.

"Did you see that?" I ask her, pointing to a spot where two beasts are standing together.

Her mouth is open. "It replicated itself." The scientist in her is nearly vibrating, but this time, in fear. "I've never seen anything like it. Anywhere."

The angel beside us huffs. "Aren't you going to do something?"

"We're waiting on you. Lead the way," I say with a bland smile, well aware he's too scared to go down there.

"I need to find Gabriel," he says haughtily.

Tempted to knock his head off, I restrain myself and flip him the bird.

"Let's go, Evren," I tell her, leaving him to do whatever the hell he's going to do.

Evren nods and grips her dagger tighter. When we land, she moves into place between the beasts and the humans clustered to the right of the square, prepared to protect them if any get past me.

With her out of the way, I release the power I've been holding back to immobilize two of the beasts while I take on the third. My sword slides between its eyes, and it drops to the ground. The minute it does, a row of beasts swivel around to face me. When they start rushing forward, I pull the two strands of power and slam the beasts into the group.

Several fall, giving me a precious few seconds to focus my attention on those that are still standing. I whirl, sword thrusting, dancing in and out of their reach. I wince. Or almost out of their reach. I slap a hand across the claw marks on my right side and cauterize the wound. Blood only makes them more animalistic.

With the first ones down, the next group approaches. Needing a brief second, I wave a hand and open the ground to take out the first couple. They drop into the deep hole, and I close the ground. Swiveling to face the next two, I dispatch them easily.

A black blur plows into me, driving me off my feet. The beast lands on top, its jaws open wide. I conjure a hellfire ball and toss it in its mouth, then use my strength to hold its jaws shut while it burns through the roof of his mouth and into his brain. It takes at least a full twenty seconds for this one to die. Too long. The others could have replicated by now. I shove the dead carcass off me and reach for my sword, only to find it gone.

The minion from earlier is holding it above his head. "I've got it." He calls out to the other angels. "Our swords don't seem to be near as effective as yours. It's only right that we have the best sword to defend ourselves."

I laugh and stand up. "You mean defend the humans, right?" I look past him to check on Evren. She's still in front of the humans, her feet shifting from side to side. There's one dead beast beside her.

"The sword only answers to me," I inform him. "And if we didn't need every single one of us right now to clear this town, I'd kill you for touching it. It's mine. I don't share." I hold out my hand in the sword's direction and it appears in my hand.

Infuriated, he stalks toward me and raises his sword. "We're angels. Chosen and beloved. It's disgusting that we have to work with you."

"Careful," I caution him, my patience wearing thin. "I saved their lives. Something you were too afraid to do."

He glances nervously at his fellow angels. "I told you. I had to find Gabriel." He points behind my shoulder.

Unwilling to let any of them at my back, I step to the side and eye Gabriel. "Is this the type of angel you're mentoring these days? A cowardly little shit who is too afraid to step into a fight?" Between one blink and the next, I move until I'm standing at Evren's side.

The little shit glares at me.

"We cleared out the other streets. These were the last of them," Gabriel's clipped voice rings out over the square. "You can go now." His eyes linger on Evren, but he waves a dismissive hand toward us both.

Surprised, I frown. I count the number of beasts we've killed here and along the way. Added to the number the angels killed, it's significant. But my instinct is telling me there's more. I wish I had better intel. Too busy closing the portal earlier, I didn't get an accurate count.

I tilt my head and study Gabriel. Most would believe that sincere look on his face, but I don't buy it.

Uneasy, but unwilling to stay and figure it out, I place a hand on Evren's back and guide her out. We pass by the spot where I was standing earlier, and I wave a hand. The ground opens and the two beasts from earlier spring out of the ground, right into the middle of the angels.

That should keep them busy.

Pulling her close, I shimmer to the edge of town and appear right between my men and the herd of beasts charging up the hill toward them.

TWENTY-FIVE

<u>EVREN</u>

That bastard Gabriel drove the beasts out of the city, knowing Lucifer's men were here waiting for him. I grip Lucifer's dagger and ready myself to fight.

Lucifer grabs my arm and the field disappears. We reappear behind the group. "Stay here. It's the safest place." He lets out a piercing whistle, and a massive green scaled man... demon... rushes over. "Your only job is to protect her. Got it?" He grabs me close and plants a hard kiss on my lips. "Stay safe."

I blink and he's gone. Leaving me with tingling lips, and a whole lot of guilt and anger. Damn it. He's changing the rules. First with that kiss earlier, and now this. It's not fair. I haven't had a chance to tell him everything.

The booming sound of the demons and beasts clashing whips across the desert. The demon in front of me bounces back and forth, his hands clenching and unclenching, as if eager to get into the fight. When his eyes flick to me, I expect to see them full of resentment, but instead, they're full of respect and pride.

My brow dips down in confusion, but I shake it off. The fighting is intense. Unlike the angels' elegant and choreographed movements earlier, the demons are brutal and fierce. They fight with little inhibition, going all in to destroy their opponent. Several even change into their demon form to fight monster against monster. Most of them know how to kill them, but I see a few who don't.

"Aim between the eyes!" I yell over and over, almost a rallying cry to remind them of where to strike. I pace back and forth behind my protector, the adrenaline surging in my veins, while I watch them take down the beasts one by one.

A movement in the sky startles me, and I shift my attention. It's the angels. They're watching the battle from up above. Furious at their arrogance, I mimic Lucifer's actions from earlier and flip my middle finger to the sky.

The demon next to me chuckles and flips them off, too.

A beast breaks through the line, heading straight toward us.

Knowing my demon protector won't be able to turn in time, I throw the dagger the same way I did earlier, and the beasts goes down.

He whips around and stares at it. "Thank you. Although I think I'm supposed to be protecting bring you." Bending down, he tugs it out and tosses it to me.

"We'll protect each other," I tell him. When I look back at the fight, there's a considerable number of demons and beasts on the ground, but it's still too close to call a winner. We need to step in and fight.

I motion to the demon in front of us. "Tell him to let the next one through."

The demon hesitates, but I can see he's already come to the same conclusion. Unintelligible words come out of his mouth, and the demon standing in front of us steps aside to let the beast charging him pass.

"Take my dagger," I urge him.

He shakes his head. "Don't worry, I've got this." With a smooth twist, he brings his sword up and over his head, driving it straight into the beast's head.

The beast stumbles, but it doesn't go down. He pulls it out and strikes again. It falls to its knees and dies.

He glances at the dagger in my hand.

"It's Lucifer's. He bespelled it," I inform him, needing him to trust the weapon. "It will take them down in one shot, but you have to hit them between the eyes."

The demon swells, becoming larger, and moves into place in front of me. "If something happens to me, you pick it up and keep fighting. Got it?"

My hands shake slightly. Defenseless and in my human form, it makes the danger feel closer than ever. While I watch from behind, he takes them down one by one. He's fast and efficient and never seems to tire. My fear slowly dissipates.

Kill by kill, we gain ground. The beasts become fewer and fewer until the last one drops to its knees. A resounding cheer goes up from the group.

I smile and look up with a sense of victory toward the sky. It's empty. Uneasy, I look around. Gabriel never gives up.

Lucifer strides over and claps the demon in front of me on the shoulder. He eyes the beasts on the ground around us and whistles. "I can't believe we didn't hold the line."

With a strained smile, I reach out and clasp the demon's hand to shake it. "Thank you. You did a fantastic job of defending us." I pause. "Lucifer forgot to tell me. What's your name?"

He flashes a worried smile at the fierce male behind me. "Moge. And it was my honor." When I pull away, he slips the dagger into my hand. "I couldn't have done it without the dagger. So I think we saved each other."

"You gave him your dagger?" a dark voice hisses behind me. "What did I tell you about leaving yourself defenseless?"

It's time. I've been dancing around this subject for days. I whirl around. When I see the deep claw mark on his shoulder is dripping blood, I cut off a piece of my shirt and press it against the wound. "About that... you see. I'm not defenseless. Not really. I mean, I am in this form, but not in my real form. I probably should have told you already, but it was too dangerous to tell you in the beginning, and there didn't seem to be another moment." I stop and think about it. "Well, maybe when we were at The Abbey, and I was recuperating. That probably would have been a good time."

"Breathe, Evren," he says with a chuckle. "Tell me."

"I'm in hiding. If Gabriel's—boss—knew I was here, it would be bad. Very, very bad. We're banned from here. You see, I'm a go—" I start, but am interrupted by the fury rolling off Lucifer. He's already mad, and I haven't finished what I was saying.

His head swivels to look at his men, while his lips move to count their numbers. "He's lost his fucking mind," he roars. "Retreat. We'll regroup and return with a larger force." The demons start disappearing one by one.

Lucifer grabs my arm. "We've got to go."

I shake him off and turn to face the object of Lucifer's fury. It's another herd of beasts. Fury burns through me. How can Gabriel say I'm a danger to the human race? Not when he only sees them as collateral damage in his personal war against me and the Druids and whoever else lands on his naughty list. Gabriel only cares about his agenda.

I look around at the demons who are littering the ground. Unlike humans, most of them will regenerate, but not all of them. The images of the bodies in town run through my mind, especially the one at the little girl's feet. Was that her mother? A sister?

Aurora and Becca. John. Thirty-seven supernaturals who were only at the club for a night out. Those deaths are on me. But Lucifer's right. The rest belong to Gabriel.

I look up at the sky and take a deep breath. So much for trying to remain incognito.

Lucifer shakes me. "What's wrong? We need to leave."

I slip from his grasp. "I'm sorry. I should have told you sooner and explained my reasons, but it's too late." Closing my eyes, I release the restraint on my true self. The human shell I've been wearing falls away, and I exhale as my true form emerges.

When I open my eyes, everything is sharper and ten times brighter. In this form, I can hear the tiny beetle scurrying into the brush and smell the decaying bodies in town. I swivel around to face Lucifer and catch my breath. If I thought he was handsome before, it's nothing to what I see and feel now. He's utterly magnificent. Power is radiating from him... along with a serious amount of rage.

Millions of hooves strike the sand behind me. "After I do this, can you take me to the warehouse and my bedroom? This will take almost all of my power, and I can only fully regenerate at home. Not this world. There's a portal in my bedroom that will take me to my true home." Without waiting for his reply, I turn and face the herd. Guilt, bitterness, sorrow, and rage. The emotions have been building inside me for days. I bathe in them, saturate myself with them, until they become the perfect fuel for my power.

Inhaling sharply, I hold the breath for a second longer to let the beasts get closer, then on the exhale, I release the power gathered inside me and hit every single one of them. They fall to the ground, dead.

Hellfire shoots past me and burns it all.

I sway. My power is completely depleted. The sky darkens and rumbles. I look up.

Lucifer steps beside me and tilts his head back. His brows crease with worry. He pulls me into his arms, and I hold him tight, relieved to see he hasn't abandoned me.

The world blurs around us and stops. It's not my room at the warehouse.

"Where are we?" I ask, swaying from the toll it took to release all that power at once. I look around and see black marble and a throne made of bones. "Underworld? Why did you bring me here?"

He pulls away from me to pace. "Why didn't you tell me? I would have kept your secret. It's not as if I'm on the best of terms with the man upstairs."

I sink down to the floor. "Honestly, I didn't intend to reveal myself at all. My mother always told me the consequences would be severe if I did." A derisive laugh escapes. "Besides, why should I trust you? The betrayed only out for revenge against his betrayer."

His head rears back. "I never lied to you about my reasons for protecting you."

My throat tightens, and I shake my head. "No, but you made me believe you cared. That it wasn't all about revenge." A tear slips down my cheek. "I need to go home. Take me to my portal."

His hand sweeps the hair off my face. "I do care. Even when

I thought you were human. I cared. And believe me, that is the absolute last fucking thing I wanted to do!" he yells, his voice raw. "Humans only survive long enough to steal your heart. And yet, I still couldn't walk away from you. It was driving me crazy."

I stare at him. "You're lying. I heard you in the hall with Daire. Yesterday. Thousands of years you've been waiting for this moment, remember?" My voice cracks. "And when you showed up to save me, for some reason, I still believed you cared. But you do one thing and say another. I don't know anything for sure. I need to go home. I can't do this with you right now." I lie down on the cold marble floor to rest for a second.

Alarmed, he picks me up. "I've got you. Just hang on, okay?"

I nod.

"Are you coming back?" His voice is hoarse as he stares down at me.

I think about all the things that still need to be resolved, including whatever this is between us. This thing drawing the two of us together.

Soon we're standing in my bedroom at the warehouse. The second my feet touch the ground; the sky starts rumbling in protest.

Hard lips press against mine. "We're not finished. Do you hear me? Go home but come back. Finish what you started here."

The building starts to shake, and he holds up his hand to keep the ceiling from falling on us. "Go now."

Emotions swirl in his blue eyes making them glow, but I turn away. I can't tell if it's his need for revenge driving him or if he actually cares. I grab my backpack and stumble through the portal.

TWENTY-SIX

LUCIFER

The strike from above completely obliterates the building, leaving nothing but a crater in the ground. His wrath knows no bounds. The instant I saw the sky darkening in the field, I knew what was about to happen. He tolerates no other gods or goddesses in his domain. Even knowing this, I can't help but hope she returns. Not for the revenge. I meant what I said. When she's near, I find myself watching her, wondering what she's thinking or feeling, and sharing things I've never told anyone else.

Turning away from the destruction, I take myself to The Abbey. It's the last place I want to be, but I need to tell Arden about Vargas.

When I arrive, Vargas is already pacing beside her. Unseen, but there to help, and to shoot silent daggers at me. He doesn't want Arden or Solandis to know his current condition. He keeps stating he needs to find a body, yet none of them are good enough.

I think he's concerned their mate bond won't be there. He worries she won't feel attracted to him when he appears as someone else. His idea is to arrange a "chance" meeting to see if she falls for him again. If she doesn't, I have a feeling he'll throw himself in every battle until his new body is destroyed, and he stands on the shores of the River Acheron again.

Theron hands me a bourbon, the glass frosty with his anger, and I wince when I take it. My eyes dart from one furious cadre member to the next, their faces set in stone and eyes burning with anger, then fall on Arden. Hope burns bright in her green eyes. She leans forward eagerly, hands clasped together, waiting for me to give her the news.

I hold up a hand. "Let me get through everything, then you can ask questions." When she agrees, I begin. "After last year's attempted coup, I promoted Vargas to second-in-command and asked him to take a guardian blood bond with me. It was the assurance I needed to avoid another insurrection."

My eyes find the translucent demon standing beside Arden. "Always loyal, he didn't hesitate. In the battle against the light Fae queen, he truly died. In normal circumstances, that would have been the end. But the bond between us had unforeseen circumstances. It gave him a choice—continue on to the places of the dead or turn back and embrace life again. He chose to return."

Arden's brows lower and her mouth turns down. "So, where is he?"

I clear my throat. "He's trying to find a suitable body. One, I think, he believes Solandis will find pleasing. Apparently, there's been a shortage recently." A thought occurs to me. "Although we had several demons pass during our last battle, so maybe there's a candidate amongst them."

Angry, she jumps to her feet. "I can't believe you." She waves a hand at me. "Not you." Planting her hands on her hips, she speaks to the air beside her. "Vargas, Solandis and I have been mourning you. Hurting every day. So has Callyx. Our hearts completely broken without you."

She furiously scrubs at the tears rolling down her face. "Your reasoning is flimsy at best and not fitting for a demon of your caliber. Get your shit together, Vargas, and return to us. I'm giving you a week. Then I'm telling her. And if you think I'm angry, wait until she hears about your cowardice." With those final words, she stalks off with Valerian and Astor following her.

Vargas flips me off and disappears.

I sigh. They needed to be told. Arden's right. He should have damn well found a body and returned to them by now. Not to mention, I need him by my side and running things, too.

Daire grips my hand. "Does this happen to everyone who takes the guardian bond?" Hope glitters in his eyes.

That's right. I forgot. Daire took the same bond with Arden, and now, they're all wondering if she will get the same choice. I shake my head, killing the hope in their eyes.

Confused, he tilts his head. "Why Vargas?"

"I don't know. I had never bonded with an immortal until Vargas. His DNA reacted differently than humans in the past. It changed him," I tell him.

His jaw firms, and he sits back in defeat.

Theron looks from him to me. "I'm not sure I understand. Arden and Daire are immortal."

Daire looks at me and raises an eyebrow.

I nod.

"Lucifer's not immortal; he's eternal. If his body dies, he can simply return. In the same body or another. When Vargas took the oath, he unknowingly gained the option to return.

Although it sounds like he has to find a new body," he explains to Theron and Fallon.

The tension falls from them. Both glance at me, then get up to follow Arden. Neither of them says goodbye. Their only thought is her.

I stand and look down at my only son. "Would you take the bond with me? Knowing what it could offer you?" My words are even, but the pounding of my heart clearly reveals how much this means to me.

His keen ears pick up on my rapid heartbeat. Daire smiles and places his hand on my chest. "Thank you for the offer, but no. I want to go wherever she goes, not hang around with my old man for eternity." Knowing his refusal will hurt, he throws his arms around me and squeezes tight.

I hug him tightly in return, knowing one day he will be gone like everyone else. "Let me know if there's anything else I can do for Arden. In the meantime, I'll push Vargas to quickly find a body." I hesitate for a second. "I love you, Daire."

He pulls away and heads toward the door. "I love you too. Although you don't always make it easy on me."

I chuckle in response, but when I get in the portal to go home alone, my smile disappears.

TWENTY-SEVEN

<u>EVREN</u>

Time runs differently on Viridian than on Earth. I've been here for at least three weeks wallowing in a pit of emotions. While my powers replenished quickly, the rest of me is stuck.

Viridian is cold and sterile. Everyone's focus is on the science, not emotions or helping others. When I was a child, my mother would bring me here to replenish our powers and teach me what it meant to be a Viridian. I loved it and hated it too. I loved the science. The advancements. Earth was primitive compared to Viridian. It still is.

But I hated the utopia of it all. Everyone has a purpose and a job, and strict rules that must be followed. Emotional outbursts are not tolerated. They are deemed ineffectual and unproductive. With few children, there was no playtime for me. It was lonely. My mother tried her best to show me the positives of our race, but she refused to hide the negatives.

After my father died, we returned to Viridian, but I think it was too much for her too. So, we traveled across the galaxies to observe and capture the essence of life. After we saw the seer, she jumped at the chance to return to Earth. I've been alone ever since.

Now I can see why she wanted to go back. Not only did the thought of helping humans evolve entice her, but she knew the loneliness would go away.

Not once did I feel lonely on Earth. Instead, I felt energized by the life around me. The emotions perfuming the air and the teeming life sustain me in a way science can't.

A tall blond warrior with a dimpled smile pops into my head. With a sigh, I plop down on the bed. I lied to him. Hid things from him. He had to know. Yet, he asked me to come back. Because if I don't, he won't get his revenge? Or is it more?

When I close my eyes, I see him watching me from across the room. His intense blue eyes studying me as if I'm a puzzle he has to solve.

Lucifer's beautiful and seductive, but it's the glimpses into his heart and mind that intrigue me. There's so much depth to him and I can't help but wish for more time to explore all his facets.

I chew on my bottom lip. If there are no lies between us, what will we find?

It's not only Lucifer, though. Those mangy beasts and the danger they represent to everyone, not just humans, weigh heavily on my mind. So do the Druids and their near extinction. The race my mother created. Can I let them go extinct?

In Viridian, our sun is closer to our planet and much more vivid. Every morning, I sit on the highest peak and hold my breath, waiting for the first rays to streak across the sky.

Sunrise has become my favorite time of day because it reminds me of him. Golden and magnificent, it rises in the sky every morning, ready to defend the world.

Most would look at Lucifer and think only of the darkness he's capable of wielding, but he's so much more than the world he lives in. When that last herd headed over the horizon, he could have retreated with his demons and left the world to fend for itself. Instead, he vowed to return with a larger force.

I can only do the same. Return. With a larger force. Not more Viridians, but with more answers. Knowing there is a solution to everything and needing the diversion, I run experiment after experiment.

Viridians are a superior race born of the God, Creatus. We've been around for ages, but there are only a few of us… less than a hundred… and it's been that way since my birth. Unfortunately, our species can only procreate with other races, and even then, we rarely produce offspring. As scientists, we've studied every race in every galaxy, hoping to find a way to cure ourselves. We finally came to the conclusion that the answer had been there all along. Our continued existence depends on other races.

This is the theory that drove my hypothesis for the humans, but I looked at it the wrong way. By changing the perspective, I successfully run several tests and arrive at a new conclusion. One I know to be true because it's based on Druid history.

Turning my focus to the beasts requires me to step out of my comfort zone. During the battle with Aurora, Cormal told me the beast smelled me. Not him or Daire. It was fleeing but stopped because of me. Using that theory as my base, I know I need to return and get rid of the beasts for good.

My mother is responsible for the existence of both the Druids and beasts. As her daughter, it's up to me to clean up our mess. Then power tripping assholes like Gabriel will have to learn how to fight their own battles and leave humans out of it.

WHEN I RETURN, the date on my laptop tells me only two days have passed on Earth. It's a good thing I chose to return here instead of the city. The cave my mother dwelled in is a much safer option. Unlike me, she only has one form, which means the cave's spell kept her hidden.

Unwilling to risk exposure, I use my power to whisper to the wind. Given this is the birthplace of the Druids, there must be a few who live close to here.

The next morning, a middle-aged woman comes to the cave. Wearing a simple white blouse and blue skirt, she looks like every other human, but the power humming inside her is pretty strong. Her eyes are huge in her small face when she steps into the cave, but her hands are steady, and she holds her palms out, ready to defend herself.

I wave to the stone across from me. "I'd offer you a proper seat or refreshments if I had any to spare, but as you can see, it's pretty bare in here."

She stares at me for a long minute, then slides onto the edge of the stone seat. "Who are you, and what do you want?"

"I'm Evren, the daughter of Viridis, and I need your help," I explain to her, hoping she knows a least a little something about her origins. "You are?"

She dips her chin but says nothing. Druid secrecy at its finest. I know she can feel the breadth of my power, but she refuses to yield an inch.

"My mother gave her blood to Brennus to create the Druid race. Once, there were thousands of you. Now, you're almost extinct. If you want to save yourselves, I'm here to tell you how, but I need you to drop the stoic act and help me," I tell her, smothering the irritation rising inside.

Interest flickers in the depth of her eyes. "You can really save us?"

Carefully crafting my words, I answer her. "I know how to save you." Whether it's something the Druids will embrace, I'm not sure, but I don't say those words to her. "I want you to send an invitation to the ten families to come here. The day after tomorrow."

She frowns. "Six. Six families," she corrects me. "I'm Fiona, head of the Brennus family. Can you not let me pass along the information or spell?"

No wonder she has more power than most Druids I've run across. "Six? What happened to the ten?"

She purses her lips, then murmurs, "Beyond the natural way of life, some meddled in things they shouldn't have and were killed by the beasts they created. Others met their end at the tip of an angel's sword." She smooths trembling hands down her skirt.

It always returns to Gabriel and the beasts. "We're going to solve that problem, too," I assure her. "While we wait for the families to arrive, I'm going to need some supplies." Stuffing my hand in my pocket, I pull out several large gems and pieces of gold. "I think this will be enough, but if not, let me know."

She cups her hands and holds them out to me. "My network can get you anything you need, especially if it means getting rid of those beasts."

I take a deep breath, hoping I'm not about to blow the small trust I've built with her. "I'll provide you with a list of the items." I pause. "I'm also going to need you to send two messages to the Underworld. One to Cormal, and one to Lucifer."

Her head shakes back and forth vigorously, and my heart sinks.

"No, I refuse to send a message to Cormal. Druids banned him long ago. We're forbidden to have anything to do with him," Fiona vehemently informs me.

My eyebrows arch in disbelief. Her issue is with Cormal? I thought sending a message to the Ruler of the Underworld might be an issue, but never dreamed she would refuse to send one to Cormal.

"Can you send a high-ranking demon to me? I'll craft my own messages to send to the individuals in the Underworld."

She carefully considers the compromise I'm proposing and dips her chin. "That will work. Anything else?" Her voice has an arrogant tone to it.

"No, that's all," I reply, handing her the list. "Thank you. I knew I chose this cave for a reason. It's almost as if Brennus himself answered my plea for help."

Fiona preens, then laughs. "You don't have to lay it on that thick. I've already agreed to help you." She taps the gems and gold in her pockets. "Although, I'm keeping the change."

Laughter spills out of me. I wonder if this is what my mother saw when she spoke to Brennus? A willingness to fight and stand up for his beliefs. My eyes water at the thought of her. Through all of this, I still haven't found one clue to her whereabouts. I turn away when a tear leaks from the corner of my eye. When did I become so emotional? I used to be more like the woman behind me, stoic and analytical. Secretive. I sigh.

Brushing it away, I swing back to her. "I agree. You should keep the rest. I'll see you soon."

TWENTY-EIGHT

EVREN

The demon arrives an hour later. With black, leathery-like skin, it appears to be locked in its demon form. Apparently, Fiona had to trap it to get it to do her will. I wince.

"You're a high-ranking demon?" I ask, needing to be sure my messages will get through immediately.

Smoke rolls out of his nostrils. "I'm a High Demon."

Unsure of what that is, I stare at him. "Do you have enough clout to get a message to Lucifer?"

He raises an eyebrow. "I can, but whether I will is up for negotiation."

Unable to help it, I roll my eyes, which as far as I can tell, only seems to piss him off further. "What about Cormal? Do you have access to him, too?"

Tired of dancing around his ego, I get into his face. "Look, I only need to know if you can get a message to those two individuals. If you can, name your price. I'll let you know if I can match it."

He looks around the cave and laughs. "I doubt it."

Knowing what I need to do, I sigh. I hate using my power like this, but I don't have time to be nice or find another demon. Releasing the tight grip on my power, I wrap it around him, smash through his barriers, and take hold of his mind. I sift through all the delightful memories of earthquakes and find the nugget he's so carefully hidden.

"Your daughter, Ruby. Do you think she would take a message to Lucifer and Cormal if I held her dad hostage?" Full of power, my voice echoes through the chamber.

He tries to slam his barriers close, but I hold them wide open.

The ground begins to tremble, and I realize why all those earthquakes were stored so lovingly in his memories.

"Tsk, tsk," I admonish him lightly. "I haven't given you permission to throw a tantrum, have I?" With only a tap of my foot, I stop the trembling. He must be a Calamitas Demon.

"I'll do it," he replies in a rush of fear.

I pat his cheek to let him know I heard him. "Price?"

He blinks. "Stay away from my daughter."

"Good answer," I return with a smile. Releasing him from my power, I hand him the two messages I wrote earlier. "One more thing." I walk over to the chest in the corner and find a small sapphire necklace. "This will protect your daughter from those who wish to harm her."

He hesitantly takes the necklace from me. "What's the language on the back?"

"It's Viridian," I reply softly. "If you want to be sure it's a protection spell, ask Lucifer. He knows the language. Thank you. You may go now." My words release him from the Druid's hold, and he disappears.

Will he come? I'm not sure. Cormal will definitely be here because he wants to know how to save the Druids. I could see it in his eyes when we spoke in this cave. Lucifer, I'm not sure. I kept a pretty big secret from him, and he was livid the last time I saw him. But he also told me to come back. I cling to that thought.

The next few hours fly by. The sky darkens from day to night, and I stand at the entrance to the cave, welcoming the Druids into my little sanctuary.

Each of the six families sent several delegates, so the small intimate meeting I envisioned ballooned into a much larger gathering. The heads of the family take a seat upfront in the chairs Fiona managed to procure for me, but the rest of the room has to stand. I glance at the man in the hoodie leaning against the far wall. Cormal knew his presence would cause an uproar, so he chose to stay incognito. I wait to see if Lucifer will come, but when nobody else enters, I start the meeting.

"Thank you for coming and welcome. I'm Evren, daughter of Viridis," I begin slowly. "I came here with two intentions. To save Druids and help mankind evolve, and to look for my mother. I accomplished nothing."

I look into the eyes of each one of the leaders. "Whether we like it or not, all of us rely on other races for our continued existence. I know this from my race's own experience, and I see it again in you."

I pause for a second. "When I came here, I incorrectly came to the wrong conclusion. I thought if I found the answer to how my mother made you evolve from human to Druid, I could replicate it in other humans. My first experiment was a colossal failure. I gave dying humans Druid blood. Thankfully, most of them passed peacefully. Unfortunately, two did not.

Those two turned into ravenous beasts and killed thirty-seven supernaturals and an innocent human. Forty dead because of me."

Several Druids shift uncomfortably on their seats while others give them hard looks.

"The fact that Druids knew about this and never wrote it down or passed that knowledge to others astounds me. The lives that could have been saved by your actions have to number in the thousands. But you believed maintaining your secrets was more important than letting the world know of this danger." The even tone of my voice slips for an instant and power fills the room.

The crowd takes several steps back.

I take a deep breath to calm myself.

A young Asian man, his back ramrod straight, stands up. "Your mother gave us a secret gift and explicit instructions. The knowledge of our race, and our power, was not to be shared with the world. We did what she suggested and trapped them on the other side of the portal. It did not enter our minds to question the one who created us," he admonishes me, then sits down.

I dip my head toward him. "You're correct. She did all of that and shares in the blame for both crises—the near extinction of the Druids and creation of the beasts. She couldn't find a way to jumpstart your evolution, so she created an entirely new race. One that is now at the brink of extinction. Thanks to Tadg, the bard, I figured out what she did to create Druids. She gave you a diluted transfusion of her blood. Viridian blood. The blood of a goddess. You didn't evolve. Her blood has power. She essentially gave you some of her power."

The crowd whispers furiously. The leaders sit stiffly in the front row. I guess not everyone possesses the same level of knowledge.

"I considered giving you my blood, but I realized it would only result in the same outcome. Your numbers are greatly reduced, and within another thousand years, you would again be facing extinction," I say with a shrug of my shoulders. "It also doesn't solve the main reason my mother gave you this power. Her intent was to help the human race evolve. According to a very powerful seer, humans will need to evolve in order to defend themselves from what's coming. They are outmatched in power and strength."

"What's this got to do with us?" a voice calls out from the crowd.

"You have the power to save yourselves and help the human race evolve, but the decision is yours. Free will, I believe Lucifer called it. The power lies in your hands. To save the Druids, you must give up your insular ways and procreate with non-magical humans," I inform them.

The crowd roars and starts shouting a million questions at me. I hold up a hand, but it does nothing to quiet them. With a wave of the same hand, I silence the crowd and look at the leaders.

"This is your answer? I'd rather you give us your blood and let us figure out how to stop ourselves from going extinct in a thousand more years," a rotund man with a large mustache yells at me, his face red with anger.

Surprisingly, Fiona looks like she's actually thinking about it.

Two of the other leaders are also shaking their heads, adamantly against it.

The young man from earlier stands. "If we procreate with humans, our powers will die out. We're already seeing generations with fewer and fewer powers, and those children are born from Druid parents. Plus, isn't the mixed blood the reason the beasts exist?"

"Your powers are dying out because of the inbreeding," I explain to him. "The mating of individuals or species that are closely related through ancestry causes detrimental effects." I pause. "The beasts are created because the Druid blood overpowers the human blood when it's given as a transfusion. When a human and Druid produce a child, it gains equal parts of both their DNAs. It's balanced."

Stunned, he sits down.

I look at the crowd. "If you can contain yourselves, I'll release you." When they agree, I wave a hand and lift the ban of silence.

My eyes return to the young man. "Even diluted, Viridian blood is dominant. It will carry through to your children quite easily. The proof is in your blood." I look at Cormal. "When each of the families was created, my mother gave her blood to the male. Who do you think the first Druids procreated with to create two hundred children? A *non-magical* human female. It is only later, probably the third or fourth generation, that you had enough Druids to become insular, which was entirely the wrong decision. A couple of generations later, and you were already in a decline. You just didn't know it."

The silence is deafening. To realize you had caused the decline of your race is humbling, especially to these proud people.

"So, that's the answer. You have the power to save yourselves. Your race is dependent on humans. The natural evolution of humans is dependent on you. If you decide not to pursue this path, then based on my calculations, the six will become zero in one more generation," I reveal.

"Also, I'm working on a plan to take care of the beasts, but my warning is for the leaders. When you accepted my invitation and sat in those chairs, you became bespelled. If any Druid attempts to create a beast, on purpose or by accident, you will lose all your powers." The leaders blanch. "Go ahead, turn them over."

They scramble up and turn the chairs over to look at the Viridian I wrote on the bottom. A couple of them show the crowd, who begins to back away from me.

"Thank you for coming," I call out, waving a hand at the departing group.

Four of the leaders immediately rush to follow the crowd. Fiona and the young man stay behind.

He dips his head. "I'm Haru Minako. If there is anything we can do to assist you in your task to take out the beasts, please don't hesitate to ask." With one last glance at Fiona, he heads over to the group waiting for him.

A tall man stands near the entrance of the cave, wearing non-descript dark clothes, with his face hidden in the shadows. If it weren't for the waves of power rolling off him, I'd think he was another Druid waiting for Fiona or Haru. My heart stops. Could Lucifer have come after all? I raise my hand to tell him to wait, but he turns and stalks out the door. I start to follow, but Fiona pats me on the shoulder.

"Well, you certainly know how to stir things up," Fiona says with a chuckle. "I suspected that was the answer, but I'm relieved to hear you say it. We've been trying to tell them for years that the inbreeding was causing us to lose our powers, but nobody was willing to take a chance with a human. Not even me."

I turn my attention to her. "It's the right path."

She agrees. "Yes, it is. Oh, did the demon come by?"

"Yes, he was here and happy to deliver my messages," I confirm. "Thank you."

She raises a snarky eyebrow. "I bet that took some negotiation. He doesn't do anything for free."

"Only a little pressure," I assure her with a silent snicker. "What about the rest of the stuff on my list?"

"We'll deliver it first thing in the morning. I wanted to be sure you kept your end of our bargain," she admits with a shrug. "I've got to go. With your little announcement, I realize I'm not getting any younger. If this family is going to have a future, I need to get busy. Maybe I'll swing by the pub and see if Liam has any plans tonight." Pink splashes across her cheeks and a giggle escapes.

When everyone is gone, I look over at Cormal. "What do you think?"

"Some will embrace the decision; others will die out. Either way, Druids will slowly rebuild their numbers. It's more hope than they had yesterday," he admits gruffly. "Did you really bespell the leaders?"

I give him a droll look. "Of course not."

While he may not be mortal anymore, he'll always be Druid, and he cares about their survival. With a sigh of relief, he reaches into his coat and grabs the item I requested from him. "What are you going to do with the torque?"

"I'm going to exponentially increase my power and trap it into five bombs," I tell him, ignoring the sheer look of incredulity on his face. I reach into my pocket and pull out the latex glove I stashed there earlier. "Don't worry. I've already tested one. This is going to work. If Lucifer doesn't help me, I'll figure out another way." I hold out a gloved hand for the powerful object, and he gives it to me.

"Lucifer?" he asks hoarsely. "Does he know about this?"

"He will when he gets the message I sent him," I assure him. "Although I think he was here tonight." I tell Cormal about the man I glimpsed earlier.

He looks at me strangely. "Lucifer wasn't here tonight." He

grabs my hand. "I know if he received a message, he would have been here."

The uncertainty I'd been feeling eases. Maybe he didn't get it?

If it wasn't him, who was watching my little presentation? It wasn't Gabriel. He wouldn't have been able to contain himself with so many Druids in one place.

CHAPTER
TWENTY-NINE

<u>LUCIFER</u>

Vargas appears three days later... still translucent.

When I see his current state, my patience leaves me. "This has gone on long enough. You have a family waiting for you. Arden isn't kidding. She'll carry out her threat to tell Solandis. Do y—"

Vargas waves a hand to cut me off. "She's back. In the cave. Conducting experiments."

"She's what?" I roar, trying to understand why the hell she would come back and conduct more experiments. "Has she learned nothing? Her experiments are going to get her killed. Goddess or not."

Vargas shakes his head. "What do you want me to do?"

A thousand options lie before me, but I realize I can't allow myself to follow any of them. Free will. It's the very basis of my power and beliefs. She makes her own choices. If she's hellbent on changing the course of human evolution, there isn't a damn thing I can do to stop her. But I'll be there to help her after it's done.

I force myself to pick up the pen lying on my desk. "Nothing. You need to find a body. Four days, Vargas. The clock is ticking." He remains standing in front of me.

"Don't let her do something stupid. 'Free will' doesn't mean shit if you're alone. Take it from me," he urges.

"Dismissed." This time, my voice is implacable. After a second, he leaves.

Security escorts Cormal into my office ten minutes later. "It took you long enough."

He throws a pissed off look in my direction. "Since you upgraded your security, I had to go through the entrance like a common visitor. Can't you set me up with special privileges or something? I hate walking through this monstrosity. It's dark and dreary and full of unpleasant memories." He shudders.

"Are you always this dramatic when you don't get your way?" I scoff.

"Do you want to hear what I have to say or not?" he says in a snide voice.

Irritated myself, I narrow my eyes at him. "I wouldn't have ordered you here if I didn't. Where have you been? Did you know Evren's back?"

Cormal sits down with a sigh. "I do. She summoned all of the Druid leaders, and I went to hear what she had to say."

He takes the bourbon I hand him. "She told them the way to save themselves was to procreate with humans. When they questioned her, she explained their roots came from human and Druid pairings." He goes on to tell me the rest. It's apparent by the admiration in his eyes, he likes the decision she made not to give the Druids her blood.

He starts talking about her plan to place bombs in the portal to kill the beasts and all my good feelings go right out the fucking window.

"She's going to do what?!" I yell, throwing my hands up in the air. "What the hell is she thinking? They'll devour her." It took everything Gabriel and I had to close the portal when he opened it. There's no way she'll be able to do it, goddess or not. She's reasonable, right? I only have to talk to her. Urge her to reconsider, or at least take a while to think about it. A few millennia, maybe. After all, the beasts aren't going anywhere.

"She thinks you're going to help her. Said she sent a message to you," he reveals, raising an eyebrow. "Did you get her message?"

I whip around and look through the papers on my desk, but I don't see a note. "Nothing. Who was your messenger?"

"Calamitas Demon, named Hadeon," he replies. "He delivered Evren's message to me this afternoon."

I call Vargas on our private channel. If anyone can find this demon, he can. He doesn't answer.

Uneasy, I look at Cormal. "You did not see this." With a wave of my hand, I bring up a map with millions of red dots. I hover my hand over each section and search. When I find the one I want, I pluck the dot from the map and throw it in front of me.

The demon falls to the floor with a thud. His bloody body is a mass of bruises and deep wounds, the kind made from a sword. I bend over and check to make sure, but he's definitely dead.

Fuck.

Cormal scrutinizes the demon. "Calamitas Demons are high in the food chain and tough to kill. Plus, Hadeon was well liked. He took care of his little girl and kept to himself. For a demon, he had few enemies."

"Whoever did this was clearly pissed off." I point to the wounds in his chest. "They stabbed him repeatedly." None of the wounds came close to piercing his heart. Frowning, I roll him over, and look for the kill shot, but find nothing. "He's not beheaded. He's not burned. I didn't kill him. So, how did he die? A spell?"

Cormal gets on his knees and sniffs. "Smell him. What does he smell like to you?"

Giving him an incredulous look, I bend down and sniff. An acrid smell burns my nose. "What is that?"

"Holy water. He was either drowned or injected with holy water. It burned all of his internal organs and killed him," he explains matter-of-factly. "I've only seen it once, but based on the screaming, it was an excruciating way to die."

The fact that he knows the method isn't surprising, but I can't help but wonder if it's firsthand knowledge. "At least there's a body for his little girl to burn. I'll have one of the staff prepare the funeral pyre and bring her here. If he has enemies, she'll be safe until I can find some relatives to take her in."

I pull the pouch off the demon's body and turn it over. A gold sapphire necklace slides out. I pick it up and hold it up to the light. "Perfect stone." An odd choice for a demon, though. Maybe it was a present for his daughter? I flip it around in the palm of my hand. A spell written in Viridian is on the back. "It's a protection spell. Evren might have given him this piece as payment. She's one of the few who actively uses the language."

The words stop me in my tracks. She knows the language because it is her language. If the ancients spoke it, that means the Viridians were here long before humans were created. I wonder how old she is.

Cormal pries open the demon's clenched fist and shows me the scrap of ripped paper left in his palm. He was definitely carrying another message, and whoever killed him received it instead of me.

"My message had her location on it," Cormal murmurs. "Do you think...?"

I'm gone before he can finish the words.

WHEN I ARRIVE at the cave, the surrounding mountain is caving in on one side, and as a result, the cave's opening is partially collapsed. Not wanting to alert anyone to my presence, I quietly slip through the opening and hit a wall. Not a literal wall, but one made of magic. The cave's protected.

A deafening sound fills the air, and the mountain shifts a fraction of an inch. Rocks and debris rain down on top of me. I stride out to see what's happening and find Gabriel using his borrowed powers to throw massive boulders at the mountain.

He stops when he sees me, and his brow lowers. "Get the fuck out of my way, Lucifer. She's a goddess, and that gives me all the permission I need to use force to remove her from this Earth." With his palm down, he pulls up another giant rock from the ground, hauls his arm back, and throws it like a baseball toward the mountain. Another boom rocks the air, and a piece of the mountain caves inward.

"You're pathetic. Let you borrow a little power, and you think you have the right to do whatever the fuck you want without consequences. Do you think this promotes the greater good? What about forgiveness and love for your neighbor? Maybe you should reflect on these things while you visit some of Underworld's worst," I snarl at him, trying to get him to shift his attention from the mountain to me.

"That's rich coming from you. You couldn't care less about forgiveness," he snorts.

"Did you kill Hadeon? The Calamitas demon?" I ask softly. "He had a little girl, you know. Apparently, he loved her very much, and you took him from her."

"What's one demon in the thousands that still exist?" he muses, crossing his arms. "Besides, it only makes us even. You killed one of my angels in a cave similar to this one not too long ago. Remember?"

Having recently attended the funerals for all the demons lost in the last battle with the beasts, rage encompasses me. "We'll never be even. Not until you fall from grace."

He laughs and reaches his palm out for another rock, then tosses it forward. This one barely hits the side of the mountain. Enraged, he stares at the offending rock until it explodes into tiny pieces.

With him distracted, I subtly weave my fingers, bringing a special set of chains up behind his back. Created by Hades himself, their purpose is to pull monsters down into the Underworld and trap them there. I usually keep them in my dungeon, as I've found them useful for a variety of reasons. Maybe Gabriel should see a little of my world. While I can't hold him indefinitely, two or three weeks is nothing. A blip so short few will notice he's gone.

When his palm moves to hover over another rock, I quickly swirl my fingers and hands around and around, guiding the chains over his wings and down his body.

He lifts a link and laughs. "These wouldn't hold a cherub. You're getting soft in your old age." His hand grabs the chain to swing it over his shoulder and it becomes increasingly heavy until he can barely lift it an inch. Panting, he lets it drop. The moment it falls into place, it becomes light again.

"Hades' chains," I inform him cheerfully. "Only I have the

power to remove them." I laugh when I see his fury. "I'm going to send you on a little trip to the Underworld. You need to realize how this world really works. You think Evren and Hadeon are evil? I'll show you what real monsters look like. When you're in the deep, staring into their eyes, you'll feel them devour your soul, piece by piece. It won't be real, but you'll swear it is. Your body will be in agony while your spirit cowers in the corner of your mind. Maybe the next time you feel the urge to kill one of my demons, you'll remember we're the only things standing between you and those monsters."

My hand circles the ground, and a long dark passageway opens underneath him. He immediately starts shouting obscenities and trying to lift the chains from his body. Bringing my fist up into the sky, I yank with all might and hurl him into the passageway. Down, down he goes. Past the fluffier levels of hell and into the belly of the beast. Hellfire is the only light in that place, and there's not a lot of it. He lands and the shadows close tightly around his body. This is the place where nightmares come to breed. My hand circles again, and the ground closes.

I stride toward the cave and find Evren standing there with a solemn look on her face. It punches me in the gut. Seeing her. Wanting more. Not knowing what she's thinking or feeling.

"Did you kill him?"

My lip curls. "Much to my disgust, no. Gabriel will only wish he was dead. The Devil bred the worst of the worst, and those monsters are the result. He quickly realized he wouldn't be able to control them, so he trapped them in the deepest part of the Underworld. If they were to ever escape, the world would end." I stand at the very edge of the entrance drinking her in.

She walks closer to the edge. "Why are you here?" Her body

leans toward mine, but her feet never leave the protection of the cave.

"To save you, of course," I reply softly. "I know you don't need a savior, but I need to be one. For you. Will you let me save you, at least for a little while?" My heart slows with my breaths, and my world narrows to this one moment.

"Are you still angry with me?" she asks, her eyes searching mine.

Am I? Yes. Probably not for reasons she might think. "Yes."

"Good. I'm angry with you too," she reveals. "And you're late."

"Gabriel killed your messenger," I explain softly.

Her jaw clenches in anger. "I'm glad he's gone, or this might have pushed me past my patience. He almost destroyed this cave with his latest tantrum." She looks behind her. "I only stayed this morning because Fiona is bringing me supplies."

"I'll post someone to intercept her," I tell her.

She takes a deep breath, steps out of the safety of the cave, and wraps her arms around my neck. "Yes, save me. Be my wicked savior. Show me your world. At least for a little while." Her lips reach up and capture mine in a kiss so filled with longing, it eases something tight inside of me.

The sky begins to darken and rumble, and I lift my head. "We need to go."

<u>EVREN</u>

Without a portal nearby, we shimmer to Lucifer's home. The power of displacement is only given to those in the Underworld. One minute you're standing in one spot, then suddenly your entire body disappears from existence and reappears in a different place moments later.

My insides feel scrambled, and when I open my eyes, the world is still spinning. I quickly shut them.

Lips skim the rim of my ear, making me shiver. "Keep them closed until your equilibrium returns." He continues to stand there with his arms loosely looped around me.

A few minutes later, I open my eyes and look up, only to find a small smile on his face. "Are you making fun of me?"

Surprise flashes across his face, then he laughs. "No, just

thinking about how nice it is to have you here. In my world. Something I never imagined would be possible."

I glance around the room we're standing in. "What's this place?" A large fireplace burns along one wall. Tall shelves are filled with books and weird-looking glass jars. A beautiful wood desk sits against the back wall near a window.

My brows come together. "How do you have sunlight down here?"

He chuckles. "Cormal. When you were recuperating at The Abbey, he installed the 'sun' he designed for his own office."

I walk over and look out, but all I see is sunshine. It even feels warm as if real sunlight is coming through the window.

When I give him a curious look, he raises a hand. "I don't know how it works. You'll have to ask him, but I missed the sun. Now I have it."

I turn from the window to the shelves. The books lined up in an orderly fashion call to me and my inner need for knowledge. The first book title is *Princes of Sin*. I skim the others in the same row. *House of Envy, House of Gluttony, House of Sloth*. The theme continues for the next four books, then it changes to *Calamitas Demon, Vindicta Demon, Chaos Demon*, and so on.

"Do these books catalog all the citizens of the Underworld by species?" I ask, pretty amazed at the collection in front of me.

Lucifer clears his throat. "Yes, I can't take the... credit... for them, but I'm glad you find them interesting." A bewildered look sits on his face. "I was actually thinking of getting rid of some of this outdated stuff."

I run a finger down the spine of a book on the Hellhounds' genealogy. "Fascinating. Viridians are scientists who specialize in the study of life in all its forms. Over several millennia, we've collected samples from millions and millions of species across the universes. Our fascination started because we were trying to solve our own fertility problems, but the collection has saved more than one species from extinction."

He leans against his desk. "I never really thought much about what gods do. I guess I only attribute creation and destruction with them." His voice is gruff with memories.

I stare at him for a second. "We preserve and study life, but I guess technically, we help create it, too. Everything comes from something. It's why I asked for your blood—to see what species were included in your creation—and to figure out how you have evolved from your original genetics."

He slowly stands up. "You mean as an angel? You think we came from a mixture of different species?" Laughter shakes his large shoulders.

I raise an eyebrow. "You think you poofed into existence? Really?" Stalking over to the desk, I hand him the letter opener I spied earlier. "Give me your blood, and I'll tell you which species went into your creation."

He stops laughing to stare at me. "You're serious."

"Gods talk," I inform him haughtily. "We know when a new species is being created. Gods frequently come to Viridian with a list of their requirements. We pull the samples for them."

"Did you pull samples for the angels?" he asks hoarsely.

"We pulled samples at the request of the god who created angels and humans. We didn't ask for specifics," I reveal. "My mother delivered the original samples. When she returned to extract samples from the new species, she met my father. He was human. She fell in love."

His eyes crinkle with confusion. "Are you a demi-goddess?"

I shake my head. "No, I'm a god or goddess, whichever term is preferred. Personally, I like goddess because it celebrates my uniqueness, and it's more modern. A lot of the old gods are old-fashioned males who can be patronizing." I wrinkle my nose at the thought.

"Viridian blood is dominant. But the human shell is another form I can wear," I explain. Another thought hits me. "You can take another form, right? I know angels have a human form, but their main form is less corporeal."

He hesitates for a minute, then moves closer to me. Bending down, he murmurs in my ear. "I have four forms. The one you see now—my human form. My angel form—it's larger, casts a golden glow, and is less corporeal, as you describe. A demonic form that is sort of a mix between human, angel, and demon with a few additions... wings of flame, horns on my head, and red eyes. And the Lightbringer, which is simply a column of light." He lifts his head to gauge my reaction.

I try to tone down the excitement thrumming through me, but his laugh tells me I failed to hide my emotions. "Sorry. It's ingrained. I don't know how to turn it off."

He tucks a piece of hair around my ear. "I don't want you to change." Then he laughs. "You did, though, didn't you? I'm not imaging the differences?"

"Between my human form and this one?" I ask with a mischievous grin. "Yes. I'm taller, my facial features are more defined, and..." I look down at my chest and hips. "There's a bit more padding in specific places."

The palms of his hands skim down the sides of my body. "Both are stunning, but I have to admit, this form fits you better. Stronger. More reflective of your personality. Although I do miss the cute freckles."

I slide in tighter and fit my taller body to his. "Definitely a better fit."

With a groan, his hand slides around my back, and he presses my body into his. His sharp blue eyes never leave mine as he slowly dips his head closer and closer. "Are we done talking yet?"

Instead of answering, I close the distance between our lips. When I was watching those sunrises on Viridian and bathing in all the light and heat, all I could think of was kissing him again.

His pouty lips taste of sunshine and darkness, like a warm drop of honey with a smoky flavor beneath it, and I can't get enough. I run my tongue across them, and when they open, I dive in to taste more of him. My tongue captures his in a dance as old as time. Wrapping my hand around the back of his neck, I hold him to me.

His lips harden on mine, becoming more urgent, as if his only thought is to devour me. I can't help the shiver that cascades down my body at the thoughts this brings to mind. Me sprawled beneath him as he feasts on every inch of my body.

A low moan slips from me.

"Evren," he groans, pulling his lips from mine. "Hold on."

Seconds later, we're somewhere else. The dizziness hits, and he eases me into a sitting position. When I open my eyes, he's kneeling in front of me, with a fire crackling behind him.

I glance around and spot a massive bed piled high with pillows and luxurious bedding and smile. The rest of the room begs to be explored, but the desire thrumming in my veins is too insistent.

Turning my attention to him, I wrap my hands around his jaw and pull him toward me for a kiss. Picking up where we left off a minute ago, I pull him in tighter, wanting his hard body against mine.

Large hands pull me to the edge of the sofa, and he slips between my legs.

I widen them, wanting to feel his hardness against my core.

Firm lips continue to dominate mine, but the kiss isn't rushed in any way. He kisses as if he has an eternity to do so. His tongue stokes the fire inside me, over and over. My legs wrap around him, and I slide my body against his, adding fuel to our already burning kiss.

Finally, his lips leave mine, and he stares down at me with his beautiful blue eyes. "I know you can't stay and live in my world forever, but while you are here, I want to pretend that this is more than a temporary interlude while the world is on pause. I want you to be mine in every way possible. What do you say?"

I think about the possible implications and the hurt that will inevitably come later, but I don't care. All I want to do is throw caution to the wind, and grab onto him with both hands.

I lean forward and place my lips at his ear while my hands continue further south to grasp the hem of his shirt. "Yes. Before the world intrudes again, I want you, and this moment. Everything you have to offer. Show me what's important to you." As I lean back to look into his eyes, I pull his shirt up and over his head.

Flames burn his blue eyes. With one swipe of his hand down my body, my clothes disappear.

I laugh. "Cheating, are we?" My breath catches when he does the same to his pants. "Mmm, there's a definite advantage to using a little magic."

Strong arms pick me up and place me down on the soft rug before the fireplace. He leans up and stares down at me while phantom fingers trail over my body. A glint of satisfaction appears in his eyes when they find a sensitive spot. His magical hands feel so good, but they're not what I want.

My finger runs over his lips. "Taste me, feast on me. I want to feel your lips everywhere."

Red rims the blue in his eyes. "My pleasure, my goddess." Invisible manacles pull my arms up and lock them into place above my head. When his lips descend, I'm already panting with desire. Sprawled beneath him, my body is an offering, one for him to do with whatever he wants. The feeling of being at his mercy only amps up my desire, and the air fills with my slick perfume.

His tongue and mouth are relentless. Licking, sucking, and tasting every inch of me. This is what I've dreamed of for so long. Someone hungry for my body whose only thought is to devour me. I arch into him, taking all that he's offering and basking in it.

Only seconds after his tongue licks between my legs, a wave of pleasure hits me, and I dig my heels into the floor. It continues to roll over me for several more seconds. When the first one is over, he starts again. His tongue brings me to the edge several times, then he finally lets me fall again. I moan when the second orgasm hits stronger. Waves of desire spread like fire through my body until it finally dissipates.

Chest heaving, I stare at him through eyes glazed with desire. "Incredible. Now unlock me so I can taste you."

His cock twitches.

An invisible manacle releases one of my ankles, and he positions himself at my entrance. "I'm too fucking impatient and turned on. All I want is to be inside you, feeling your slick body gripping my cock." With one smooth thrust of his hips, he slides in to the hilt, filling every inch of me inside.

He gives me a second to adjust. Releasing the restraint from my other leg, he stares down at me. "Wrap your legs around me. Tight. I want to be as deep as possible."

My body clenches at his tone, and I quickly do what he says. He slips a little deeper, and I gasp.

"That's it. Feel me deep inside you?" he asks, flexing his

cock until I nod. He slides out until only the tip is inside me. Using shallow thrusts, he teases the spot inside my entrance with little thrusts until I'm digging my heels into his back. Then he thrusts in hard.

When he pulls out again, my eyes drift down to watch the two of us, then swivel up to meet his. "Why does this feel so good?" The question is both real and rhetorical.

He shakes his head and grips my hip. "It's about to feel better." With those words, he starts moving harder and faster.

The pleasure builds and builds. "More," I plead with him.

As if he were only waiting for the word, he thrusts faster and faster. His hand slips down my body and strokes the very heart of me.

This time, it's as if the stars go supernova. Blackness flashes for a second, then I fall over the edge and into the abyss he created for us. Moments later, he follows, his body pulsing as his release hits.

We lie there for several minutes, catching our breath. The firelight flickers over both of us. The weight of his body on top of mine is a memory I store away for later.

"You are a wicked, wicked savior." I stroke a hand down his back. "Good thing neither of us needs sleep."

He chuckles and lifts his head from my breasts. "We're only getting started, love."

THIRTY-ONE

LUCIFER

Hours later, I make myself move farther than two feet away from her. When I return with a glass of bourbon for us to share, she's lying on her side, staring into the fire with a smile on her face. My eyes skim her creamy skin, noticing the faint marks of my possession everywhere, and satisfaction fills me.

I jokingly groan. "Are we already back to reality? What are you thinking about in that super smart brain of yours?"

A blush steals across her face, surprising me.

I hand her the bourbon, and she takes a sip and wrinkles her nose. "No, thank you. Why do you drink that stuff?"

I laugh and take a sip. "I like the taste." And the taste of her. "Are you not going to tell me what you were thinking about?"

She places an arm across her eyes. "Nothing clever or smart."

Sensing her discomfort, I sit down and rub a hand down her arm. "You can tell me anything. Even if it's dumb." I deliberately use the word to get her to look at me.

Her arm whips across and smacks my shoulder. "Nothing is dumb." She sighs heavily. "If you must know, I've never been with someone equal in power to me."

My brows draw together in confusion. "I haven't either, but I'm not sure I understand why it's important."

Her cheeks darken. "When you took control, my mind knew it was true, and it lent a certain... It let me be demanding, but it let me also give in to you. It was freeing." Her words are rushed, but I understand what she's trying to tell me.

My lips graze her ear. "I love having you at my mercy." She shifts to clench her legs together. "And being able to use my full power and not hurt you is new for me, too." I blow in her ear. "Mm, what fun we're going to have when we get back."

"Back?" she questions, her eyes glazed with passion.

"As delectable as these hours have been, I have some work to do, and you're going with me. I want to hear what you think," I tell her, although my cock vehemently disagrees.

A spark of interest ignites in her eyes, and she stands up. Waving a hand over her body, she washes herself, but then stands there naked. "What should I wear?"

"Preferably nothing, but since I can't blind every male in the vicinity, clothes would be best," I reply, standing and quickly washing and dressing in black pants and a button-down shirt.

"Do you own anything not in black?" she asks, with a frown. Black pants and a green silk blouse appear on her, along with some boots. With a deft twist, she pulls her dark red hair into a smooth bun at the base of her neck.

I bend down to place my lips on my favorite spot. "Black hides blood. It's ominous-looking, and it suits my mood." Maybe not today, but most days. I'm a broody bastard. "You look beautiful. Ready?"

She grimaces.

When we arrive, she grips my arm for a second, but gains her equilibrium a little quicker. "It's getting shorter, isn't it?"

Her eyes are already darting past me to the construction site. "Yes. Where are we? Is this one of the habitats you were telling me about?"

The corner of my lips twitches, and I turn to face the project Cormal started while I was helping Evren recuperate. "It is. We decided to tackle the largest one first. There are a lot of merfolk and other creatures from the water who have made this city their home. We want to give them something that suits all their needs."

I pull her to the edge of the large hole in front of us. "Some depths resemble those of the ocean above, but the water will slowly rise for the creatures who require shallower depths."

She points to the middle, where the hole stops on one side and begins again on the other. "What is that for?"

"When we spoke to the people, we realized some like cold water and others need tropical or warmer waters. The divider allows us to give them two mini-oceans with both options," I reply.

She bends down and sifts the soil between her hands. "Will this support the vegetation they will expect in this replicated environment?"

I smile and point to the huge pile of plants in the far-right corner of the construction lot. "Yes. If it hadn't, we would have brought in new soil."

The Nemean Lion spots us and comes striding over. Orlo's eyes shift inquisitively to Evren, and I possessively slide an arm around her. She's taken asshole. "Evren, this is Orlo, the site manager. Are we hitting our deadlines and budget?"

He cocks an arrogant eyebrow. "Things are coming along great. So far, we're hitting each milestone in the timeline. Do you want a tour?"

Evren moves her head up and down before I can decline. "Yes, please."

The damn lion flashes her a bright smile. "Wonderful. Follow me." He strides off toward the plants in the corner, with Evren following, and me bringing up the rear. For the next hour, he explains all the different components of the project to Evren, who continues to ask question after question.

It's extremely informative, and I find myself altering my opinion of him. When we get to the end and Evren's asked her last question, I dip my head. "You're doing a great job here. I don't know if Cormal's shown you the scope of the project, but I'd like you to consider taking on the role of lead supervisor."

His lip curls in disdain, but he says nothing.

"It's a great opportunity, and I know you'll do a fabulous job. Congratulations," she tells him, ignoring his rude behavior. "This is a terrible question, but what is that symbol on your neck?"

Orlo looks at me and smirks.

"It's my mark," I tell her, silently berating myself for not covering it up when I saw him walking toward us. "We had a spat when we first met. This was the penalty."

She shoots a murderous glance at me. "I see." Turning to Orlo, she shakes his hand. "Thank you so much for the tour. It's magnificent."

He beams and bends over to kiss her hand, but the snarl on my face stops him. "It was a pleasure meeting *you*. Come again." Turning around, he stalks off without a word in my direction.

Insolent asshole.

Evren pulls me around to face her. "Do you mark everyone who pisses you off?"

"Only those who use physical force against me," I retort. "It's fine, Evren. Do you want to go see the campus next or continue to argue about Orlo?" Crossing my arms, I stare down at her with my best "don't fuck with me" look.

She squints at me for a second, then nods. "You could remove it, you know. Now that you've made your point."

I glare down at her. "Out of the question."

She steps into my arms. "Fine, let's go."

Exasperated, I take her to the area where we're going to build the campus. She briefly closes her eyes, but when they open, she's glaring daggers at me.

Ignoring the look, I turn her around to face the valley. "We decided this would be a great place for the campus. It's sheltered from the harsh winds that can sometimes come down from the nearby mountains, and the natural barriers deter random visitors. What do you think?"

She waves a hand and brings up the sketches I showed her in The Abbey. "Where will each building go? Show me."

I chuckle. She might want to be a little submissive in bed, but out of it is a whole different story. Using my own magic, I place the imaginary buildings over the land in front of us. "The main buildings will be in the center of campus and accessible to everyone. It will contain the food halls, dorms, gyms, and other common areas. The science building will be here. English here, math, languages, and the others."

"Did you find experts to help you?" she asks, staring at the science building with longing.

"Surprisingly, there are quite a few demons, and several dead humans, who have the knowledge we require and are eager to help us build the school," I tell her, still surprised by how many. "Although none have your level of expertise in science."

She squints up at me as if assessing whether I'm telling the truth.

I look at her in disbelief, but she sniffs and looks away.

"Would you be willing to sit down and detail out everything we would need for the lab and classes? Think about it, and name your price," I say, dangling the idea in front of her. I can't help wondering what she'll ask for... my help with the bombs?

She tilts her head to the side to study the science building. Her mouth opens, then closes. "If I do this, can I build the lab and study your blood?"

Surprised, I stare at her for second, then agree. "Done. Are you ready to go? I have court this evening."

Delighted at my answer, she smiles. It's so breathtaking, it makes me clench my jaw. "I can't wait to see your court."

I grimace. I wonder what she'll think of it. "Ready?"

She steps stiffly into my arms.

Irritated, I detour to the habitat and stalk over to Orlo. Waving a hand, I remove my symbol from his neck. "Not a fucking word."

He gives me a solemn look, but I see him blow a kiss to Evren behind my back.

"Insolent bastard."

Her lips curve in a broad smile, and she drapes her arms around my neck. "Let's go finish our discussion from earlier."

The feel of her body brushing intently against mine drives every other thought out of my head.

THIRTY-TWO

<u>EVREN</u>

Court is much more interesting than I thought it would be. The people present cases for him to review and determine a ruling. A dispute with a neighbor over land, a demon who failed to pay taxes for the last five hundred years, and an illegal gambling hall wagering with souls instead of gold. He deals with them efficiently and fairly.

The people at court are interesting, though. Some are there to watch the sessions or extend a sexual invitation to Lucifer, which I ignore, but the rest are waiting for their case to be called. I wonder how he determines which one to hear?

The council sits in their seats, whispering back and forth, but never asking a question or throwing out a suggestion. Why are they here if they're not going to help?

Once he's dismissed everyone, he turns to me. "Thoughts?"

"It's tough to fairly judge your court on one session alone," I start. "It feels like there are a lot of surplus people here with nothing to do."

I stop and check to see if he's offended by my observation, but he waves his hand for me to continue.

"How do you choose the sessions?" I ask him.

With a surprised look, he shrugs. A second later, a small blue demon appears before us. With large floppy ears and whiskers on his chin, he almost looks like a grumpy puppy.

"Sonders, how do we choose which sessions to hear?"

The demon lifts his chin. "I choose them based on their level of importance. Many people apply to court, but their grievances are too petty and not worthy of your consideration, my benevolent ruler."

I frown. "If he only hears the most important cases, then who listens to the others?"

Sonders swings his dark eyes to me, then back to Lucifer without answering the question.

Lucifer leans forward. "She asked you a question."

Sonders swallows hard. "Nobody."

"You've done a great job of picking the largest disputes," I assure him, guessing he takes his position very seriously. "Do you have any ideas about what to do for the small grievances? Also, do you have suggestions on how to make the process more efficient for everyone, including yourself?"

His dark eyes light up and he bobs his tiny head up and down. "Yes, I've given it a great deal of thought, but these sessions were established based on his orders. It's not up to me to change them."

At that statement, I give Lucifer a look. It's his court.

The corners of his mouth twitch. "Send me your suggestions. We'll see what we can do to make things better." He waves a hand to dismiss him.

Sonders bows deeply. "Thank you, Sire." He swings to me and dips his chin. "Miss."

When he's gone, I hesitate to add another suggestion, but he did ask. "What does the council do?"

The near smile on Lucifer's face disappears. "They advise me on matters of state and political alliances."

"They didn't do anything in today's session. Was that an anomaly, or is that the norm?" I ask him, unsure what's bugging me about them.

"They rarely interfere in court sessions," he replies gruffly.

It hits me. "They look like the old gods we used to have on our council. As our numbers started to dwindle, we knew we needed a new council. So, we asked them to take over certain duties. Unfortunately, when they couldn't perform the tasks we set for them, they had to step down and let another take their place, someone willing to work harder for our people." Once appointed, we couldn't get rid of them, because it would have caused a lot of uproar and anger the god. It was better for them to step down using their own judgement.

Lucifer stares at me with dawning comprehension. "Clever. I have been thinking of getting rid of them but putting them to work is a better idea. There are plenty of items on my list I can delegate to them." He eyes me. "Anything else?"

"Your bone chair is very fitting for the ruler of the Underworld," I tell him. "You should invite other leaders here. Let them see you in your domain."

"I've tried, but none will come. Besides, if they did, I'd have to attend one of their insufferable balls," he says, laughing at the expression of outrage on my face.

Irritation blooms. "That's rude. They may need you one day."

He gives me a lazy look, which tells me he couldn't care less.

"The nymph was very beautiful and sexy," I blurt out, unable to stop myself.

He stands and stalks toward me. "Mm, what nymph?"

I narrow my eyes. "Good answer. What's next?"

He tugs me up from the small, tufted chair he had placed next to his throne and pulls me into his arms. "A surprise. Ready?" The smile on his face pulls at something inside me.

Breathless, I raise my head for his kiss. Hard lips press on mine as he whirls me away. When we get to our destination, I realize I'm no longer plagued by the dizziness from traveling that way. I open my eyes and pull my lips from his.

The room we're in is full of stainless-steel counters, beakers, and an assortment of machines. My mouth drops open. "How did you get all this? I haven't given you a list."

"No, but you gave Fiona one," he replies with a chuckle. "When she arrived with the supplies, the sentry I posted alerted me. I let Fiona know you were safe, but in hiding. Then we transported everything here." He runs a finger across my mouth. "I also had a team transport the items from the lab at The Abbey."

That's why there is so much stuff here.

"My mother's cave, actually," I correct him, still thinking about what I can do with all this at my disposal. "My mother was the one who gave the Druids her blood and started the entire race. There wasn't an evolution of human powers, as I originally thought."

I've been completely avoiding this conversation, not wanting the realities of the past to intrude on our little bubble, but I've been in the Underworld for three days now. If I don't get started on building the bombs and devising a plan for their delivery, Gabriel could end up unleashing more of those beasts on unsuspecting humans and supernaturals. I doubt he's learned anything during his little vacation with the monsters.

"Cormal told me what you said at the meeting. If I'd known you invited me, I would have been there," he admits, raking his hair back from his face. "I'm glad you took the path you did. If the Druids want to save themselves, they will."

Expelling a sigh of relief, I look over the items Fiona delivered and spot the canisters I specifically requested.

I open my mouth, but he jumps in before I have a chance.

He picks up a beaker filled with a dark substance. "This is my blood. Run whatever tests you want, but promise me, you'll burn it when you're done. I don't want anyone else getting a hold of it and casting a spell or using it for dark magic."

The trust he's giving me with his blood tells me more than any words. "I promise. Thank you," I tell him, putting it in the small refrigerator. "Once I'm done with this lab, you can use it for the school. It has everything you need to get started." Even as I say the words, a pang of sadness hits me at the thought of leaving him.

I clear my throat. "I think the books and specimens on your shelves would make great additions to the science department. You could ask your people to donate samples of their DNA for further study and match them to the books. Not only would it be helpful for the science department, but history, and medical, too," I stop, aware I'm babbling now.

He laughs. "Does your brain ever stop?"

"Viridians are hard wired to question everything until we can find solutions to problems. It's probably why I was so stubborn about the Druids. And why I need to finish what my mother started and end those beasts. Did Cormal tell you about my idea?" I ask, unwilling to avoid the discussion any longer.

"He told me," Lucifer replies in a hard voice. "It's ludicrous to think you can destroy all of those beasts with a few bombs.

The portal is teeming with them. Every time we open the door, they spill out of there. It's not a solid plan."

Insufferable man. "You don't know the plan," I retort, anger rising to the surface. "Do you want to hear the details or would you rather I leave you out of it?"

He swings around furiously. "Fine. Let's hear this grand plan."

I lift my chin, refusing to let my own anger take over. "Using the five points of a pentagram as our guide, we place five bombs at equal distances from each other inside the portal. This will exponentially increase our chances of covering the outer rim of their little world, which is the widest part."

I walk over and open a canister to show him the hundreds of smaller canisters inside. "When the bombs detonate, they will not only take out the beasts on the edges, but these smaller bombs will also disburse and eliminate the remaining beasts in the middle."

He rubs a hand on his chin. "How do you plan on getting the canisters set up?"

"By using my power to push them back from the portal entrance while someone flies in to place the bombs at the designated points," I tell him, a little unsure about this part.

"What happens if the beasts knock them over? Or the flyer drops one into the herd?" he retorts.

"These are capable of holding nuclear material. They're pretty indestructible. Plus, the beasts don't have magic to pry them open," I state firmly, more confident about the method of delivery than any other part of the plan.

"The beasts are fast. One flying person, even one as fast as me, wouldn't be enough. You need to think of a different plan," he informs me, arms crossed over his chest.

I shake my head in agreement. "Maybe. Also, I originally thought you might be able to help, but I can't ask you now.

These people... this world needs you. If you were gone, they could end up with someone like the Devil." I shudder. "I'll take what you said into account about needing more than one flyer to deliver the bombs and figure out an alternative plan."

"You're not doing this," he snarls.

"I am," I state firmly. "It can't wait any longer. You saw it yourself. They're replicating at an astonishing rate. How long do you think we have until they can no longer be contained? Or what happens if Gabriel loses his mind and releases them all? He doesn't care about anyone."

"Fuck!" he roars, sweeping an arm across the top of the nearest counter. Beakers and pipettes smash on the floor below. His eyes flash from blue to red and horns appear on his head.

My eyes widen. and he whips a hand up and runs it across his hair, his eyes closing when he finds the horns.

Something guttural comes out of his mouth and he disappears, leaving me to clean up the mess he made.

Unable to help myself, I sweep another beaker to the floor in anger. I wait for the satisfaction to wash over me, but all I feel is guilt. With a wave of my hand, I fix all the beakers and place them on the counter. There. I dust my hands together. That feels better.

I roll up my sleeves and turn to the only constant in my life. Work. Good thing there's a lot to do.

THIRTY-THREE

EVREN

Once the lab is together, I start testing his blood. Viridians know all of the superior, or god-like races, in the universe. It's the first thing we teach our children. Once they can recognize those races, we expand their education to include less powerful species, like humans and others across the worlds.

Only the most superior races were used in the creation of angels, but the percentages and composition likely differ between angels. It's why some have powers that are unique to them. Like Lucifer's ability to kill angels.

For hours, I pipe blood into small tubes and place them into the centrifuge. Methodically moving from one step to the next, I extract and spin until I have multiple samples. Ready to view the first one, I search the room for the electron micro-scope and a few other machines.

Once it's set up, I place the first glass rectangle into the sample holder. Peering down, I find a unique combination of the most powerful races, as I expected. Grabbing a piece of paper and a pen, I write them down one by one. I won't be able to tell the percentages of DNA with this equipment, only their original source.

Hours pass while I look at the different samples. The results are consistent across all the tests. They're also very interesting.

Power enters the room, but it doesn't feel like Lucifer. Tensing, I slowly raise my head to confront the intruder... and find Cormal leaning against the wall.

"Do you enjoy sneaking up on people?"

He lifts a shoulder. "You should be more aware. Are you ready to go?"

"Go where?"

"Back to the palace," he informs me. "Lucifer said he told you before he left."

Ah, those must have been the sounds he spit out.

"I'm not ready to leave. It will take me several days to build the bombs. Can you return tomorrow and check on me?"

I'm not avoiding him, I assure myself.

He studies me intently. "I'll be back tomorrow."

As promised, I burn the samples.

Closing my eyes, I call the torque to me. Minutes later, it lies on the stainless-steel countertop, the gold gleaming against the silver backdrop. Carefully preparing each of the containers, I hover my hand over the torque, hesitating for a split second, then pick it up.

Power instantly builds inside me. It doubles, triples, increasing over and over. Sweat breaks out on my forehead, and I grit my teeth. When I can no longer contain it, I focus on the container in front of me and pour the power into it, then seal it shut with magic.

I repeat this five more times. Lucifer was right. I can't plan for all contingencies. Something could happen to one of the canisters. It's better to have a back-up.

Once the last one is done, I drop the torque onto the surface in front of me and slide down to the floor. Maybe I should rest. It's the last thought I have for a while. When I come to, I'm lying on the cold floor. Disoriented, I push my way into a sitting position.

It's rare for me not to be aware of time passing. The only reason I can deduce is my power was so completely depleted, I passed out. I must have put more than I realized into each container. Placing my hand on the wall for balance, I slowly make my way to my feet.

"I didn't think goddesses slept," Cormal's amused voice says from the corner.

"We don't," I retort, irritated at the idea of being so vulnerable in front of anyone with power. I glance at the torque on the counter, then back at Cormal. He stares steadily at me in return. Knowing him, he probably used the torque, but there's not much I can do about it, nor do I really care. "I thought you were coming back tomorrow?"

His eyebrows arch high. "It is tomorrow. You've been here for two days."

Two days? And Lucifer still hasn't come to check on me? I can't help but wonder if my determination to carry through with my plan has ruined things between us.

"Thank you, Cormal. I'm really behind now. Do you mind giving me one more day?"

After he's gone, I wipe away the stupid tears that roll down my cheeks.

Stop being so human, I admonish myself.

The ache in my heart refuses to listen, but thankfully, my mind is better at obeying my commands. Focusing all my attention, I methodically transfer some of the power into the smaller canisters. When each of them is full, I pour the leftover power into the larger canister. I repeat this until all six are done.

He hasn't come to check on me once. Angry now, I carefully store the canisters in individual steel boxes to ready them for transport. I'm adding the last one when Cormal arrives.

I swivel around to face him, and he holds his hands up. "Don't shoot the messenger. Or in this case, your ride."

"Do you know where he is?" I ask in a determined voice.

"He wants you to return to the palace. As soon as he's done, he'll meet you there," he informs me, his voice carefully neutral.

"Take me to him," I order him, then backtrack a little. "Please."

"He said—"

Fists clench, I step into Cormal's face. "I don't care what he said. Take me to him."

Cormal's eyes study mine, then he nods his head in agreement. "Don't let him kill me."

I give him a dismissive shrug. "Who would miss you? Who do you have besides a group of criminals who would mourn you for five sad minutes, then fight to take over your empire? Meri? You're like a lone wolf circling her, but for some reason, you won't commit."

A choked laugh escapes. "Harsh. True, but harsh." He slides a glance at me. "Who would miss you?"

The loneliness of my existence has hit hard over the last couple of days. Maybe because I didn't know what it was to truly be with someone until Lucifer. "Touché."

Instead of the glossy black marble halls of the palace, we

land in a field full of grass, dirt, and a few strange looking animals that resemble cows. I turn in a circle. There is nothing around for miles and miles except a ginormous arena. Similar to the domed arenas used by humans for their sports, it stands tall, at least six or seven stories high, and several hundred feet across.

Cormal grabs my arm. "Are you sure you want me to take you inside?"

Intrigued, I nod. "Yes."

A half smile appears. "This should be interesting."

When we arrive inside, I see Lucifer high above in the center of the ceiling, shouting orders to the males flying at dizzying speeds below. "Faster. He's gaining on you. Place the stone. On the marker. Now!"

The males drop something on the ground, then shoot up in the sky, barely avoiding the beast behind them.

"Done!" Lucifer shouts, clicking something in his hand. "One minute, twenty-two seconds. It's closer. Pick them up and we'll run it again."

Daire flies down to pick up the stone but stops when he sees me.

"What's the hold up?" Lucifer shouts from above.

Daire's icy blue eyes are lighter than his father's. The last time I saw them, they were filled with loathing. He inclines his head and moves across the arena to where the dragon is hovering in the sky.

Daire, the dragon who I assume is Valerian, a phoenix, a griffin, and a wyvern hover uncertainly in the air. Lucifer immediately swoops down and lands in front of Cormal and me. He strides forward, his eyes locked on Cormal, and I step in front of him.

"I ... I thought you were avoiding me. I ordered Cormal to bring me to you so I could give you a piece of mind, and I find you training flyers for the bombs. Damn it." The rest of the words are lost to the knot in my throat. I'm so used to working alone or with my mother, it didn't occur to me he would take charge of this part of the plan. I was so mad and had all these great lines prepared in my head. A laugh escapes.

"Cormal, leave. Everybody else, take a break," Lucifer orders, and every one of them disappears. He yanks me into his arms. "I'm sorry, love. When I left, I was so angry, and I didn't want you to see me that way. It took me a while to calm down. When I did, I was so consumed by the thought of you doing this on your own, or finding a worse alternative, that I knew I had to try to find a solution."

I reach around and grip him tightly, fisting his shirt in my hands. "It's the sweetest gift. Thank you." Leaning forward, I nibble on his lips. "You're going to have to release Gabriel soon, and I'd rather do this while he's out of the picture. I've been worried we wouldn't be able to prepare for everything, but this saved us."

He threads his fingers through my hair and pulls my head to his. "I'm a ruler, you know. Used to being in charge." Laughing out loud, he combs my hair using his fingers. "We're good together. What do you think of splitting your time between Viridian and here? As long as you stay away from his domain, you should be safe. It also allows you to go back and replenish your powers or check in with your people."

I bite my lip, considering it. The thought of leaving him in a few days is already tearing at me. Time passes differently in the two worlds, but that might be an advantage. "Yes. I want to figure a way to be with you, even if I need to spend time in two places, like your Hades and Persephone."

His lips settle on mine, and I cling to them, letting them soothe the sting in my heart from his absence.

With a heartfelt sigh, he pulls away and jerks his head

toward the arena. "I think we have a plan that will work. Want to see?"

When I nod, he puckers his lips and whistles loudly. The five creatures from earlier fly out into the arena.

"If we can figure out a way to get all the flyers in simultaneously, we can place the canisters at the exact same time in a little over a minute. I'd like to keep trying until we can get it under a minute, though. The beasts are fast, and they're predators. The more time we give them to think, the worse it is for us," he explains, tossing the stopwatch to the large griffin. "We need five of us to hit the targets. All six are training, though, in case we need a back-up."

He motions to a seat. "Stay up here." When I sit down, he flies to the center of the ceiling where the rest of them are hovering. Lucifer, Daire, the dragon, wyvern, and phoenix fly out and hover over a spot on the ground, waiting for the signal.

When a sharp whistle pierces the air, all five take off, flying impossibly fast. Surprisingly, the beast below is maintaining the same incredible speed. They all move faster and faster until the griffin yells "now!"

"Wait, stop!" I yell, but they don't hear me.

They dive for the markers on the ground and drop the stone. The beast comes out of the shadows at one of the markers and clamps his jaw around the leg of the phoenix. He cries out.

Lucifer lands next to the beast and waves his hands to distract him, but the beast refuses to let go of his prey.

"Fuck. He isn't going to release you. Do it!" he orders.

The phoenix places his hands on the beast's head and incinerates him. Lying on his back, I watch in awe as he regenerates his leg right in front of me.

Lucifer is cussing up a storm.

"What is it?"

"The beasts have lethal instincts. They're confused when they first see us run the scenario, but they are always ready the second round. We tried to use teleportation instead of flying, but not all of us have the ability and by the time we shimmered to the second spot, they were spreading out to cover the entire edge of the perimeter," he states wearily. "Thankfully, they caught the phoenix who can regenerate. We'll have one shot at this. We'll pick it up again tomorrow."

The phoenix transforms into a startling good-looking young man, with dark red and black hair, and beautiful tan skin that has been inked with numerous tattoos. I can't see his eyes because he keeps them turned away, but deep lines of sadness mark his face. The griffin turns out to be a tall woman with long blond hair, deep brown eyes, and golden-brown skin. She smiles at me. They both quickly disappear.

Shockingly, Ishkova is the wyvern. He laughs at the expression on my face, then bows respectfully, before he too leaves.

Daire folds his black wings into his body. I find it interesting that they're black instead of white, but given his father's genes, it's not surprising.

The gigantic dragon transforms into Valerian. He walks forward and leans down. "I admire you for taking charge of the situation, and I apologize for the way we all behaved at The Abbey." He steps back and looks at Daire.

Daire studies me carefully, then looks at his father. "I also apologize for what I said at The Abbey. I was upset about more than the beast, and I made you the target of my anger. I'm sorry. Truly. Hopefully, this makes up for it. Not just to you, but for the supernaturals who were under my protection."

They both leave via a portal in the far corner.

"Zephyra, the griffin, volunteered for the spot and beat almost all of the other contenders. She doesn't speak to anyone. One of the beasts wiped out her family long ago, and she took a vow of silence because of it. I'm hoping their deaths will allow her to move on," Lucifer explains, stroking my hair from my face. "Your hair is so beautiful. I'd love to see it fanned out across my bed."

He picks me up, and I automatically wrap my legs around him.

"And the phoenix?" I ask, sliding my arms around his neck.

"Cormal brought him here. Said he needed a purpose. His name is Rivan," he murmurs in my ear. "I've missed you in my bed. Come home with me?"

My heart soars. "Always."

THIRTY-FOUR

LUCIFER

After three days away, my need for her is almost feral. I slam her against the wall and thrust into her slick heat. Her body opens like it was designed for me. Swiveling my hips, I revel in the feel of her wrapped around me. I pull her down until I'm as deep as I can go, and she's grinding on me.

Cheeks flushed, she grips my hair and digs her heels into my back. "Horns. Show me your horns again."

I growl. "I'm barely holding on to the edge of sanity. The horns will send me over the edge."

She licks the side of my neck. "I won't break, remember?" Her body flexes tightly on mine. "They were so... sexy."

With every word out of her mouth, I can feel the demon rising in me and taking over. When the horns come out, she sighs and runs her hand over them.

If she keeps that up, I'm going to come hard. Pulling her off the wall, I place her on her hands and knees in front of me and slam back inside her. Setting a hard pace, I thrust into her body until I feel her release. With her body milking mine, I carefully pick her up and carry her over to the bed. Once her body loosens, I flip her over and start again.

My cock swells to its largest size, and she catches her breath, trying to move and adjust to it. I bend over and trap her beneath me. Her body is mine to command. Shallow and deep, I start and stop, coaxing her orgasm to the edge, then toppling her over. When she catches her breath, I start again. Joined together so tightly. I can't feel where she ends and I begin.

Sweet words fall from her lips, begging me to come. Unable to resist her request, I finally release the torturous hold on my body and fall over the edge with her. Breathing hard, I lie on top, my body skimming hers with delicious friction.

When my body returns to its normal form, I slide out and lie beside her.

Her green eyes glitter with satisfaction. "Maybe we should fight more often."

I skim the back of my finger across her cheekbone and down her jaw while I try to think of the words to put things in perspective. "We'll see. I don't like seeing you in the state you were earlier," I confess to her. "I'm sorry. I'm not used to telling anyone what I'm doing. When I was married, my wife couldn't visit the Underworld, so I rarely shared this world with her. Our whole life revolved around Daire and Danica, and the moments we lived for in our little bubble by the lake."

Her hand comes up and caresses my face.

"Sharing all this... with you... has been incredible. I've felt like I had a partner by my side, someone to help me solve this kingdom's problems, even the ones I didn't know I had," I say with a chuckle, thinking of the new protocols we'll have to set up for court and the tasks I need to find for the council. "Have patience with me. This is new to me, too."

When she bites her lip, I use my thumb to make her stop.

"I've never been in a relationship," she reveals slowly. "I don't know what's right or wrong, but I didn't like you shutting me out. It's not very fair of me, though. I'm sorry, too. I've hidden things from you all along. I'm still hiding something."

I raise an eyebrow. "What is it?"

"My mother disappeared during her time on Earth, and I haven't been able to find any trace of her. I've looked everywhere, including other worlds to see if she might have moved on, but there's nothing. She must be here. The seer showed me a dark-haired angel. It's not Gabriel, but maybe one of his minions."

I sit up and look down at her. "Unfortunately, there are a lot of angels that fit that description. Most of us have the same blue eyes. About half of us are blond, the other half are dark-haired like Gabriel. There are a few redheads." I smile, wrapping a piece of her dark red hair around my finger. "None with beautiful hair like yours." I spread it out over my sheets.

"I won't give up looking for her." She stubbornly insists.

"I'm not asking you to give up, but if you stay up there, he'll eliminate you. I'll help you search for her. We'll enlist Cormal's help, too. His network is impressive, if a bit shady. We'll find her," I promise, pulling her into my arms for a hug.

She pushes me onto my back and slides up against my side. "I tested your blood. It was very interesting. Just as I thought, your blood is mix of gods and various advanced races. With a couple of exceptions. You have Viridian in your blood. My guess is it gives you the power to kill the angels." She lifts her head to look up at me. "It isn't the gold knife, or the spell engraved on it, that kills the angels. It carries my blood, which has the power to kill many species. The spell on the knife helps me do it in one hit. As I said, I'm not the best fighter. My mother made sure I didn't have to be."

Stunned, I think about the angels who also have that power. "Michael and Mercy can both kill angels. They must also carry your blood."

"Maybe. There are a few races out there with the power to kill gods, so it could have been one of those species instead of a Viridian," I caution him. "The only DNA I couldn't identify was the one you added while you've been here."

"My demon," I state softly. "It was the only way to get the people to accept my rule and stop the fighting."

"It's also the reason Daire's wings are black, and his birth created a new race," she murmurs quietly. "Does he know?"

"Yes, I told him when he was a young boy," I reply with a reminiscent smile. "He could never tell Danica or his mother. But after the incident, Danica could feel it in him. It drove her mad, and he's been carrying that guilt around forever."

"What happened to her?" she asks, her hand stroking my chest.

The image of my beautiful blond-haired, brown-eyed daughter flashes in my mind. "She was full of life and laughter, always playing jokes on the three of us. But because of me, she grew up sheltered from the rest of the world. I didn't want anyone to use her as a bargaining chip. We knew we had to tell her who I was, but I kept putting it off. Then, it was too late."

"She was kidnapped by a demon gang when she was nineteen. The leader didn't know she was my daughter. He simply saw her in the village with her mother and took her. If she had known what to tell him, he would have left her alone." I clench my fist, thinking about that day.

Evren pries open my hand and laces her fingers through mine, then grips it tightly.

"The things they did... broke her. Her mind never recovered. When she was twenty, she walked into the lake by our cottage and drowned." My voice is hoarse with pain, even now, hundreds of years later. "They took the light in our lives. All three of us were shells of our former selves. Existing, but not living. It's only recently that Daire has begun to open up again. All because of Arden."

She's silent for a moment. "Thank you for telling me about her. I know it wasn't easy." Her green eyes stare up at me, and I can see the thoughts swirling around in them. "Maybe you and Daire should sit this one out. We can find two other flyers. Look how much you two accomplished over the course of three days. There is time to train a couple of new flyers."

I sit up, dislodging her from my chest and rolling over to trap her under me. "If you think you're doing this without me, you've lost your magnificent mind. Do you hear me? If I asked you to wait on the sidelines while we destroyed them, would you?" My breath catches while I wait for her reply.

She immediately shakes her head. "No, but I don't have a son or a kingdom. Who would miss me if I were gone? Although—"

I plant my lips on hers to stop the words flowing from her mouth. After a second, I lift my head and whisper, "I would miss you, damn it."

THIRTY-FIVE

<u>EVREN</u>

When General Ishkova knocks on the door early the next morning, Lucifer speaks to him quietly for a few seconds, then swears loudly. A wry smile appears on his lips. "Ishkova reminded me that tonight's the Celebrationem Peccari, or the celebration of sin. It's the annual anniversary of the night the seven princes of hell founded the Houses of Sin. The princes needed a way to build their power base, so they created a house that most reflected one of their seven sins—sloth, pride, envy, anger, greed, gluttony, and lust."

He runs a hand through his hair. "I've got a million things to do for tonight. We need a new beast for the portal. Ishkova is going to lead that effort. Once it's in the arena, they'll run a few practice drills. Do you want to come with me or watch the practice?"

"Do you think Ishkova can capture three beasts?" I ask him, my mind flipping to the problem with our current plan.

He grins. "It's doable, although we might have a pissed off general on our hands later."

"Good. I might have an idea on how to distract the beasts so the flyers can enter, but I need to build and test it out," I inform him. "Should I meet you here later?"

"If you're ready, I'll take you now, then ask Cormal to escort you from the lab to the arena," he offers, holding out his arms.

Waving a quick hand over my body, I clean and dress in seconds, then walk up and loop my arms around him. "Let's go."

Once in the lab, I start stripping down a few of the machines to find the parts to make a launcher big enough to hold three of the small canisters. It takes a couple of hours to get the mechanism right and strong enough to hold the three. When it's done, I lay the short round barrel weapon on the counter and reach for one of the mini canisters.

Removing the power I added yesterday, I absorb it into my body. Then I do the same with the other two. I pull open a drawer and grab the supplies I need. Sitting down on a nearby stool, I prop my elbow on the counter and slide the needle into my vein. The plastic bag begins to fill with my blood.

Once the bag is full, I carefully fill each canister with a third of the bag. After each one has the desired amount, I burn the bag to prevent my blood from being used by anyone else.

With the open end of the barrel pointing up, I carefully load each canister into it and flip the lever to hold them inside. With several towels in hand, I pack it in a crate to take it with us.

"Did you build a gun?" Cormal murmurs quietly beside me.

My eyes dart to him. "It's a good thing your power always precedes you, or I'd probably accidentally stab you with my knife. I built a launcher for the small canisters."

"A gun," he confirms with a wide smile.

I glare at him. "Guns are weapons. This will only launch objects. It cannot be used to kill anyone." My irritated tone finally gets through to him. "Are we going?"

He holds up his hands. "Do you want to carry the launcher or should I?"

I ease the crate on its side and grasp the handle. "I'll do it."

He takes my elbow, and we shimmer directly into the arena.

When Ishkova sees me, he glowers at me.

I wave him and the others over to the bleachers. Ishkova practically stomps toward me, but the others approach a little more cautiously. When they get close, I lay the crate on the ground and open it.

Valerian darts a glance at Daire. Rivan says nothing, but a smile hovers at the edge of his pouty lips. Zephyra looks confused. Ishkova's jaw slackens.

I pick it up and point the barrel over their heads to the top of the arena. "With this launcher, we can open the portal and shoot the canisters into the center of the ceiling where they will explode and rain blood down on the beasts in the middle. According to Cormal, they love my blood. Let's see what happens when it covers their own brethren."

I eye the general, who's still looking stiff. "Thank you for getting the extra beasts. I know it wasn't easy, but if this works, we will have what we need to safely get the flyers inside the portal."

His eyes dart to his fellow flyers. "It's worth a shot." He moves to the center of the arena and transforms into his wyvern. Flying to the left of the circle, he stops. "With only two beasts, we need to get them in the center."

I put the stock up to my shoulder and push my power into the chamber I designed for it. It loads smoothly, and I give the flyers a thumb's up.

"Release two of the beasts!" Ishkova yells.

Daire and Valerian flip the latches holding the beasts in two of the iron cages.

Charging through the gate, they look around and sniff. Ishkova whistles at them, and they immediately shuffle to the center.

They circle Ishkova from below, stalking his every move.

He raises an arm and brings it down.

I launch one canister toward the ceiling where it detonates. Blood rains down on the two beasts below, and we collectively hold our breath.

They stop eyeing Ishkova like he's their next meal and swiftly turn on each other. Their ravenous teeth tear into fur and limbs. Each one fighting to get to the blood that's driving them mad. One of the beasts falls to the ground, unable to get up, and the other beasts sinks their teeth into its belly. It stops and backs up, spitting out the chunks it just ate.

It circles the beast on the ground, smelling the fur, then the belly. A deep howl erupts from its throat, and it snarls at Ishkova.

It knows the beast is its sibling and refuses to eat it.

"Twenty to thirty seconds," Ishkova calls from the ceiling. "Unfortunately, once we shoot the canisters, we'll have to close the portals. We'll be blind. If the distraction doesn't work and we open the five portals simultaneously, we could have a massive problem on our hands."

Disappointed, I lay the launcher in the crate.

A whistle blows. "This will be a tight run. It's already

pissed off and ready to pounce, but we'll be facing a lot more than one on the day. Everyone ready?"

The five flyers get into position, but the beast never takes his eyes off Ishkova. Tense, I grip the bars in front of my seat.

"Begin!" Ishkova orders.

The five fly in tight formation, faster and faster, but the beast only tracks Ishkova. I pull out my gold knife and hold it by the blade, ready to throw it the instant it goes after Ishkova.

"Now!" Ishkova yells.

All five flyers dive and place their canisters. The beast leaps straight toward Ishkova. I raise my arm and toss it as hard as I can.

A blue tail whips in front of the beasts and impales it on an impossibly long stinger.

"Ishkova, move!" I scream.

With a hard push of his wings, he whirls around, withdrawing his tail from the beast, and the gold knife embeds itself in the exact same spot.

Relief drives me to my knees.

"What the hell?" Ishkova roars, furiously rushing over to me. "I'm a general in Lucifer's army. Do you think I didn't see the beast tracking me? It was my battle, and you almost took it from me." He pulls my knife from his belt and moves his finger to the blade.

"Don't. It will kill you," I reveal. "It's why I screamed at you to move." When he holds the knife out, I take it from him. "And you're right. I should have never interfered. You're a season warrior, and a high-ranking demon. I apologize."

He eyes the gold knife in my hand. "Don't interfere again, or I'll have you removed from the arena. Understood?"

Humbly nodding my head, I give him the only answer he wants. "Understood."

Cormal chuckles softly behind me. "Killing Lucifer's

second-in-command would have earned you a hell of a lot of enemies. Ishkova is well-respected."

Rolling my eyes, I turn to him and mockingly wave my knife in his direction. "Don't tempt me." I slide into my seat.

He takes a step back. "Don't worry, I've seen what that knife can do." With an elegant twist, he unbuttons his suit jacket and sits down beside me. "Do all the women in your family get a knife, or is this something special between you and your mother?"

Pulling my brows together, I look at him in confusion. "My mother designed them and had one made for each of us. Why?"

He gives a lazy shrug. "Just curious. It's the only weapon you both carry."

I blink at his statement. It is the only weapon we both carry. Cormal recognized it as the same. And so did... Gabriel when we were in the cave.

<u>EVREN</u>

Numb to the world around me, I can't help but wonder what lengths Gabriel took to get rid of my mother. Unlike me, she had no human form and no way to shield herself outside of the cave. She could spell a structure to provide her cover and hide her god status, but on the move, she would be nothing but a target. He knows more than he's saying.

Eager to tell Lucifer, I rush back, but his office is empty. I return to the bedroom hoping to find him there, but the only thing I see is a large package on the bed with a red bow on top. I stroll over and finger the card on the outside.

Evren,

It would be my honor if you accompanied me to the ball tonight. This dress is guaranteed to bring me to my knees.

Lucifer

Laughing, I lift the lid off the box. Nestled in the delicate tissue paper lies a red dress so dark it almost looks black. Grasping the bodice by the edges, I pull it up and hold it out in front of me. It's magnificent and fierce. On one side, a sharp point tapers from the bodice into a single strap over one shoulder. The other shoulder is bare. Cut-outs, lined with diamonds, appear in strategic areas along the waist. The dress cascades down to the floor with a split on one side.

It takes seconds to put on the dress. The mirror beckons, and I move to stand in front of it. The hair cascading down my back in waves is the only brightness against the luxurious fabric. The dress is dark and moody and simply spectacular, and it fits my body like a dream.

Who is this goddess looking at me? I don't even recognize myself. But it's not the dress. It's me. For the first time, I feel like a goddess. Powerful and confident. The faint hollow look of loneliness is gone. Instead, my eyes sparkle with life and happiness.

I stride back to the box and find a pair of diamond heels glittering inside, so I slip them on my feet. As I finish, there is a knock at the door.

With a large smile, I open the door, expecting to find Lucifer, but instead a stranger stands there. With rich, chestnut brown hair and light green eyes, he's immaculate in his perfectly pressed suit. Surprisingly, he's not a demon, but Fae, I think. He certainly looks Fae, but his magic feels different in some way. Uneasy, I drop my hand to find the knife strapped to my thigh.

Green eyes flick to my hand, then crinkle with approval. "Right idea. Although, I would practice to make it more subtle." He runs his hands casually down his hips, as if smoothing the material, then whips his hand up. "See."

I raise the knife in my hand and point it toward him. "Good tip. Now, who are you?"

He chuckles. "Vargas, Lucifer's commander. I'm here to escort you to the ball."

I study the man in front of me. He's not even remotely close to what I expected him to look like. "Proof please."

"You haven't seen me because I haven't had a body, but I watched over you, even led Lucifer to find you after Gabriel plunged a needle into your neck. And you're right to ask for proof. I used to look different," he admits with a heavy sigh. His body and face transform into a tall, ferocious looking man with dark hair, a dark complexion, and massive muscles. "This used to be me. I was much more terrifying and fit the role of Lucifer's commander, don't you agree?"

I slide the knife into the holster on my thigh. "Yes, this fits your role better, but your new face is incredibly handsome." With a pat on his hand, I try to reassure him. "And personally, I'm a huge fan of green eyes." I wink at him to show him mine.

"You think so?"

"I do. Change back for a second," I order him. When he does, I study the physique of the Fae and compare it to his old one. "Ok."

"Well?" he asks, desperate to know what I think.

I tap a finger on my chin while I try to figure out how to explain the similarities and differences. "Your old body is fierce with an almost raw masculinity that hints at the brutality underneath. The new one is dominant with a subtle, lethal edge. Warriors, both. Although there is a curious blend of magic with your new body. Demon and Fae, but unique. What is it?"

He leans closer to murmur. "Chameleon. He was part Vindicta Demon, part Dark Fae. It's an extremely rare trait to inherit. I'm not sure why the combination of Fae and Demon sometimes results in a Chameleon. Maybe you can study it for me and let me know."

My lips twitch because he's not wrong. I find myself intrigued by this rare genetic variation. "Maybe. We should go. I'm sure the ball has started by now."

He changes into his old body. "It's better if I remain in this form while I'm here in the Underworld. I've spent too much time cultivating the right amount of respect and terror." With a twist of his arm, he holds his elbow out for me to take.

"Thank you for the escort," I tell him, taking his arm. "Is there a reason you're escorting me instead of Lucifer?" Disappointment flares.

A sheepish expression crosses his face. "My fault. I sent Lucifer a note to let him know you would meet him at the ball. I've been watching you for a couple weeks, and I wanted a chance to speak with you. Alone."

He pauses for a second. "Bringing you here, into his world, and sharing his plans... it is a huge leap of faith from him. It also puts a spotlight on you. Everyone now knows you are different. Don't be afraid to be a goddess here. They'll respect you more for it. Demons like to show off. Humility isn't a trait we admire."

His feet slow. "If you want all this, including him, don't hesitate to claim it. He's never had anyone fight for him. If they did, he'd be theirs forever."

I stare up into his dark eyes. "Forever is a long time."

"I hope so," he returns with a wistful smile. "I'm counting on it for myself."

THIRTY-SEVEN

LUCIFER

The upper class of the Underworld is decked out in its finest tonight. Dresses of silks and satins, iridescent scales, demon skins in a variety of color, glitter, and paint everywhere. Old jewels laden with enormous stones are draped over every inch of their bodies, some barely covering the necessary parts. Lords and ladies with color coordinated ensembles compete against each other with a ferocity usually reserved for battles.

The ballroom is lit with millions of red and black candles to lend ambiance to the event and showcase the vignette designed by each House of Sin. Lust is a lush red boudoir, complete with a bevy of beauties from Cormal's brothels. Envy is dark green and filled with the rarest luxuries of life like Unicorn tears. Fluffy beds with downy white comforters and soft pillows fill the sloth area where patrons can lie down and be waited on hand and foot. Wrath is a boxing ring only the most fit dare to enter. Gluttony is the finest of restaurants where everything is on the menu. Greed is a gambling hall only open to the wealthiest patrons. Last, but certainly first, is Pride, where showcase is the name of the game. Lords and ladies use their most powerful talents to compete with each other until one is crowned the best.

Where is she?

Speculative side glances at the chair beside me tells me where my guests' interest lies, as if there were any doubt. I'd hoped to arrive with her on my arm, but her note begged me to go without her. Unable to sit still any longer, I stand.

A familiar red catches my eye, and I swing all my attention to the center of the dance floor. The music starts, and the crowd immediately moves away from the couple, a tinge of fear on their faces. Evren's companion twirls her into a polished waltz, and she laughs. Astonished, I narrow my eyes, wondering who I'm going to have to kill tonight. Everybody knows she's mine.

I step off the dais and walk intently toward them. The crowd scrambles to get out of my way. But when I get to the edge, a big green brute of demon refuses to move. His eyes are locked on the couple in the center, and when I try to push past, he raises his arm. A guttural growl comes from deep inside me.

Brows lowered, he turns and shoves me. The crowd collectively inhales, riveted to the scene happening right in front of them. The demon's small beady eyes widen in his large face when he sees me, and he drops to his knees.

"Your benevolent Majesty."

Intent on getting to Evren, I rein in the urge to flatten him. "You want to fight?" I ask him, flashing my pissed off smile. "I'm sure the Duke of Furor would love to see you in the Ring of Wrath."

His eyes dart nervously to the ring where the Duke lounges against the ropes. "I'm not much of boxer, Your Majesty."

"You are tonight. Go," I order him. When he's gone, I look around at the crowd gathered and raise an eyebrow. They quickly find other things to interest them.

With a clear view of Evren, I inhale sharply at the sight of her. The magnificent blood red dress she's wearing enhances every curve of her bewitching body.

Tearing my eyes from her to focus on her asshole dancing partner, I meet the laughing dark eyes of my most loyal commander and friend. "Vargas?"

He bows. "Sort of. Myself and... more."

On our private channel, he tells me he found a Chameleon and shows me the true Fae version of himself. "So you won't kill me if I forget to change into this one."

I pull him into a tight hug and slap his back hard. "Have you been to see Arden?"

He nods. "I went first thing this morning, but we decided not to tell Solandis. I'll explain more later." His eyes dart to the crowd listening nearby. "Would you like to cut in?" He slides Evren's hand from his arm to mine. "I've made my point."

Acceptance and protection. The same thing I did for Arden when she came to the Underworld. I incline my head in gratitude.

He stalks off toward the Ring of Wrath, an irritated look on his face.

"Is he okay?" Evren asks softly.

Staring into her green eyes, I find myself. "He's going to make sure the demon I sent over there receives a good beating or two." My fingers caress her bare neck, and seconds later, a ruby and gold necklace graces her throat. "A goddess with or without it, but it goes perfectly with your dress."

She reaches up and places a hand on the elaborate necklace. "Between the dress and necklace, I'm feeling lavishly spoiled. Thank you." Her lips meet mine, and the entire ballroom goes silent.

When she's done kissing me, she leans into me and whispers, "Faux pas?"

"Staking a claim on me in the middle of my ballroom?" I tease her, wrapping my arms around and pulling her close. "Completely acceptable. Dance with me."

She locks her eyes with mine, and the world narrows to the two of us. Head held high, her body moves sensuously to the music. The goddess in her is on full display.

"Magnificent," I murmur, enthralled by this side of her. I get the feeling she rarely allows herself to be a goddess, preferring to hide behind the science.

When the dance ends, her chest is heaving, and I glance down at the creamy globes propped up by her dress. Temptation.

She laughs up at me. "What are you thinking?"

"That there are too many fucking people in my house tonight," I growl, reining in the urge to throw them all out. "I need to make an appearance at each of the showcases to give them a token. Care to join me?"

She takes the elbow I offer. "So, who decided there would be seven sins?"

"There used to be seven Princes of Hell. Each had a sin they preferred. Whenever someone committed the sin, their power increased. To ensure a continuous supply of followers and power, they created the Houses of Sin," I explain. "Even though they were killed in the battle against the angels, the houses live on in perpetuity."

We enter Lust's boudoir, and I hand the Duke of Lust a gold token. His mouth turns down in disappointment, but he bows and thanks me for the visit.

After we leave, Evren leans in and whispers, "Why was he upset?"

"It's a contest. First prize gets a trophy and bragging rights for a year. All other houses receive a gold token for their participation," I murmur in her ear. Unable to help myself, I place a kiss on her neck.

She shivers. "Ooh, I can't wait to see which one you pick and why."

I chuckle. "Only you would want to know why."

We make our way to Wrath's boxing ring. Vargas stands shirtless, sweat dripping off him, above the green demon who shoved me earlier. I dip my chin to acknowledge the win even though I had no doubt who would come out on top. When the Duke of Wrath comes over, I hand him a gold token.

The demon immediately gets angry, but Vargas claps him on the shoulder to remind him to be respectful. He chokes down his rage and inclines his head toward me.

"Thank you, Your Majesty."

Without replying, I turn and escort Evren to the House of Sloth's showcase. We walk over to where the duke is lounging on one of the beds. He holds out a lazy hand for the token, which I hand to him.

"Thank you, Sire," he says. With a huge stretch, he returns his attention to the male feeding him grapes.

Evren's eyes dart between the two of us.

"Sloth never tries to win the trophy. It's too much work," I explain.

Her brow furrows, but she says nothing.

"Not everyone enjoys working as much as you do," I remind her with a smile.

Greed and gluttony each receive a gold token. The prize is down to Envy and Pride.

Ultimately, Envy wins the trophy this year. They usually

use showcase beauty, but I liked the extra effort they brought this year with the rare items. Instead of shouting and screaming about their win, they enlarge the trophy until the entire ballroom can see it.

The Duchess of Pride sniffs when I hand her the token instead of the trophy. "Thank you, Sire." She turns to Evren with a calculated gleam in her eyes. "Care to demonstrate your power? The trophy we award rivals no other."

I chuckle. Pride couldn't let a loss go without a dig.

Evren strokes my arm. "It wouldn't be fair of me to compete but thank you for inviting me."

The duchess smirks. "Of course. It would be bad for Lucifer's... guest... to be defeated so easily."

Evren squints at the duchess for a second as if she's examining her under a microscope and purses her lips in thought. She extends her arm until her hand is in front of the duchess's face, then snaps her fingers.

The entire showcase with everyone in it disappears.

Delighted with her show of power, I roar with laughter.

The crowd begins to gather around us.

She wraps her arms around my neck and gives me a long, deep kiss. "You should laugh more often." Her eyes dart to the people around us. "Or maybe not. Everyone looks terrified right now."

Demons love nothing more than power. "They're terrified of you, my divine goddess." My lips find the sweet spot between her neck and shoulder. "I've done my duty and given out all the prizes. I'm ready to leave and spend the next few hours holding you. Tomorrow will be here too soon."

"I'm ready," she assures me. She snaps her fingers, and the entire showcase reappears, along with the duchess and the rest of her people. "You should be grateful I'm not a vengeful god."

The duchess bows deeply, then shouts. "The winner is...

Lucifer's goddess!" Her red eyes are twinkling when she turns to Evren. "I'll have the trophy delivered to his office tomorrow. Thank you for participating in our showcase. It was a prize I wasn't expecting."

Evren raises an eyebrow but says nothing.

"Unexpected, but well played, love," I murmur as we walk away.

"Advice from Vargas," she reveals with a sparkle in her eye.

When we reach the edge of the ballroom, I shimmer us to the balcony outside my bedroom. Shielded from the world, I point to the dark sky. Less than a minute later, fireworks shoot into the air, filling the darkness with colorful displays of light, but all I see is her.

I wrap my arms tightly around her. Tomorrow is only hours away. For the rest of the evening, I hold her close.

THIRTY-EIGHT

EVREN

My gloved fist grips the torque hard. Six silver canisters are lined up like soldiers near the entrance to the portal. We simplified the plan. Open, push the beasts back, flyers enter and place the bombs simultaneously, then fly out. One minute and fifteen seconds. That's all we need to end this threat once and for all.

The five going in will be Daire, Valerian, Lucifer, Rivan, and Zephyra. Ishkova stands calmly beside me, but the tick in his jaw tells me he's not happy to be the one staying behind. After Lucifer and Valerian, he's the third fastest. It was the only plan that made sense, which is why, after a lot of cursing, he suggested it.

I close my eyes and take several deep breaths. When I open them, I can't help but search his for added strength.

Lucifer leans down and places a hard kiss on my lips. "Stay safe."

Because I'm looking up, I spot them before anyone else. "Incoming. The sky is full."

Lucifer whirls around and stares at the sky for a brief second. "Legion!" he roars.

Valerian and Daire enter into two different portals.

Ishkova grabs Rivan and Zephyra and shimmers out.

"Steady," he tells me.

I move to his side. We'll face them together.

The corners of his mouth curl up, but he never takes his eyes off the angels landing on the Earth in front of us. "Five thousand. I haven't seen this many angels here since the war with Satan. I'm impressed."

I'm not. I bite the inside of my cheek to help steady my nerves.

A portal opens to our left and Theron steps out wearing formfitting dark armor and leading at least a thousand Dark Fae soldiers behind him.

Theron dips his chin toward me and Lucifer. On his other side, four more portals open simultaneously. Valerian leads a flight of dragons onto the field. Astor and Arden step out surrounded by a small group of witches. Daire and several hundred vampires arrive next. And in the final portal, Fallon and a large brute of a man lead another thousand or so stoic warriors, who move as if they're a single killing machine.

The angels slide their gazes to our allies and raise eyebrows in challenge.

Lucifer raises his arm and the cloak of glamour behind us falls. Ten thousand ruthless demons and creatures of the Underworld army, including Vargas, Ishkova, and Moge, stand ready to move on Lucifer's command.

"Now, that's impressive," I murmur to him.

Lucifer crosses his arms and waits for the angels to make the next move. "I like to be prepared."

Five almost identical-looking angels step forward. All tall, fierce warriors, but there isn't much to distinguish one from the other. "We fight in Gabriel's honor. But first, we command you to give us his body so that he may be laid to rest as befits his status."

Lucifer tilts his head. "Who said Gabriel was dead?"

The angel from the town square pushes through the front line, his chest puffed up with pride. "I told them. You can't deny it. The ground opened and swallowed him whole."

Lucifer chuckles. "I merely forced him to take a vacation. He's alive. Maybe a little worse for wear mentally, but alive." He motions to the canisters. "As you can see, we're in the middle of something. Once we're done, I'll send him to you."

The five look at each other, then up to the sky. It begins to fill with more angels. Some continue to fly above us, while others join the ranks on the ground. It's double their original count, making us almost evenly matched.

"How many more can they call?"

"Enough to cover the Earth," Lucifer murmurs.

Frustrated, I heave a sigh. "Give them Gabriel. It's not worth the lives of you, your men, or allies. We'll figure out a way to do this another time." He looks at me in disbelief. "As you've said, the beasts aren't going anywhere."

He searches my eyes and finally dips his chin in agreement. Before leaving, he signals to Ishkova to remove the canisters. We don't want that much power in anyone's hands.

"I'll return shortly with Gabriel," he informs the angels, then shimmers out. Seconds later, he appears as promised with an almost unrecognizable Gabriel.

If anything, he's worse. Unkempt and hunched over, he's a

shadow of his former fastidious self, and the maniacal gleam in his eye has an edge of darkness now.

He stalks over to me, and I flip the knife into my palm. Upon seeing it, he laughs. "Just like your mother. Stab first, talk later. Look what good it did her. She's gone. Didn't even say goodbye. Now, here you are, trying to repeat her mistakes. Why couldn't you die?" he roars.

I step into him, face to face. "Tell me what you did to her."

He shakes his head, as if it's sad I don't know. "She went into the portal." He points to the entrance of the beasts. "Her plan was to annihilate them. She failed. Never came out."

Lucifer grabs my hand and squeezes.

I turn my head to look at the portal. She sacrificed herself. I exhale in relief and smile. I needed to know what happened to her, and now I do. And it's more than I hoped. When she returns, I'm going to give her a big hug and tell her how proud I am for trying to right the wrong.

Gabriel snarls. "Did you not hear me? She's dead."

With an apologetic glance at Lucifer, I shake my head. "She's eternal. Sometimes it takes a while for a god to return, but one day, I'll see her again."

Lucifer leans down and whispers, "And you?"

Before I can answer, a loud scream of outrage pierces the air. Gabriel. I turn to face him, but he shimmers out of sight.

"Fuck," Lucifer whispers. "He must have traded the monsters for that piece of knowledge. Do you see him anywhere?" His head swivels around to look for his nemesis.

He reappears in front of us with Ishkova locked in his arms. Jerking his head, he calls forth the five angels from earlier. "What is in those canisters?"

Lucifer hesitates.

Gabriel jerks his chin in an unspoken order, and the five angels from earlier grab Ishkova.

"They're bombs," I reveal, glancing at Ishkova. "We can get rid of the beasts. Forever." I hold my hand out to Gabriel. "Take me. Return Ishkova."

Lucifer grabs my hand and pushes me behind him. "You won't fucking touch her, or I'll end you forever, Gabriel, just like I did Satan."

Several of the angels look surprised at his statement.

Fury rises like a storm in Gabriel. "Kill him."

"Don't," Lucifer orders. "You kill him, and we go to war. I'm tired of dancing around this ego trip of yours. One day, you'll abuse your power and he'll take it from you forever. Then what will you be? An angel. That's it. Nothing more or less."

Vargas leads the demons closer.

The angels begin to spread out to encompass the entire battlefield.

"Do it," Gabriel orders, his eyes locked on Lucifer. "You don't rule this world. I do. The humans belong to the one I serve. You chose your side." He tosses his head toward the demons behind Lucifer.

"You're right," Lucifer states loudly and firmly. "I chose to take a stand and eliminate Satan. For years, I blamed you. But I caused my own downfall. I used my free will. I knew I could save the world, so I did. It's that simple. I had no desire for power. It was only when the waters rose, and the people were gone, that I chose to enter Underworld and take it for my own."

He holds his arms out wide. "I didn't choose the side of evil. I chose the shades of grey. All the races, including humans, who stand in the in-between. Neither good nor evil. All of them, like myself, flawed and imperfect. Full of free will. And truly brilliant creations. But I also inherited the deepest of sins, the blackest of evil, and all those void of humanity or a speck of grace."

He looks into the eyes of the angels behind Gabriel. "I accept and claim all of them as mine. And when the end comes again, I'll stand for them—against you and whatever army comes to end them. Tell me, Gabriel, is today the end?"

His voice dies.

Gabriel stands there, swaying in the hot sun.

The sky rumbles and darkens. Both Lucifer and I shoot a worried glance at the sky.

Gabriel laughs and walks over to Ishkova. He motions for the angels to release him, then slings an arm around his shoulders. "No hard feelings, right?"

Ishkova snarls at him and tries to jerk away. Gabriel grabs his arm and holds him, then plunges the small gold knife into Ishkova's heart, killing him instantly.

"No!" I scream, sending a stream of power to knock Gabriel away from Ishkova. The angels move toward me, and I strip the glove off my right hand to grasp the torque.

Gabriel laughs and eyes the dagger in his hand. "You would not believe what it cost me to get this knife. Luckily, one of the monsters was willing to bargain for it." He points it at Lucifer. "You're next."

With a roar of outrage, Lucifer charges forward and grabs Gabriel by the neck, swinging him to the ground. He holds him down and punches him repeatedly in the face. His fury is unending.

Gabriel is laughing maniacally. His arm goes up, and he slams the blade into Lucifer's chest.

Lucifer grunts. With a curled lip, he pulls it out and throws the knife on the ground near me. He raises his fist and brings it down.

Vargas' warrior yell, along with several others, echoes across the land.

Gabriel's gaze swings from the knife to Lucifer. "Why won't you die!?" He screams and shoves Lucifer off him.

I pick up the knife and add it to my belt loop. The five angels from earlier stalk toward Gabriel and Lucifer, who are now circling each other. With a wave of my hand, I hold them in place.

Angry, they order their army to advance against us.

The ground begins to tremble from the stampede of feet running toward each other. The air above fills with fire, ice, and shadows as the dragons release their magic. Angels fly in deadly formations, weaving in and out, brandishing swords, spears, and arrows. The war begins.

THIRTY-NINE

EVREN

My power reaches its threshold, and I turn toward the angels and their army. I take a deep breath to release it, and the world stops. It literally freezes. Everyone and everything is motionless. Even the fire in the sky has stopped moving toward its target.

The only ones who aren't frozen are Gabriel, Lucifer, and me.

Lucifer immediately moves to my side.

A rocket plunges to the ground from above, landing directly in front of us. The Earth trembles from the impact, and a large crack appears between us and the angels. When it stands up and expands its wings, I see it's an angel unlike any other.

Most angels are beautiful and perfect looking. Elegant. And

even though they're warriors, their fighting retains a civilized edge. A formal dance choreographed by their leader.

This beast of an angel stalks forward. Features that might have originally been perfect and symmetrical have been broken and realigned. A large scar runs across one eye and down his cheek. It's not alone. There are scars all over his body, as if he wasn't able to return to Heaven quickly enough for them to heal perfectly.

He's the epitome of war. He's also the dark-haired angel the seer showed me.

Cold and menacing, he studies the scene around us, his eyes taking in every detail from the canisters remaining by the portal entrance, to Ishkova, to the power crackling inside me.

"Can you maintain control of the power while I clean this up?" His voice is guttural, as if he lost his majestic voice long ago.

Gabriel begins to protest. "This isn't your domain, Michael. Don't you have a secret mission to run?"

"I've been sent to clean up your mess," he replies with a hard look at Gabriel. "The power isn't yours to use as you wish. You command his armies and send them against his enemies when he gives the order. Your duty is to protect mankind and promote the greater good, but all the things I've seen over the last few weeks tells me you can no longer carry out your duties. I'm stripping you of his powers and reassigning you. But first, we're going to fix things here."

Gabriel's face whitens.

Lucifer shifts nervously beside me.

Michael studies him. "The arrogant angel has turned into a halfway decent warrior and protector. It suits you."

Closing his eyes, Michael's hand weaves an intricate pattern in the air. Everything around us begins to rewind, including the magic I generated from the torque. Until he gets to Ishkova's death. He stops.

"I can't undo his death," he informs us, glaring at Gabriel.

Michael places a fist on his heart, and three more rockets land beside him.

These angels are cut from the same brutal mold as Michael, but their DNA differs dramatically from his. One angel has light green scales across his arms. His gold eyes are slits, and fangs protrude from his mouth. Another looks like a mythical shadow warrior with his black skin and equally dark eyes. Unlike all the other angels, he has no luxurious locks, only a sleek bald head, and his wings are black, not white. The last warrior looks similar to Michael until his eyes find yours and you feel yourself falling into nothingness. When he sees me sway, he looks away.

"Guard him." Michael flicks a hand toward Gabriel, and the three angels press their fists to chest, then move into place around him.

Michael releases the angels first. They stop in confusion when they see their enemy frozen. With a wave of his hand and a simple command, the angels file into formation and return home.

Once all the weapons and magic are removed from the sky, he releases each group.

Lucifer immediately holds up his hand, and the demons stop moving forward. "Vargas, return the army to the Underworld. Transport Rivan and Zephyra here."

He opens a massive portal and marches the army through it to the other side. Rivan, Zephyra, and the other three canisters appear when the portal shuts.

Each of the cadre releases their warriors and sends everyone back. Theron, Astor, and Arden also return, although her eyes can barely move from the two men she's leaving behind—Daire and Valerian.

Michael raises an eyebrow at Lucifer.

"We have a plan to rid the world of the beasts for good. Are you intending to stop us?" Lucifer asks, pointing to the canisters. He explains the canisters' purpose, the dual delivery method, and the purpose of the flyers.

Michael looks at the three angels with him, silently communicating, and lifts a shoulder. "We won't stop you. In fact, we'll help you, won't we, Gabriel?"

"I'm not helping them," Gabriel sneers at Michael.

The shadow angel takes Gabriel to the ground in three moves and holds him there.

"Wrong answer," Michael rasps, looking down at him.

Gabriel's face crumples. "I can't."

One of the angels swoops down and picks him up, but Gabriel starts yelling "No wings! No wings!"

A crease appears in Michael's forehead. "Turn him around." When they turn him around, Michael lifts up Gabriel's shirt, and we all see bloody stumps where his wings used to be. "Who did this?" Michael swings around to us.

Lucifer holds up his hands. "My guess is he traded them for the knife so he could kill me. Isn't that right, Gabriel?"

"Too bad the knife won't kill him," I reply with confidence. "It won't kill anyone with Viridian blood. My mother didn't want someone using the knife on me or her. Based on the genetic testing I did, Lucifer has Viridian blood."

Gabriel drops to his knees and screams until the angel with the scales knocks him in the head and jerks him to his feet. He hangs between two of the three.

Michael walks over to me.

Lucifer steps in front, but I step to his side.

"Well, that's unexpected, but not unwelcome," Michael

drawls, his eyes bouncing between the two of us. "I heard what you said the other day in the cave. You made the right choice. The Druids have to help themselves to survive. Your mother couldn't quite grasp that concept. She did try to kill the beasts, though, and I'm sorry, but she didn't make it."

I shake my head. "She's not gone. Viridians are eternal." My eyes slide to Lucifer, and a flame appears in his eyes.

Michael eyes Lucifer. "Makes sense now."

Daire also looks shocked for a second, but then a broad smile appears on his face. For the first time, he looks at me with something more than grudging respect.

"I'll make the run," Michael informs Lucifer. "You'll go as well. Pick the other three."

"Rivan's phoenix is faster than Zephyra's griffin, but she needs this more than him," Lucifer states firmly. "Daire, Valerian, Michael, Zephyra, and me. Everyone, grab a canister."

I use the glove to grab the torque and carry it over to the portal. All six of us line up in front of the entrance.

When Lucifer gives the nod, I drop the glove and grip the torque to build upon the power I pulled earlier. I let it roll through me, filling every inch and more. Locking my jaw, I give a short nod to Lucifer.

He opens the portal wide.

Beasts stampede toward the opening, but I push them back and hold them. Five flyers rush in.

Rivan steps to my side and counts out thirty seconds. "Now!"

The five flyers dive, placing the canisters at the edge of the beasts below. One of the beasts catches Zephyra in the leg with its jaws. Lucifer dives down and kills it. The jaws fall open, releasing her, but she's still on the ground. Daire lands nearby and uses his vampiric speed to get to her and lift her up into his arms. He takes off just as the rest of the horde reaches the area.

"Out," I whisper, barely able to say the word. My body shakes as I use every last drop of power to keep the beasts at bay.

Rivan eyes the trembling in my hands. "Out now!"

Michael's angels move toward the opening, swords drawn, to help any who might need it or to fight the beasts who slip from my hold.

The flyers escape one by one.

With one last push of power, I shove the beasts back, and they slam the portal shut.

Rivan catches me when I start to fall. "Feel my power flow through you. Replenish you." A reddish-orange glow travels from him to me, and my strength returns.

"Thank you," I tell him, reaching out a hand to pat his arm, but he quickly moves away.

Everything rocks around us and the portal in front of us bulges but holds.

The shadow warrior moves to open the portal.

"Stop," I order. "There's a second detonation."

This one is much quieter.

Lucifer strides over and opens the portal a sliver, then flings it wide to show the rest of us. Beasts lie on the ground for miles and miles. He lays hellfire down to burn them all. It dies a few minutes later. Nothing remains. It's completely empty of life.

Taking out my knife, I inscribe the portal with a spell to stop anyone from ever using it again.

I look at Michael. "What about me?" Even if I'm banned from here, I can still travel between Viridian and the Under-world. From a distance, I can help the Druids and humans.

He closes his eyes and listens. "You may stay or go, as long as you don't interfere in the evolution of humans. This is his most successful experiment. Every day we fight to keep other worlds from taking what is ours."

Michael turns to Lucifer. "Do you think he didn't know the path you would choose? The choice was yours. He secretly applauded you for it. By taking that path, you took on the role of protector, freeing him and us to fight the constant threats from other species who want to destroy this world. With you here, humans have a chance."

Lucifer steps up to Michael and bares his teeth. "Remember that when the end comes, because I'll fight for them all." His blue eyes swing to Gabriel, anger burning in their depths. "What happens to him?"

"He needs purpose. Something hard and meaningful. It's past time he learned our true enemy. There are worse things than monsters out there," Michael says, his eyes reflecting the horrors that await Gabriel.

"Take the last canister," I urge, uncomfortable with the idea of owing him a favor. "Remember, there are two deto-nations."

He flicks a hand, and the angel with the scary eyes picks up the canister and shoots up into the sky at near impossible speeds.

"One day," he promises Lucifer. He, too, takes to the skies with the other two carrying the wingless Gabriel between them.

<u>LUCIFER</u>

All this time, I blamed Gabriel for losing my place amongst the angels, but he never ordered me to kill Satan. He only stated that his loss would restore the balance, but I knew what needed to be done. And a part of me wanted to do it. The idea of Satan gaining a foothold over the humans burned in my blood until I could think of nothing but eliminating him.

Sorrow and regret came later. I never dreamed I'd lose my home or my brothers. Cast out and vulnerable, I lived here with the humans. They taught me about strength and fear, love and hate, and the ability to hope beyond the boundaries of logic. Until the flood, when all hope was lost.

No matter what happened, though, I couldn't let go of the past. If only Gabriel hadn't said anything, I would be above where I belonged. The thought consumed me until I could no longer think of anything else. Alone again after the flood, the thought of revenge became the air I breathed every day. It fueled my rise to ruler of the Underworld.

Seeing Michael again, I realized it wasn't revenge fueling me, but anger. Anger at my actions, the loss of my home, the devastation of humans, and everything else.

Michael was right. The reason I believe in free will so much is because I used it to choose my path, and I continue to use it every day. Listening to Michael preach the same tired narrative to Gabriel that he only exists to serve at the whim of another, it reinforces the freedom I've found by using my free will.

Did I expect this outcome? To become ruler of the Underworld and protector of humanity. Never. But I regret nothing now. Nor am I filled with the need for vengeance. Instead, all I see are possibilities.

Evren's red locks are blowing in the breeze, and her fierce smile is free of the strain she's carried the whole time she's been here. When I thought her human, I tried to separate my feelings, but even then, they refused to be contained. I was already trying to figure out a way to keep her safe, and accessible, in a nearby world.

She bends down to help Valerian stabilize Zephyra while Rivan and Daire work on healing the griffin's leg.

Her green eyes dart to mine. They were the first thing I noticed, but certainly not the last. Overflowing with emotion and hope, they are the windows to her soul and the key to her mind.

Daire finishes healing Zephyra's leg and strides over to me.

He slaps me on the back. "I used to think you were the scariest thing on two legs, but not anymore. Michael's in a whole other league. And the three with him might be worse."

"Reassuring to know they're fighting to keep the real

monsters at bay," I reply firmly. I turn to face Daire so he can understand the importance of what I'm about to say. "I know you have doubts about her, but Evren's everything to me. Beautiful, courageous, incredibly smart. She challenges me to be the best person I can be, not just for myself, but for the people I rule and protect." I pause. "It doesn't mean I'll forget your mother. She was my first love. But if Evren will stay, she's my eternity."

Daire searches my eyes with his own. "I know. I see it now. You're happier than I can ever remember. With her, you don't have to worry about keeping your two worlds apart." His eyes dart to Evren. "I used to worry you would be alone when I passed, but hearing her say Viridians are eternal, it comforts me. Not that you need it, but I give you my blessing."

Daire signals to Valerian, who walks over and shakes my hand. "Thanks for all the fun. I might have a few nightmares over the scary-as-fuck angels I saw today, but I guess it's good to know they're standing between us and the big bad. Call if you need anything. Arden's family is our family." His phone pings, and he looks at the screen, then laughs. "Arden is requesting you join us for dinner soon and bring Evren. You know, she gave us all hell, especially Daire, when she heard how rude we were to a guest in her home. It took us a while to get out of the doghouse, so make sure you don't wait too long."

Once they're gone, I stroll over to Ishkova's body and call Vargas to me. "Before you leave, can you help arrange a funeral for him? Full honors. He died a hero, and I want to celebrate his years of service and loyalty."

"I'll get it done," Vargas states firmly, a harsh frown on his face. He bends down and picks up the body. "How did you know I was leaving?"

I lift an eyebrow. "The body you chose. It's perfect for what you're planning to do." I glance at Evren and see she's ready to go. "Do you mind helping Rivan and Zephyra get home, too?"

He agrees, and I walk over to thank the two valiant flyers. "Zephyra, I hope this helps soothe the anguish of the past. What you did today was heroic and brave. If you ever want to work for me in a different capacity, contact me."

She silently dips her chin, but I can see the impact my words have on her.

I turn to Rivan. "Thank you for taking Ishkova's role in this mission. He would have been proud of you." My eyes dart to Vargas. "If you find yourself in need of a friend, there is none better."

Rivan stiffens. "Thank you." He walks over to stand with Vargas and Zephyra.

Unable to wait any longer, I pull Evren into my arms and capture those luscious pink lips of hers. An intense feeling swells inside me. "You were incredible today. Brave, powerful, and strong. A true goddess."

I comb my fingers through her luxurious strands. "I'm sorry about your mother. Even if some part of you knows you will see her again, it's still hard to hear she's gone."

Her smile is tinged with sadness. "I've had over two thousand years with my wonderful mother." Her shoulder lifts. "No matter how small or great the number of years, there's never enough time. I do the only thing I can do and take solace in the fact that we're both eternal and will see each other again."

I shift my hands to cup her face. "Do you know what it means to hear those words? Eternal myself, I thought I'd come to terms with the fact that I'd spend most of my life alone and without love. Then you come along, and I find myself fascinated and full of hope again. This last week with you has been incredible, but I want more. Stay with me? Forever?"

Her green eyes dance with happiness. "Forever's a long time."

"Damn right it is, and it still won't be long enough."

A mischievous grin lights up her face. "Yes, but with one condition."

"Anything."

"I want to run the science department. And I want to catalog the DNA of every Underworld citizen. Think of what we could do with that information..."

My lips cover hers to stop the flow of words. She immediately surrenders with a sigh. Shimmering to our bedroom, I undress us both and proceed to show her what she means to me. My forever love.

SHE SMOOTHS down the short silky blue dress. "What do you think?"

Her long legs are on full display beneath the very short scrap of fabric she's wearing. "It's terrible. Instead of looking at you, I'm going to be watching all the males around us. The color looks gorgeous on you, though."

She laughs. "The color reminded me of your eyes." The dress flares when she twirls. "It's perfect for dancing after dinner with your family." Nervous, she continues to look at the dress from all angles in the mirror.

I silently groan, knowing I'm going to be in hell on the dance floor. "It's perfect. We need to go, or we'll be late." The magic word. Evren abhors being late.

Her eyes widen in horror. "Let's go."

When we arrive at The Abbey, a huge table is set up on the

dance floor. Arden is standing there with her men surrounding her.

"Thank you for inviting us," I tell her, leaning down to give her a kiss on the cheek. "You all remember Evren."

"You look beautiful. I've never met a goddess before," Arden remarks with a smile. "Do I curtsy or bow?"

Evren flashes her a puzzled look. "You've never met Theia?"

Arden glances at each of her men. All of them shake their head. "Who's Theia?"

"I met her on the bottom floor during my last visit. She's the goddess who created this sanctuary," Evren explains to Arden. "I assumed you had met her."

"Theia is the primal source?" Theron asks her. His violet eyes studying her intently.

Evren's eyes move to him. "She's a primordial god or goddess, here long before the god above, angels, and humans arrived. Her primary concern is protecting the supernaturals, but she was very helpful to me."

I lean down. "Why is she allowed to stay on Earth?"

Evren shrugs. "She said something... 'He cannot banish what was here before him.' I guess his power only extends so far."

Astor chuckles. "So you weren't talking to yourself the day I found you?"

Evren returns his laugh. "No, but it's not an uncommon occurrence. I'm sure you'll see me talking to myself in the future."

Daire and Arden's eyes dart to me.

"Evren splits her time between Viridian and the Under-world, but she's here to stay," I tell them.

Daire offers me a glass of bourbon. "Evren, what can I get for you?"

She looks at my glass and shakes her head. "Wine, please."

Arden waves a hand toward the table. "Daire usually doesn't eat, preferring to drink his meal, and I know you both don't eat, but I'm glad you joined us. It's nice to sit down together as a family."

Evren sits down at one of the chairs, and I grab the seat next to her.

"Are Meri and Solandis joining us?" I ask, taking a sip of my drink.

Arden's smile disappears. "No. The light Fae requested their presence early to determine if the Wild Hunt should be called." She fiddles with the silverware by her plate. "I don't like the idea of a trial."

I frown. "The rules of the Wild Hunt are clear. They only interfere if magic was used to manipulate the transfer of power from one ruler to the next. In order for the Wild Hunt to consider the case, the light Fae would need to bring evidence against Meri and prove she purposely, and magically, took control of the power to rule as Queen. She didn't. I doubt they will consider it grounds for a trial. Did you talk to Cormal and Vargas?"

Her sigh of relief is heartfelt. "Thank you. I needed to hear that." She takes a sip of water before continuing. "Cormal and Vargas are working on a plan."

"Those two are the most stubborn and fierce fighters I know, and they're not about to let Meri and Solandis go to the light Fae without one," I assure her.

She thinks about it for a second, then nods. "You're right."

The food arrives.

Evren turns to Valerian and Fallon. "That was quite an impressive collection of warriors you brought to the meeting with the angels. I'm guessing you're not just a dragon shifter or an elf?"

With my arm on the back of her chair, I idly play with the

strands of her hair while she bombards my family with a slew of questions. Daire looks at me with a raised eyebrow, silently asking why I didn't tell her about them, but I smile. This is the best way to get to know Evren. And it makes her happy. When Daire sees the unspoken answer in my eyes, he laughs and raises his glass in a toast.

EPILOGUE

<u>LUCIFER</u>

Vargas is waiting for me in my office, bag packed and lying on the ground beside him. As is his usual habit, he's pacing in front of my desk. The fluid way he moves and carries himself tells others more about his lethalness than the face he wears, but it's still startling to see the face of a Fae and know it's him. The light Fae guard uniform doesn't help, either.

Cormal felt the best disguise for Vargas would be to enter into the light Fae palace as a guard, and I agreed. With very little effort, Cormal had a captain of the light Fae army put Vargas on the roster and assign him as Solandis' personal guard. I scoff. And people worry about me. At least I operate in the open. Cormal's the devil in the shadows who will slit your throat for leaning against his wall.

I wonder if Solandis will be able to tell it's Vargas. I hope so. He needs her, and she needs him, but right now, Meri needs them both.

I clasp his forearm with mine. "If you run into any danger or need anything, send word via our private channel. The fewer people who know where you are, the better. Be careful. The Fae are vicious. Unlike demons, they hide behind pretty words and glamours. And don't get too cozy at the light Fae court. Half demon or whole, I don't give a fuck. You're my second-in-command and critical to the future of the Underworld. Hear me?"

His voice is gruff when he replies. "Don't worry. I know the Fae better than they know themselves. Thank you for understanding." He bends down and grabs his bag. "Take care of Evren. Give her some fighting lessons. She needs more than just a dagger."

"I will. Go," I order him, hiding the smile that threatens to take over.

I'm still sitting there when Cormal strides in an hour later. "Thank you for adding my name to the side gate. It's a hell of a lot easier to get to your office." He motions to the decanter on my desk, and I wave a hand.

Pouring a large splash, he sits down and eyes the large knife in my hand. "Did Vargas leave yet?"

"Dressed in his shiny gold light Fae guard uniform, he left about an hour ago," I confirm. I flip the knife over and point the tip at Cormal. "Don't ever negotiate with any of my men for access to this palace. This is my domain, and you will not dip the smallest toe into it without my permission. Understood?"

He jerks his chin in response.

"Good. Now tell me, what do you think Meri's chances are of getting and keeping the light Fae crown?" I ask, wondering if this is going to pull us into another war. Probably wouldn't be a bad thing. We have a reputation to keep up. Plus, it keeps the army sharp and ready for battle.

A worried look settles on his face. "My sources say they're prepared to give her the crown, but no one believes they will allow her to keep it. Meri has the power to hold on to her reign, but I doubt she'll realize it until it's too late."

"I know you'll keep a close eye on things. Let me know if we can help," I tell him.

He stands up and downs the last of the bourbon in his glass. "I will. Also, I've used the torque." Sliding a glove onto his hand, he reaches into the air beside his head and pulls the torque out. With one last look of longing, he lays it on the desk and leaves.

I stare at the torque, then wave a hand to put it into my secret vault. It will come in handy one day, when the end times are near. Until then, it will remain hidden.

THANK YOU!

Thank you for reading! Lucifer demanded to have his own story, but because of the religious references, I wanted it to be optional for fans of the series. I thoroughly enjoyed writing it and it's made me so excited to jump into Meri's book next. I'd love to hear your thoughts. Whether it's "give me more," or "I want to see a book with…" reviews help me write the next story. Please consider leaving one for this book.

*If you find an error, email me at Stellabrie@stellabrie.com.

*If you see the ebook anywhere besides Amazon KU, please send me an email (see address above) or contact me on social media. Pirating can have severe consequences, preventing authors from creating new stories.

To get a free eBook copy of my first book, My Salvation, just subscribe to my newsletter.

Website: https://www.stellabrie.com/my-salvation

AWESOME PEOPLE

Huge thanks to everyone who make my books possible!

To my readers, friends, and fans! Thanks for all the wonderful words of encouragement, friendship, and love for my books! And for participating in my shenanigans and all the other weird things I post. You guys rock! I couldn't do it without you!!!

My awesome beta readers. They catch so many big and little things, help me with names, show me such amazing friendship, encouragement, and excitement, and they can't even share it with anyone! My books are a thousand times better because of their feedback. Thank you, Nia, Bianca, Iliana, Melissa, Rachel, Sandi, and Debbie for everything!

My ARC team who gives me so much support and enthusiasm even though I drop things on them at the last minute. Ooh, look, cover reveal! Book's launching in a week! Seriously, I appreciate all of you!!

My biggest supporters—my husband and mom. I'm so lucky to have you both! Love you!

And always... a special thanks to all the wonderful authors in the writing community who support each other day in and out. Writing would be a lonely and weird world without you. It would be me and my characters sitting around chatting (drinking) while we plot the next book. Your friendship and support mean a lot to me!

ABOUT THE AUTHOR

Stella Brie lives outside of Nashville, TN, with her husband. After mentioning her desire to write a book a million times to her husband, he challenged her to sit down one day and write a paragraph. Instead, she wrote her first book, *My Salvation*.

She traded in her career in digital marketing, working on big brands, for this wildly creative one. Armed with a notebook crammed full of ideas, she's constantly thinking about bold heroines, sexy men, and HEAs. Whether it's a paranormal book full of creatures and magic or a contemporary romance full of heat and drama, she's always thinking about how she can bring her books to life.

Latest News and Updates:

Facebook Group: Stella's Stalkers

Instagram: @stellabrie_author

TikTok: @stellabrie_author

Website: Stellabrie.com - Exclusive sneak peeks, cover reveals, giveaways, and more!

BOOKS BY STELLA BRIE

PARANORMAL WHY CHOOSE

KILLIAN BLADE SERIES

The Rowan (1)

The Rowan's Stone (2)

The Rowan's Destiny (3)

The Light Falls (4) - Meri's story

The Dark Rises (5) - Meri's story

Spin-offs:

Wicked Savior - Lucifer's story (MF Romance) - Book 3.5

CONTEMPORARY WHY CHOOSE

THE SAVAGES SERIES

Savage Traitor (1)

Savage Ruin (2)

Spin-off:

Lethal Vengeance (Standalone)

My Salvation (Standalone)

To get a free eBook copy of my first book, My Salvation, just subscribe to my newsletter.

Website: https://www.stellabrie.com/my-salvation